There [illegible]

The h[illegible] quick, r[illegible] stone.

He shi[illegible] books—actual printed-on-paper books—protectively under his arm and anxiously tugged the collar of his drab, gray raincoat tighter around his neck in an effort to hide his already nondescript features.

As he reached the steps of his building, two books slipped out of his grasp and landed on the crumbling concrete stairs. He paused for a split second, almost reaching to retrieve his treasures, but the sight of three huge shadows darting toward him froze his mind in blind panic.

He dropped his remaining volumes and scrambled through the door, then half ran, half crawled up the ancient stairwell that led to his room. He threw himself into the apartment and fell back heavily against the door, panting with exertion.

With an explosion of wood slivers and plaster, the apartment door burst in and three figures dove through the hole.

They were Martian Desert Runners, he realized with growing horror. These gennies were feline; they stood well over six feet tall and were covered with fur. Their ears curved into sharp points, and their hands and feet resembled soft paws—but ended in razorlike claws. Two of them had black and orange stripes in their fur, like tigers, but the third was white with black hands. They all wore heavy leather body armor made from the hide of some Martian beast.

"Who . . . who are you? What do you want?"

The white gennie grabbed the man's head, clamped a small box roughly over his eye, and scanned the pattern of blood vessels in his retina.

"I greet you, Your Lordship," the gennie purred, then it intoned, "We're here to take you home."

BUCK ROGERS™ BOOKS

ARRIVAL

THE MARTIAN WARS TRILOGY

Book One: Rebellion 2456

Book Two: Hammer of Mars

Book Three: Armageddon Off Vesta

THE INNER PLANETS TRILOGY

Volume One: First Power Play

Volume Two: Prime Squared

Volume Three: Matrix Cubed

BUCK ROGERS
XXVc™
THE 25TH CENTURY

The Inner Planets Trilogy, Vol. Three

MATRIX CUBED

Britton Bloom

Cover Art by
JERRY BINGHAM

TSR™

MATRIX CUBED

Distributed to the book trade in the United States by Random House, Inc. and in Canada by Random House of Canada, Ltd.

Distributed to the book trade in the United Kingdom by Random Century Group and TSR Ltd.

Distributed to the toy and hobby trade by regional distributors.

First Printing: May 1991
Printed in the United States of America
Library of Congress Catalog Card Number: 90-71508

9 8 7 6 5 4 3 2 1

ISBN: 0-88083-885-4

TSR, Inc.
P.O. Box 756
Lake Geneva, WI
53147
U.S.A.

TSR, Inc.

TSR Ltd.
120 Church End,
Cherry Hinton
Cambridge CB1 3LB
United Kingdom

The Inner Planets

Earth

A twisted wreckage despoiled by interplanetary looters, Earth is a declining civilization. Its people are divided and trapped in urban sprawls and mutant-infested reservations.

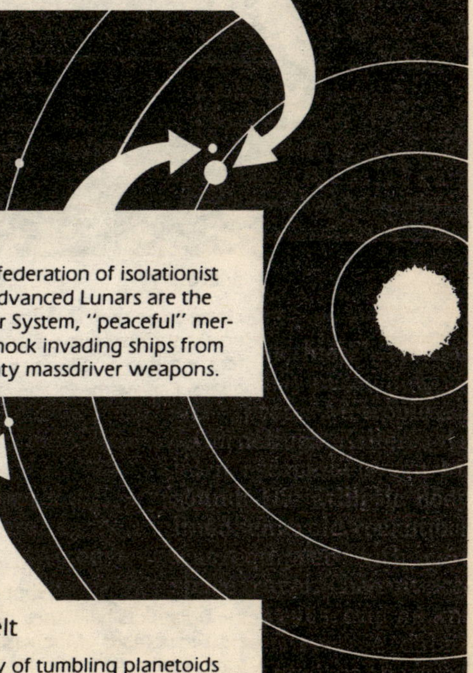

Luna

An iron-willed confederation of isolationist states, the highly advanced Lunars are the bankers of the Solar System, "peaceful" merchants willing to knock invading ships from the skies with mighty massdriver weapons.

The Asteroid Belt

A scattered anarchy of tumbling planetoids and rough rock miners, where every sentient has the right to vote, and the majority rules among five hundred miniature worlds.

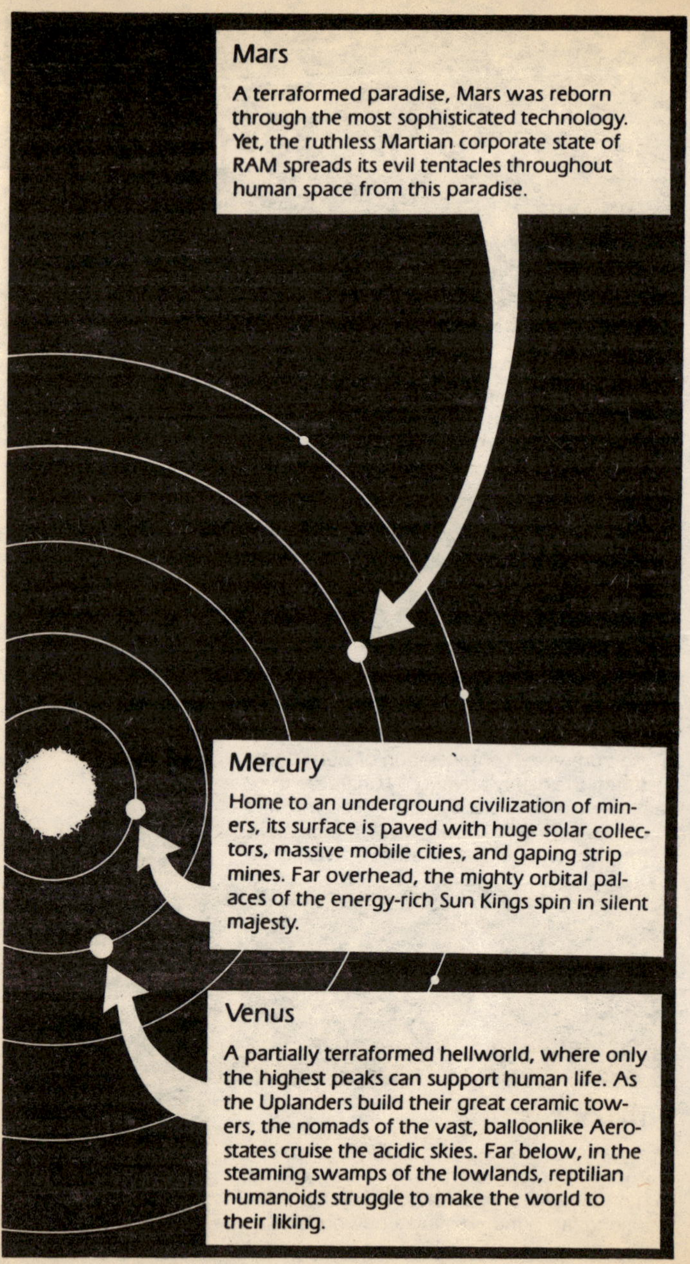
Mars
A terraformed paradise, Mars was reborn through the most sophisticated technology. Yet, the ruthless Martian corporate state of RAM spreads its evil tentacles throughout human space from this paradise.
Mercury
Home to an underground civilization of miners, its surface is paved with huge solar collectors, massive mobile cities, and gaping strip mines. Far overhead, the mighty orbital palaces of the energy-rich Sun Kings spin in silent majesty.
Venus
A partially terraformed hellworld, where only the highest peaks can support human life. As the Uplanders build their great ceramic towers, the nomads of the vast, balloonlike Aerostates cruise the acidic skies. Far below, in the steaming swamps of the lowlands, reptilian humanoids struggle to make the world to their liking.

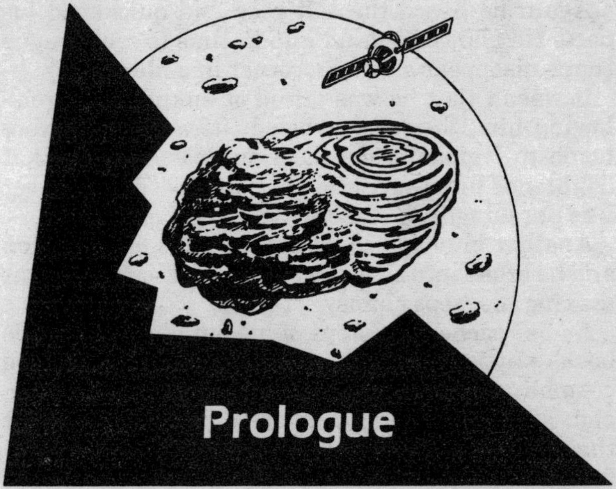

Prologue

There! he thought. There's that sound again!

The heavy-set man paused to listen and heard a quick, rasping noise, like a knife scraping against stone.

He ran his hand across the masonry wall beside him and looked nervously up the dark street. No one was visible.

He shifted the load of books—actual printed-on-paper books—protectively under his arm and anxiously tugged the collar of his drab, gray raincoat tighter around his neck in an effort to hide his already nondescript features.

He caught a sudden movement in the corner of his

eyes, but by the time he swung around to look, there was nothing to see. He resumed walking quickly toward his apartment in a dilapidated building at the end of the street.

Again he heard the soft rasp and quickened his pace. He glanced behind him in time to see a vague shape disappear around a corner in a blur.

It wasn't that he was afraid of unknown men following him; the reconstructed cities of Earth were home to legions of derelicts and castaways. What frightened him was the silence and speed of whoever was pursuing him, almost like . . . gennies.

Another blur moved across the edge of his vision and he broke into an awkward trot, his excess weight making his steps clumsy.

As he reached the steps of his building, two of his books slipped out of his grasp and landed on the crumbling concrete stairs. He paused for a split second, almost reaching to retrieve his treasures, but the sight of three huge shadows darting toward him froze his mind in blind panic.

He dropped his remaining volumes and scrambled through the door, then half ran, half crawled up the ancient stairwell that led to his room. He threw himself into the apartment and fell back heavily against the door, panting with exertion.

After a few minutes, his breathing returned to normal and he began to relax. The building was utterly silent. Whoever was following him had given up—*if* they were following. It was more than likely they were just a group of transients looking for a few coins. He chuckled at his own nervousness. Huge shadows, indeed! he thought. The dim streetlights always distorted, and sounds could . . . deceive.

He mopped his sweating brow with his sleeve and pushed away from the door. His books! He remembered them slipping from his grasp and lying on the front steps! He had searched for months for those precious paper books about knife design in the twentieth century. They might be able to link Mercury's Dancers to a specific area of old Earth.

The man immediately grabbed the doorknob . . . but a lingering edge of fear stopped him. If there *was* someone outside, it might be best to wait a few minutes, he thought.

He fumbled the lights on and stepped away from the door. His apartment was literally filled with Dancer artifacts; cases of knives and daggers lined the walls; diagrams of scarf patterns littered the floor; a large desk was piled high with computer printouts tracing Dancer ancestry on Earth.

With an explosion of wood slivers and plaster, the apartment door burst in and three figures dove through the hole. Even before the tenant could recover from the shock, the three were on their feet, spreading out to search the room.

They were Martian Desert Runners, he realized with growing horror. Generations earlier, Runners had been humans whose genetic makeup had been mixed with another species' to create a new organism designed to live in the wastelands of Mars. These gennies were feline; they stood well over six feet tall and were covered with fur. Their ears curved into sharp points, and their hands and feet resembled soft paws—but ended in razorlike claws. Two of them had black and orange stripes in their fur, like tigers, but the third was white with black hands. They all wore heavy leather body armor made from the hide of some Martian beast.

Despite their size, they moved with inhuman speed. Within seconds they had searched the apartment, tearing open the closets and bathroom door. Their furred feet made no sound as they moved. They had obviously been bred as hunter-stalkers.

"Who . . . who are you? What do you want?"

The white gennie turned to him. "You," it growled.

"There's been some mis-mistake. My name is Shor Cortel. . . . I'm a professor . . ."

The white Desert Runner took a step closer to him. "You're from Mercury," he declared.

"Yes, I'm an anthropologist studying the origins of Mercury's Dancers." The heavy man swung his arm around the room to point out the collection of Dancer memorabilia as if to confirm his story.

The white Runner suddenly grabbed the man's head, clamped a small box roughly over his eye, and scanned the pattern of blood vessels in his retina. After a moment the gennie removed the box and glanced at it. He growled at his companion, who nodded back at him.

"I greet you, Your Lordship," the gennie purred, "Garrick Gavilan, brother to His Highness Gordon Gavilan, the Sun King of Mercury."

The man backed away in terror. "There's been a mistake!"

The white gennie held up the ident box. "No mistake."

The other Desert Runners hedged in closer to him.

"What do you want of me?" Garrick asked, panic spreading through him once he realized his cover had been blown.

"We're here to take you home," the white Runner said, his lips curling back in a contorted smile.

"No!" Garrick shouted, stumbling against his desk. "I renounced the kingship years ago! I want nothing to do with Gordon!"

"Gordon didn't send for you," the gennie said, raising a heavily muscled arm.

The last thing Garrick saw was a blur of white fur.

Consciousness returned slowly. Garrick felt as though he were swimming through an endless tunnel of thick foam toward an ever-receding pinprick of light.

Somewhere in the distance he heard a soft moan and realized that he himself was making the noise. The feeling of disassociation frightened him, and he fought harder against the soft, strangling sense of numbness that filled his mind.

After what seemed an eternity of struggle, he managed to open his eyes. He could make out almost nothing around him, only shades of light and dark with vague, blurry shadows.

He tried to sit up, but his arms and legs wouldn't respond to his will. By a supreme effort of concentration, Garrick forced his muscles to work and struggled into a sitting position.

Waves of nausea coursed through him. He closed his eyes and clamped his teeth against the rising gorge of bile. It felt to him like the after-effects of a drug overdose.

He opened his eyes again and glanced at his arm. Three anestho-pacs were taped to the bare flesh of his forearm. Three! Whoever drugged him wanted to make sure he would stay unconscious. Disgusted, he ripped the anestho-pacs off. The sudden movement made his head reel, and he slumped back heavily against a rough wooden wall.

Who did this? he wondered, but his brain was too fuzzy to think clearly enough to find an answer. He shook his head to clear his mind, but the only image that came to him was a huge white . . . cat?

A Desert Runner! he suddenly remembered. No, three of them! They had cornered him in his apartment and brought him . . . where?

He looked around, but nothing seemed familiar. He was surrounded by a confusing jungle of plants, a sea of green. Could this be a garden, or a park? he wondered.

"Ah, there! You're awake, young master Garrick," he heard an old voice call.

Garrick turned slowly to the voice and saw an immensely ancient man dressed in tattered clothing tottering toward him and bearing a tray of food.

"It's good to see you again, young sir. It's been . . . my goodness, almost eighty-three years, hasn't it?"

Garrick was startled. The man looked old, but he couldn't have known him eighty years—Garrick was only fifty-two. . . .

A sudden realization dawned on him: Mercury had an eighty-eight-day year! He had spent so much time on Earth that he had all but forgotten. Garrick tried to calculate the number of Earth years the man was talking about, but his drug-dulled mind could come up with nothing closer than twenty years . . . about the time he left Mercury.

"I'm on Mercury?" Garrick asked.

"Hielo, actually," the old man replied. "We're in the royal greenhouse of Mercury Prime. Don't you remember? You used to play here as a child."

Garrick leaned forward and stared at the man's hawkish nose and bushy eyebrows; recognition finally dawned. "I know you. . . . You're Shazimar, the gardener!"

"Of course I am," the man beamed, obviously pleased to be remembered.

"I could never forget you, Shaz," Garrick said, smiling. "But how did I get here?"

"They brought you here two days ago," Shazimar explained, nodding to one side.

Garrick looked to where the gardener indicated. Two orange-and-black gennies—the same two that attacked him on Earth, he guessed—stood a few feet away.

Fear returned in a sudden wave. "What do they want from me?"

"I don't know, young sir. They just dumped you here and won't say a word to me."

"Shaz, I need your help," Garrick whispered urgently. "I've got to get out of here. Can you get me away quickly?"

The old man frowned and shook his head. "I'm afraid His Royal Majesty wouldn't . . ."

"Gordon did this to me?" Garrick asked.

"I'm sure I don't know . . ."

"My father had nothing to do with this," a new voice interrupted. "The responsibility is mine."

Garrick looked up at a young man in his early thirties, built like an athlete, with a deep chest and broad shoulders, and with an angular thatch of black hair on his head. A jet-black mustache, set above thin lips that curled back into a tight smile, gave him a cruel appearance.

"Dalton?" Garrick said hesitantly, trying to match the young man's image with the boy's he remembered. "Is that you?" He wondered at how much Dalton looked like his father, Gordon.

"Why, how kind of you to recall me, Uncle," Dalton replied with a sardonic smile.

"You had me kidnapped? What do you want?"

"Actually, I just wanted to see you, to make sure I'd really found you at last. You see, I've been searching for you for a very long time."

"Why?"

"Well, your 'disappearance' and continued absence from court has delayed several very important plans," Dalton said with exaggerated nonchalance. Despite his casual speech, something in his eyes made Garrick uneasy.

"What . . . what plans?"

"Oh, my dear uncle, great plans."

These matters are . . . trivial!" Gordon Gavilan, the ruling Sun King of Mercury, shouted, flinging a handful of papers at the assembly. "Budgets! Balance of trade . . . solar energy production . . . There are petty officials to handle such things!"

The council members muttered restlessly, with muted anger. One of the Musician delegates shouted, "That's our livelihood you're throwing away! It's not trivial—"

"Your livelihood will be worth less than your endless words if RAM turns its laser on Mercury!" Gordon's immense frame filled the throne in which he sat. If his stature didn't make him obvious, then his jet-black hair and high-contrast clothes did.

Kemal Gavilan groaned to himself. The laser again. For the last two hours his uncle Gordon had raved endlessly about *his* laser, which had been "stolen" by RAM; every topic addressed by the council for the last few days had been twisted around until it came back to the laser, every report weighed against the pressing need for the laser.

A Miner sitting beside Kemal nudged him sharply with his elbow. "What *is* it with him and that damned laser anyhow? Every other word out of his mouth is laser this and laser that!" The Miner's clothes were cut of fine fabric and tailored, but Kemal noticed he still wore the heavy boots of a surface dweller. The Miner may be a diplomat now, he thought, but he isn't far removed from the mines.

Kemal's own clothes were the finest in the inner planets. His lean, muscled body was covered in the black-and-gold uniform of the royal family. His bronze face was angular and held his father's hazel eyes. Short-cropped, light brown hair topped his head.

Although Kemal was an official delegate of the Dancers, the desert nomads had totally ostracized him since Gordon had used him to locate their secret crystal field on Mercury's surface. Despite the fact that he hadn't actually betrayed the Dancers, his own pride—and a deep sense of guilt for having planned to reveal the fields to Gordon anyway—made him accept their exile without a word of protest. He still attended council meetings as a delegate, but he always sat apart from the Dancer delegation and kept his mouth shut when the council addressed matters relating to the desert dwellers.

Kemal began to reply, but before he could say a word, the chamber erupted in a crimson explosion.

The initial flash of fire and the deafening roar

almost paralyzed him with shock. He spun around to face the front of the chamber in time to see a huge chunk of glistening synthetic stone hurtling toward him. His experience as a rocketjock during the Martian Wars had honed his reflexes to a razor's edge; without thinking, Kemal flung himself to the floor as the fragment of artificial masonry smashed into his seat just where his head had been. Shards rained down on his back, stinging as they pierced his skin.

The Miner beside him hadn't been so lucky. Kemal heard him start to shout, but his words died with a wet gurgle. Kemal couldn't see the man, but a spray of blood told him he didn't need to look.

Even before the tremors died away, a second explosion ripped through the chamber, cracking the floor. Kemal wondered for a moment if the blasts would undermine the palace structure, but the chamber was on an upper level, far from the foundation. He wrapped his arms around his head and tried to burrow into the unyielding stone.

The shattering roars left his ears ringing, so he felt rather than heard the spattering of new shards that dug into his back. When the hail of silicate fragments finally stopped, Kemal raised himself gingerly to survey the damage.

The chamber was a shambles.

The council room had been designed as a large amphitheater, with rows of tiered seats arranged in ever larger semicircles that focused on the Sun King's throne. Rows of columns throughout the chamber supported a balcony reserved for the public.

Kemal saw that the explosions had come from behind the throne, showering the entire room with debris in a deadly spray of shrapnel. A gaping hole yawned in the wall to the rear of the throne. There was no sign of Gordon, only a pile of rubble where he had been a moment before.

As the echoes of the explosion faded, there was an eerie moment of silence, then the survivors began a low keen of pain. Someone screamed in agony.

The sound seemed to galvanize Kemal. He leaped to his feet and vaulted over the seat in front of him.

"The king!" he shouted. "See to the king!"

Royal guardsmen were already pouring into the chamber, but Kemal reached the throne before them. Without thinking, he began pushing aside the rubble and pulling at twisted support beams with adrenaline-enhanced strength.

Kemal dug with his bare hands, frantically scraping the debris away. Then his hands struck the solid back of the throne.

"I've got it!" he shouted at a guardsman who kneeled beside him.

Together they cleared the gravel away from the enormous seat, until they saw Gordon's limp arm twisted awkwardly in the dust.

Kemal drew back at the sight, suddenly puzzled at why he was rescuing the Sun King whose tyranny threatened the well-being of a whole planet . . . the man he believed had killed his father.

For a moment, Kemal couldn't decide if he hoped Gordon was alive or dead. Then one of the Sun King's fingers twitched.

"He's alive!" the guardsman beside him shouted. "Sergeant! Send more men!"

The throne was a huge stone seat, ornately carved and inlaid with gold. It's high back apparently had protected Gordon from the initial explosions, and when it had overturned on him, it acted as a shield against the deadly rain of stone shrapnel.

The other guardsmen arrived and pushed Kemal aside as they dug to free Gordon. For the first time, Kemal looked at the gallery, seeing the chaos and destruction among the delegates.

Bodies sprawled across the seats, and wounded delegates moaned, clutching their heads or broken limbs. Guardsmen were already among them, helping the survivors out of the room.

Except for the Dancer delegation.

No one approached them. They stood apart, nursing their own wounds. One figure remained aloof from the suffering: Corianne, the second-ranking member of the Desert Dancers' ruling council. Kemal had never met her, but he had seen her picture often enough to recognize her, a short, dark woman with a stern, uncompromising face. Despite her short stature, she held herself erect with an imperious strength even Gordon would have envied.

Kemal met her gaze. She was staring at him, her face cold and hard, a deep contempt blazing in her eyes. Kemal felt himself wither under her scrutiny.

He rose slowly, watching her still figure amid the destruction. He started to take a step toward her, but a trickle of dust from above drew his attention. He looked up in time to see several large chunks of stone detach from a pillar supporting the upper floor.

"The balcony!" Kemal screamed, pointing above the Dancers.

The delegates followed his arm and cried out in panic as the pillar began to crumble. The upper floor started to sag dangerously over their heads.

Kemal froze while the horrifying scene seemed to play itself out in slow motion. The Dancers scrambled out of the way . . . except for Corianne. Her hard eyes burned into Kemal, almost through him, he felt.

The balcony began to crumble. Jagged blocks of stone crashed down on the empty seats just behind Corianne. Slowly she looked around as the falling rocks raised a cloud of dust that enveloped her; she watched the chaos with a look of disdain.

Kemal saw another section of the upper floor crack.

"Run!" he shouted at her. "Get out of there!" He leaped across the throne and ran toward the Dancer but knew he would never reach her in time. Already a rain of dust and stone chips swirled around her.

Suddenly another Dancer rushed into the cloud and dove at her. He caught her around the waist and carried her away just as a shower of rocks and steel collapsed on the spot where she had been standing.

By the time Kemal reached them, Corianne was on her feet, dusting herself off.

"Are you all right?" he panted.

She turned on him, her face a cold mask. The man who had saved her wrapped his arm around her, and held Kemal away with his other hand.

She stared at him for a long moment. Then slowly she said, "I've heard about you. The stories say that you betrayed us to Gordon. I didn't believe, not even from Duernie's own lips. Such things can be misunderstood. But now . . . when I saw you run to your master's side . . . I know, now."

Kemal drew away involuntarily, her words bursting inside his head like the explosions of moments before. "Does Duernie believe I betrayed her?"

Kemal thought Duernie understood what had happened at the crystal field. She had crept through the ducts of Hielo and attacked Kemal in his apartment for the hurt he'd caused her; it was the only opportunity he had to explain what happened, that Gordon had him followed and found the field when Duernie took him there. She had seemed to accept his explanation, but Kemal felt a familiar tug of fear in his heart. If Duernie still felt he was a traitor . . .

Corianne tilted her head slightly, and an expression of puzzlement crossed her face. Then her eyes hardened again. "I have nothing more to say to you, Prince Kemal. We are of different worlds. I am a

Dancer, and you . . . you are a Gavilan!" The name sounded like a curse on her lips.

She turned abruptly, shaking the Dancer's arm from her shoulders, and strode toward the door.

"Corianne . . . wait . . ." Kemal began, but she was already too far to hear his whispered words.

Kemal watched her receding figure with a sinking feeling in his gut. He hadn't even known he had such a powerful friend, and now Corianne was convinced he was a traitor. The feeling burned inside him like a river of molten metal.

He heard a voice behind him shout, "Stop them! Don't let them leave the building!"

Kemal turned and saw a guard pointing at Corianne's back. He recognized the man as one of Dalton's bodyguards, but instead of wearing Dalton's personal livery, the man was dressed in a standard palace uniform. Kemal took a step toward him.

"The Dancers are responsible for this! Arrest them!" the guard shouted.

Kemal stared at him with open-mouthed amazement. "What are you talking about?" he cried, and stepped forward to grab the man by the arm.

The guard shook free of his grip and pushed Kemal away. "Guards! To me! Stop those Dancers!"

Kemal stumbled backward and tripped against a loose seat. He sat down heavily, scraping his back against the jagged edge of the chair. Waves of pain coursed through him, but he tightened his lips against the groan he felt building inside him. He tried to stand, but the tension and panic of the day left him weak and dizzy.

Well, he thought, maybe I'll just sit here a moment and rest . . . just for a moment . . .

❍ ❍ ❍ ❍ ❍

"Ah, Uncle, did you feel that?" Dalton asked as the ground gently shook beneath his feet.

"Feel what?" Garrick asked.

"The winds of change," Dalton replied, smiling. "The foundations of Hielo itself are being shaken."

"What are you talking about?"

Abruptly Dalton turned to the aged gardener. "Shazimar, you are dismissed."

The old man nodded slowly. "As you wish, Sire." He shuffled away as a second tremor shook the floor.

"You must have felt that, Uncle."

Garrick said nothing for a long time. Finally he asked, "What does all this mean?"

"It means that you are now the Sun King of Mercury," Dalton answered, his eyes glistening. "But I'm afraid you will have a short reign."

Garrick edged away from him, his mouth open in disbelief. "You killed your own father? My brother?"

Dalton frowned briefly, then sighed theatrically. "Gordon is . . . pardon me, *was,* a weak man, irresolute in the face of changing times. Revolution is spreading through the solar system, following the example of Earth's rebellion against Mars. Gordon wasted time and money on an obsession for a laser weapon he didn't have the strength to hold . . ."

"This has nothing to do with me, Dalton. Why are you holding me prisoner?"

"Don't you like these gardens? I find them very pleasant," Dalton said, glancing around the lush greenhouse. "The dungeons are so much more . . . uncomfortable, or so I'm told."

"And the guards would have informed Gordon of my presence," Garrick added.

"Yes, well, that's true, too," Dalton said. The mocking smile disappeared. "To put it bluntly, Uncle, you stand between me and the throne."

Garrick paled. "I told your goons here, I want nothing to do with the kingship. I gave that up years ago when I left Mercury. I'm an anthropologist now, studying the origins of the Dancers," Garrick said quickly. He could feel himself babbling out of fear. "I've found links between them and certain tribes of north African nomads . . ."

Dalton leaned over and patted Garrick's knee gently. "Uncle, Uncle, Uncle," he said, then laughed. "No one really cares." He turned aside and barked sharply, "Ral! Come here!"

The foliage parted with a rustle, and the white Desert Runner padded quietly to Dalton's side. The hunter-stalker's lips twisted into a fearful smile.

Garrick scrambled away, backing into a rough wooden wall. "On Earth I read of ancient civilizations whose rulers gained power by assassination. Is that what you want to bring to Mercury?"

Dalton cocked his head and rubbed his chin thoughtfully, as if considering the idea. "It sounds like a delightful tradition," he said mockingly, "though I think we will end the custom very soon." He turned to the gennie. "Ral, carry out your orders."

The man-cat advanced on Garrick.

"You don't have to do this," Garrick said.

"Oh, but I do," Dalton replied. "Whether you want to be king or not, you are the legal heir after my father, and the council would have to deliberate over your intentions. I don't want my reign troubled with squabbles or plagued by pretenders."

The gennie reached toward Garrick's neck with a razor-tipped claw. He tried to bat it away, but the gesture was futile against Ral's inhuman strength.

"I hope you won't think it morbid of me to watch," Dalton said casually, "but I do need to make certain."

Garrick started to scream, but the sound never left his throat as the Runner's hand quickly clamped around his neck.

Chapter Two

Kemal was dimly aware of being shaken, but nothing really registered in his mind.

"Wake up, K-K-Kemal," he heard a voice call from far away. "You've got to get out of here. This r-r-room's not safe!"

Kemal opened his eyes and saw his cousin Tix's thin frame looming over him. "Why? What's the matter, Tix?"

"There's been an explosion!"

Kemal blinked rapidly as his memory flooded back. He bolted upright, looking around at the destruction. Survivors were limping from the room while medical technicians hovered over the wounded.

"I f-f-found you unconscious," Tix persisted. The overhead lights reflected off his mostly bald head. "Are you hurt?"

Kemal struggled painfully to his feet. "I don't think so—no broken bones anyway. I must have . . . blacked out," he said, avoiding the word "faint."

"Oh!" Tix cried as Kemal turned to the door. "Your b-b-back is covered with blood! Let me get a doctor." Tix started to run toward a med-tech.

Kemal grabbed him by the shoulder. "Leave them for the seriously wounded. I just want to get out of here. Can you help me to my apartment?"

"Certainly, if that's what you w-w-want." Tix took his cousin's arm and directed him to the exit.

Tix was shorter than Kemal and had a slighter build than his cousin; he was an artist rather than a warrior. He sagged under Kemal's weight but managed to support him as they staggered out of the devastated room.

The corridor outside the council chamber looked like a charnel house. Dozens of delegates sprawled on makeshift cots and stretchers while medical teams swarmed around them, barking orders and scurrying after equipment.

"What happened to Gordon?" Kemal asked.

"That old fraud Catiff bustled him off to his chambers. He's got a few cuts and b-b-bruises, but my father is fine."

As they continued through the halls of Hielo's palace, Kemal felt his strength returning. By the time they reached the recessed alcove of his apartment door, he was walking without Tix's help.

Kemal keyed in his personal code on the lock and pushed his way inside before the door fully opened. Tix followed hesitantly.

"You really should s-s-see a doctor. You're bleeding rather badly."

Kemal looked behind him at the trail of blood his wound had left on the floor. He ripped his tunic off and threw it in a corner with a disgusted gesture. "Can you clean me up?"

"Uhh . . ." Tix began uncertainly. "I'm not sure I know what to d-d-do."

"Didn't anyone ever teach you how to make a field dressing?" Kemal asked with a grin.

"N-n-not where I went to school." Tix disappeared into the washroom and returned a moment later with several wet towels.

Hesitantly Tix wiped Kemal's shoulders. At the first touch of the cloth, Kemal arched his back painfully and a deep groan escaped his clenched teeth.

"There's a d-d-dozen chips of rock stuck in your skin," Tix said. "Maybe we should get a—"

"Just do it!" Kemal snapped.

Kemal felt a nervous finger tentatively probe a sore spot. His muscles tightened involuntarily, but he bit back the moan that formed in his throat.

"Oh, my," Tix quavered. "I feel dizzy. I think I might f-f-f—"

"Tix!" Kemal yelled through gritted teeth. "Hold on to yourself. I need your help!"

There was a moment of silence, and Kemal was afraid his young cousin might indeed have fainted. Then he saw Tix's face peering around his shoulder with an intense expression he had never seen on him before.

"Do you?" he asked, searching Kemal's face.

He stared back at Tix with the same intensity. "Yes," he answered slowly. "I need your help."

Tix regarded him a second longer, then went back to his ministrations. The hesitancy was gone from his touch, making the cleanup less painful.

"I don't believe I've ever b-b-been needed before," he said quietly.

Kemal nodded and patted his knee. "You're doing fine."

Tix quickly finished cleaning Kemal's back, then stepped into the washroom again for another towel and bandages.

"Was Dalton in the council chamber?" Kemal called after him.

"Not that I s-s-saw," Tix answered, coming back. "Was he there earlier?"

Kemal shook his head. "No. But I saw one of his bodyguards there, wearing a guardsman's uniform."

Tix stared at his cousin with disbelief. "Why?"

"Why, indeed?" Kemal said. "He started yelling that the Dancers were responsible for the bombing."

Tix froze in midstep. "The Dancers?" he repeated. "Impossible!"

Kemal stared at him until Tix became flustered and retreated back into the bathroom. He clattered among the bottles in the medicine chest, but Kemal suspected he was just trying to cover his confusion with activity.

Finally Tix craned his neck around the door and looked at him.

"Kemal . . ."

"Yes?"

"You don't think . . . Dalton was involved, d-d-do you?"

"Let's say it's possible."

Tix stared at him, his eyes wide with uncertainty. Then something in the smaller man hardened in resolve. "What do you want m-m-me to do?"

Kemal smiled. "Keep your eyes and ears open. He might let something slip around you."

Tix nodded seriously. "I will."

O O O O O

After Tix left, Kemal sat for a long time in front of his computer console, idly tapping the keys. He tried to make sense of the day's events, but too much had happened to easily comprehend.

Tix had put his finger on the point that was eating at Kemal's mind without coming into focus: was Dalton involved in the bombing?

He knew his cousin was ambitious and ruthless, but . . . patricidal? Could he kill his own father for a throne he would come to inherit anyway? It was unthinkable, but . . . possible. Terribly possible.

There had never been love lost between Kemal and Dalton; they had fought on opposite sides in the Martian Wars. The Gavilan family had sided with the powerful RAM organization, while Kemal had joined Earth's NEO forces against their Martian masters. And Kemal had bloodied Dalton's nose a bit in that campaign.

The animosity had become more personal, though, when Kemal had returned to Hielo and Gordon named him head of the laser project on the Rising Sun Station, thus replacing Dalton. It was a wily move, Kemal knew; in one stroke, Gordon had created a bitter rivalry between the two young men, potential allies against the Sun King's throne. Divide and conquer, the oldest dictum in war—and politics—was a well-used practice of Gordon Gavilan.

Is that what it meant to be a Gavilan? Kemal wondered. To use people, to pit members of one's own family against each other? Kemal thought of his father, Ossip, and his suspicions of Gordon's involvement in Ossip's death. And now a possible assassination attempt by Dalton. . . . Kemal shuddered. Yet he himself was a Gavilan.

He stared at his dark reflection in the computer's monitor screen. He had the Gavilan features: the high forehead, the straight nose, a square jaw with a firm chin. Yes . . . he was a Gavilan.

People had reacted to that name, rather than to the type of person he was, all his life. He remembered with bitter resentment the preferential treatment he had received at the Ulyanov Academy on Mars; the loneliness he felt, when boys who might have been friends turned away from him because his family outranked theirs, had cut him and continued to leave scars. Dalton gloried in the privileges granted to him as the scion of the most powerful family in the inner planets, but Kemal was always embarrassed by the deferential treatment.

Only Buck Rogers—the fighter pilot who'd miraculously survived centuries of suspended animation—saw Kemal as an individual, as himself, and not a Gavilan. Perhaps that was the way of the twentieth century, Kemal thought, or maybe it was just Buck's own values, but he judged a person by what he or she could do, not by family or social class. Buck had recognized Kemal's achievements as his own.

Duernie, too, had seen through the family name and come to know him as a person, a friend. But after Gordon used him to trace the location of the Dancers' crystal field, she saw him only as a traitor who had betrayed her trust. She came to hate him enough to attack him with a knife. He still didn't know what he said that changed her mind, but she had listened to him, and in the end she had sheathed her knife of her own will.

In his bitter heart, though, Kemal knew she was right. He had been planning to betray the field's location to regain his uncle's trust after fighting against his family in the Martian Wars.

Perhaps, underneath all his fine words and sentiments, Kemal was indeed a Gavilan as others knew the name.

He watched his face in the dark monitor screen

until he could no longer stand his own image, then impulsively activated the computer to banish the reflection.

Once the computer was on, Kemal knew what he wanted. Deliberately he typed: "kemal."

Almost instantly a holographic blur of colors solidified into the image of his father standing beside him. The computer-generated persona had been programmed by Ossip before his untimely death, and Kemal had only recently discovered it.

"You look troubled, Kemal," Ossip's familiar voice said softly.

"Much has happened today, Father."

"You mean the bombings?"

Kemal looked up in surprise. "You know about that?"

Ossip's image chuckled. "Of course. The medical computers have been clogged with nothing but trauma procedures all day."

Kemal's face darkened as he glanced away. "I think Dalton may be behind it," he said slowly.

Ossip's eyebrows raised a fraction of an inch, then knitted in thought. "Indeed?"

Kemal looked up, pain and confusion plain in his face. "Father," he said desperately, "who am I?"

Ossip tilted his head quizzically. "That's an odd question to ask a machine."

"But . . . but you're . . ." Kemal began.

"I am a program your father fed into the computer system of Hielo just before he died," the hologram interrupted. "At most I was designed to watch over you, not to answer philosophical questions older than humanity."

Kemal frowned and leaned back against the chair, wincing when the upholstery touched his wounds. "You're right," he admitted. "I just needed someone to talk to."

"It's true that I have Ossip's memories, and his feelings for you."

"You're the closest thing I have to a father now."

"That's part of your answer then. You are Ossip's son."

Kemal nodded. "But I am also a Gavilan, and there are things we have done that I am . . . ashamed of."

"You feel responsible for Gordon's and Dalton's crimes?" Ossip asked.

Kemal ducked his head, as if to avoid the accusation he carried in his own heart. "I am coming to realize that I am capable of betraying a friend," he whispered.

"You're talking about Duernie, aren't you?"

Kemal nodded miserably.

"Did *you* pass along the coordinates of the crystal farm?"

"No," Kemal replied. "Gordon had me followed, and I led him to the location."

"So you didn't actually betray the Dancers' trust."

"Technically, no, but I planned to . . ."

Ossip smiled and shook his head. "There is an ancient Earth saying that the road to hell is paved with good intentions. Do you suppose the road to heaven is paved with bad intentions?"

Kemal looked at him, puzzled. "What do you mean?"

Ossip shrugged. "The things that happen in our lives frequently have little to do with what we intend. If you didn't actually give Gordon the information leading him to the crystals, don't destroy yourself with guilt over what you *intended.* Are you absolutely certain you would have passed the information to Gordon in the end?"

Kemal opened his mouth, but no words came. He looked away. "Corianne thinks . . ."

"Corianne has her own decisions to make, her own

feelings to sort out. Leave them to her."

"It was her bitterest accusation to call me a Gavilan."

Ossip sighed and nodded. "Well, that is true. You are a Gavilan. And you are Ossip's son. But you left out the most important thing: You are also you. Gavilan is only a name. What you *do* with that name is what determines the kind of person you are and how people see you."

Kemal chuckled and felt a wonderful sense of relief in the laughter. "You sound like Buck Rogers."

"Who?"

"A friend from the war."

"He sounds like an interesting man. I'd like to meet him."

"I think you'd like Doctor Huer better. He's a computer personality that helps Buck."

"Does he play chess?"

"I'm not sure. I think so."

"Then he's the one I want to meet!" Ossip said enthusiastically. "You've no idea how boring it's been wandering around this computer net all these years."

Kemal laughed. "I'll ask him next time I see him." Kemal's face grew serious again, but not troubled.

Ossip watched him a moment, then reached toward him. The insubstantial holographic image passed through Kemal's shoulder without impediment. Ossip raised his hand and stared at it, first with surprise, then sorrow.

"I'm afraid I'm not much comfort, am I?"

"You are," Kemal whispered, "more than you'll ever know."

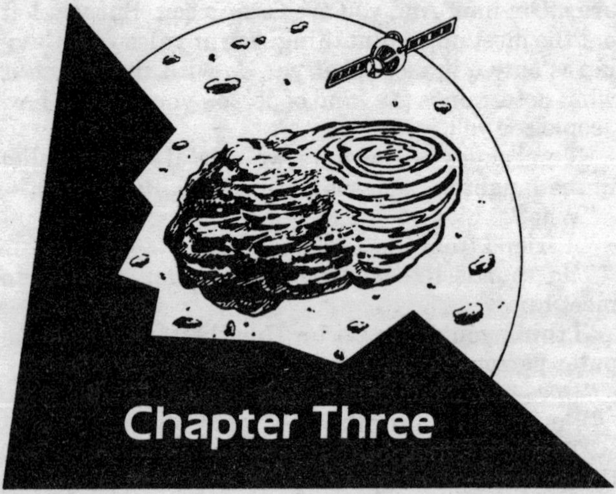

Chapter Three

That thief!" Ardala Valmar fumed as she furiously paced down a long corridor of Mars's Coprates Metroplex.

Cornelius ("Killer") Kane drew a deep breath and let it escape between his teeth with a dry, hissing sound. His athletic body was clothed in a streamlined, emerald rocketjock's outfit that, nonetheless, was equipped with various devices necessary for space travel. The suit accentuated the jade chips that were his eyes, and he knew it.

"That viper!" Ardala continued, her sharp heels clicking against the synthetic marble floor.

Kane noticed a definite rhythm in her cursing.

After ten minutes of steady raging, her tirade had begun to match the steady *click-click-click* of her steps. The effect was becoming boring.

"That Venusian slime rat!"

"Ardala . . . ," Kane ventured.

"That mutant cabbage worm!"

"Ardala . . . ," Kane tried again to stop the stream of denunciations.

"That creeping—"

"*Ardala!*"

"*What!*" Glaring, she spun around to face him.

Kane smiled. No one glared like Ardala, he thought appreciatively. Her hands were balled in tight fists resting on her exquisitely sculpted hips. She leaned forward aggressively, her eyes seemingly on fire above high cheekbones and glossy lips. Her long, black hair glistened in the faint light.

The effect of her fury was enhanced by the most stunning gown Kane had ever seen her wear. It was made of a lavender synthetic fabric only two molecules thick and clung to the curves of her body as tightly as another layer of skin. It wrapped around her from the left shoulder and fell all the way to the floor like a sheath that held a deadly dagger.

"I merely wanted to point out," Kane began in his most infuriatingly casual tone, "that you have been fuming continuously for two weeks, since Parsonawitz put his laser up for auction."

"*My* laser," Ardala interrupted.

"*His* laser," Kane countered. "Warhead built the laser. Parsonawitz is president of Warhead. Thus, the laser is his."

"And he ruined my deal!" she snarled. "I had the Gavilans eating out of my hand! Three million credits they paid me, and I could have milked them for five more!"

"Ardala, you know pirates stole your laser. It had

nothing to do with—"

"Because Parsonawitz hired them to steal it! Just so he could raise the price of his!"

Kane looked at Ardala for a moment with his sardonic smile, then started to laugh.

The sound of his laughter drove Ardala into a blind rage. Wildly she swung her hand toward Kane's face, her fingers arched into claws.

With blinding speed, Kane's hand shot up and caught her wrist in a painful grip. "Ah-ah," he said, smiling. "We don't know what kind of special polish is on those beautiful fingernails. What color is that . . . lavender? It matches your gown so perfectly."

Ardala wrenched her arm free and stalked away. Kane caught up with her in a few of his long strides, but she studiously ignored him.

Despite her words, Kane was sure she knew he was right. Parsonawitz hadn't arranged for her laser to be stolen. But it *had* been stolen; her deal with the Gavilans *had* gone sour. And it wasn't even the loss of the money that bothered her—she already had many times more than the amount she had lost.

What really galled Ardala was that she had *lost.* She had arranged a complex deal, and it had been snatched from her hands. She needed someone to blame, and Parsonawitz was a convenient scapegoat. She hated him with the same intensity that she loved to *win.*

Kane heard the soft whisk of a door sliding open behind him and his hand instinctively reached for his needle gun. The holster was gone, though; Coprates was too civilized for its citizens to carry weapons—entirely too civilized for Kane's taste.

He spun around in time to see a solitary figure step from the darkness of an office.

"Joachim!" Ardala purred with delight, a warm smile spreading across her face. Her eyes positively glowed with pleasure.

Kane glanced at her doubtfully for a fraction of a second, then turned his attention to Joachim Parsonawitz.

Even by Martian standards, Parsonawitz was tall—well over seven feet; he towered above Kane, looking down at him with a quiet air of superiority and power. Slender, lean, and angular, he wore a crisp suit with fluting ribs sewn into it that gave him the appearance of an ancient Greek column. His pale, genetically enhanced features were almost painfully beautiful, the sign of Mars's ultra-upper class.

Kane's face hardened at the sight of the Martian. A tenant on Luna, Kane was very proud of being a pureblood Terran and had no use for the genetically manipulated creatures that inhabited the solar system.

Ardala, however, had no such prejudice—in fact, Kane doubted that she had any of her original genes intact. She sidled up to Parsonawitz with her most provocative walk. The abrupt change in Ardala's demeanor from rabid hatred to slinky seductiveness was a dangerous sign, Kane knew, and he determined to watch for trouble.

"I didn't know you were going to be here," Ardala said, slipping her arm into the crook of his elbow.

"Nor was I aware that you were invited," Parsonawitz replied, squeezing her hand. "Do you have an interest in the delivery of the laser?"

"Is that what this is about?" Ardala asked. "I didn't know. I just received this." She handed him a plain plastic card that read: *Ardala Valmar's presence is requested at Coprates Court loading dock 14-A tomorrow, 1600 hours.*

There was no signature. None was needed. The simplicity of the invitation—the order, actually—meant it came from the most powerful being in the solar system: the chief officer of RAM, Simund

Holzerhein himself. If he "invited" a person somewhere, he or she went and didn't bother asking why.

"So RAM is going to take delivery of the laser today?" she continued, her voice carefully disinterested. Kane marveled at the skill of her acting.

"Yes," Parsonawitz agreed, controlling his own voice with equal care.

The three resumed walking down the nearly deserted corridor of Mars's largest population center, the very hub of RAM's political-industrial network.

In fact, where is everybody? Kane wondered, looking around the strangely deserted hallway. He suddenly had a very uncomfortable feeling in his solar plexus. Unconsciously his hand slipped back to where his missing needle gun should have been, and he cursed himself again for leaving it behind.

He glanced at Parsonawitz and caught him watching him intently as Ardala wriggled at his side. That Parsonawitz could even think of someone else while Ardala practiced her wiles further disconcerted Kane.

He peered around suspiciously, looking in the niches and dark corners of the hallways as they continued.

"One thing I don't understand," Ardala said casually, "is why Warhead—RAM's own munitions division—put its laser on public auction, only to sell the weapon to another RAM company?"

"I can't answer that," Parsonawitz said grimly.

"But surely you knew RAM was selling the laser to itself?" she persisted, an edge of anger creeping into her voice.

"Miss Valmar, I am simply a cog in the huge machine that is the Russo-American Mercantile. I do not know the details of every policy."

"Oh, but the president of Warhead must be a very big cog."

A slight movement crossed the edge of Kane's vision. He snapped his head around toward the movement but saw only shadows. Kane felt the hairs on the back of his neck stand up.

Kane looked at Parsonawitz. The tall Martian was watching him again, a slight smile on his lips.

The barest hint of a sound reached Kane's ears, like the soft rustle of cloth moving. Kane spun around as five shadows detached from the wall and leaped at him.

Even before the first black-robed figure reached him, Kane was already moving, his fighting instincts taking over. Shifting his weight, he swung his leg in a high arc that caught the first attacker on the side of his head. The man went down in a heap in front of the second shadow, who dove over his comrade, directly at Kane.

Letting the momentum of his kick carry him along, Kane dropped to the floor and rolled as the diving man sailed over him and skidded on the slick floor. Before Kane could regain his feet, the next assailant crashed into him, sending him sprawling. He tucked his shoulder and rolled, hitting the ground in an awkward tumble. As Kane struggled to right himself, the remaining attackers converged on him with incredible speed. Kane had a terrifying thought that they might be reflex-enhanced Terrines, RAM's most vicious and best-trained warriors.

A fist smashed into his jaw, driving the thought from his mind. Kane spun with the force of the blow and reeled sideways into the assassin on his right. Before his assailant could react, Kane lashed out, sinking his fist into the man's stomach.

The blow startled the man more than hurt him, but the instant of hesitation gave Kane the opportunity he needed. He kicked at his assailant's leg, feeling the bone break. The man screamed and started to fall, but Kane swung him around and threw him at the remaining attackers. The wounded man clutched at one of his companions, and they fell in a tangle of arms and legs.

The last assassin paused, studying Kane before moving. The element of surprise was gone, and against an opponent of Kane's skill, a more careful attack was needed.

The man feinted with his left, then shot a lightning-quick pile driver at Kane's midsection. Kane twisted away and counterpunched to his attacker's head. The blow connected and the black-clad assailant staggered back a step. Kane followed relentlessly, battering him with combination punches until the man was unconscious on his feet.

There was no mercy in Kane's attack. He had grown up in the toughest part of the "organized area" that had once been Los Angeles, where the law of the street was that only one person walked away from a fight. Although he was many years removed from the Los Angelorg ghetto, that instinct had never died.

Kane grabbed the assailant's mask and forced his head back to expose his throat. As Kane drew his arm back for a killing blow, another hand gripped his wrist.

"That's enough, 'Killer,'" Parsonawitz said calmly. "You don't need to prove your point by killing my men."

Kane was so deep in battle-fury that he nearly attacked Parsonawitz. "Your . . . men," he panted. "You . . . arranged this?" His green eyes flashed savagely.

"Let's call it a test," Parsonawitz replied. "The company wanted to see if you were worth the price you charge for heading security on the laser test."

"That little game is going to cost you another fifteen thousand credits!" Kane snarled.

Parsonawitz shrugged. "You seem to be worth your fee."

Kane continued to stare at him, his breath rasping heavily through clenched teeth. His eyes burned with hatred as his hands compulsively twitched.

"You've learned remarkable self-control," Ardala purred, patting Kane's shoulder. "I'm surprised Joachim is still alive."

"He owes me money!" Kane growled.

Ardala laughed lightly and turned to Parsonawitz. "Well, my dear, you'd better make sure you owe him that money for a very long time."

Parsonawitz looked at her, then at Kane. As a high-ranking official in the RAM hierarchy, he had spent his life insulated by the power of his position; he could use people as he saw fit and throw them away without a thought about consequences. No one could hurt him. But Kane was different from the mass of corporate underlings he was accustomed to dealing with. There was a touch of madness in the man. For the first time in his life, Parsonawitz felt a twinge of fear.

"And what's this about you heading security for the laser test?" Ardala turned to Kane. "You never told me about that, Cornelius."

Kane blinked at her. She never used his first name unless she was furious with him. He grinned, knowing that would infuriate her even more. "It's just a job, darling," he said. "I didn't mention it because the subject never came up."

"I hired Kane to escort the laser to a test site in the asteroid belt," Parsonawitz added. "There has been some trouble lately with lasers being stolen."

Ardala looked at him sharply, then quickly masked her eyes. "And are you responsible for any of those thefts?"

Parsonawitz looked genuinely surprised by the

accusation. "Me? No, of course not! Where did you ever get an idea like that?"

"Oh, intuition, perhaps," Ardala drawled. "I had a laser I was negotiating to sell, but it was stolen and I lost a great deal of money. That left the market open for your laser."

"I wasn't . . ." Parsonawitz began, flustered. "I didn't . . ."

Ardala reached up and stroked his face with her fingertips. "Please don't concern yourself with matters in the past," she purred. "I don't. I am more concerned that the past doesn't repeat itself. Sometimes I find it helpful to have a reminder."

Ardala's hand moved with the speed of lightning across Parsonawitz's cheek, leaving a bloody trail.

He jumped back from her with his hand clasped to his face, his eyes wide with disbelief.

"Oh, I'm so sorry," Ardala said. "I must have a ragged edge on one of my fingernails. Did I hurt you?"

Parsonawitz stared at the bloody smear on his fingers, then looked at Ardala and Kane. They took a step closer to him, Ardala all silky smooth, like a tigress ready to pounce, Kane's face and body hard, like a tightly coiled spring about to explode.

"St-stay away from me, both of you!" he quailed, backing away.

Ardala's eyes narrowed in an expression full of venom. "You never did tell me why Warhead sold the laser to another RAM firm."

"It was policy," Parsonawitz said quickly. "Orders."

"Orders from whom?" Kane demanded, taking another threatening step closer.

"From me," a voice whispered behind them. Despite the soft tone, the voice itself was as harsh and hard as forged iron.

Kane and Ardala spun around as a whirl of flickering colors resolved into the holographic image of

Simund Holzerhein.

Ardala had met Holzerhein before and always found herself fascinated by the stern old man with the thin, brutal mouth.

Yet he wasn't a man—merely a holographic projection. Holzerhein was a program in the RAM computer system. More than a century ago, he had had his mental engrams digitized and loaded into the computer network to avoid death. What remained of his body was rumored to be moldering somewhere in the recesses of Holzerhein Crag, sustained by the most elaborate life-support systems RAM could buy or develop.

The long decades of existence without a body had changed Holzerhein, and not for the better. In life he had been a cold, utterly ruthless businessman whose scruples extended no farther than expediency. As a computer personality, he had lost whatever tenuous hold on humanity he had ever possessed. A scowl perpetually crossed his face. Nothing mattered to him but his own ambitions and the twisted, intricate plans he dreamed up in the depths of his electronic boredom.

Ardala took a step forward, almost mesmerized by the cold gray eyes that never blinked.

Parsonawitz, his mouth gaping, stared at Holzerhein's hologram.

Kane nudged him roughly in the ribs. "Hey," he said quietly.

"Hmm?" Parsonawitz said, glancing down at him.

"You know, you really should have a doctor look at that cut," Kane said.

The tall Martian gingerly touched his cheek. "It's nothing," he said, "just a scratch."

"Ah, but you should know that Ardala's fingernail polish is occasionally poisonous," Kane said with a smile.

Parsonawitz paled. He swallowed noisily. "Wh-what kind of poison?"

"I believe she usually uses a neuroparalyzer," he said nonchalantly. "It's slow acting, but you should begin to feel the first symptoms any minute."

Parsonawitz whirled and bolted away, his long arms and legs pumping wildly. Kane started to laugh, a deep roaring laugh that echoed through the halls of the Coprates complex.

"Mister Kane," Holzerhein said, his unblinking eyes still locked on Ardala. "The Warhead Laser XIV is currently entering its landing pattern. Be so good as to oversee the touchdown and transfer to a transport ship."

"That's what you're paying me for," Kane said with an insolent smirk.

"Then earn your money," Holzerhein said, turning his gaze chillingly on Kane.

Kane nodded and waved in a mock salute as he backed away and around a corner.

"You're still here?" Holzerhein said to Ardala.

"So are you," she answered.

"I am . . . everywhere. Part of me is here, while another part is waiting at the dock to receive the laser and say a few words to the multitudes who are waiting to catch a glimpse of the most destructive weapon this solar system has seen, the weapon they believe will give Mars back the prestige it lost in the Earth rebellion."

"Why the elaborate game of the auction, then? Why sell the laser to yourself?"

Holzerhein chuckled, a dry, rattling sound that only vaguely resembled a laugh. "You're more intelligent than that, Ardala Valmar."

"Very well, then. Who is it that you wanted to inform that RAM has the laser?"

Holzerhein nodded with satisfaction. "The House

of Gavilan."

"I was about to sell the Gavilans my—" Ardala began angrily.

"Your laser was a toy compared to the Warhead XIV," Holzerhein interrupted. "But it was a destructive toy that would have interfered with my plans."

"Are you saying *you* arranged for pirates to steal *my* laser?"

"No, but I knew they would."

"How? Those scavengers are the most unpredictable thieves in the solar system."

"They are players in the game."

Ardala watched him for a moment. "Players? . . . Game? What are you talking about?"

"A card game I played when I was young," he said with a thin, reptilian smile. "It was a game from Earth called Poker. You bet that your cards were better than your opponents' cards. A simple game, really, but the skill came in knowing your opponents. Oh, sometimes the cards ran against you, and then there was nothing you could do. But more often, if you *knew* the people you were playing against, knew how they thought, how they would bet, you could defeat them."

"And win all the money?" Ardala said sarcastically. "What do you need with money, Simund?"

"The money was unimportant. It simply told you how badly you beat your opponents. The important thing was *knowing* how your opponents played."

"Holzerhein, what do you want from all this? You can't want power—you are already the most powerful man in the history of humanity. There is enough money at your disposal to buy anything in the solar system. And if what you want doesn't exist, you can order your army of scientists to invent it."

"I doubt that you could understand what I want."

"Try me," she said, leaning forward hungrily.

"I want my plan to *work,*" he said.

"Your plan for what?"

"It doesn't matter what the plan is, as long as it works. I want to understand my players well enough that I know what they will do before they know. I want to manipulate my players into positions so that their actions will advance my plan." Despite Holzerhein's flat, emotionless eyes, Ardala heard an edge of mania in his voice.

She stared at him for a long moment. "I don't think there is an entity in the universe that can know and control so many factors."

Holzerhein shrugged. "You asked what I wanted. That's it."

"And am I one of your 'players'?"

"Of course you are, Ardala Valmar. I *know* you, better than you know yourself."

Ardala frowned, angry at the idea of being manipulated by Holzerhein. "That makes me want to see your plan ruined."

"Even if your success will advance my goals?"

She paused, shaking her head. "I don't like being controlled, Simund. Have you calculated that in your grand plan?"

"I'm counting on it, Ardala."

The two of them stood for a long moment, studying each other.

"As long as we understand each other so well," she said at last, "shall we begin the game?"

Holzerhein replied, "We already have."

Chapter Four

The next morning Kemal stepped from his quarters and nearly tripped over what appeared to be a large pile of rags huddled in the dark alcove of his doorway.

"What . . .?" Kemal began, regaining his balance.

"I beg your pardon, young sir." The bundle of dirty clothes started to move, unfolding arms and legs. A colorless face lined by innumerable wrinkles and creases emerged. "Do you think you could help me up, young sir?" he asked. "The body isn't as spry as it used to be."

Stunned, Kemal could only reach down wordlessly and grasp the man's thin arm.

"Thank you so much," the old man said, struggling to his feet.

"Were you here all night?" Kemal asked.

"That I was," he answered. "Must have dozed off. I wanted to see you. Very important."

"Why didn't you just knock?"

"Oh, I didn't want to disturb Your Highness. Morning's a good enough time for the likes of me."

Kemal frowned. There it was again, that deferential treatment shown him by another man who should have been able to approach him as an equal.

"Well, come in and have some tea. Then you can tell me what's so important that you had to wait outside my door all night to see me about." Kemal stepped back into his room, and the old man shuffled after him.

"That's very kind of you, young sir, to make a fuss over me like this."

The man's excessive humility was beginning to irritate Kemal. "First of all, I'd like to know who . . ." he began, more harshly than he intended. Seeing the ancient man's face up close, Kemal paused, a flicker of memory stirring. "Wait a minute. You're Shaz, aren't you?"

The man's bushy eyebrows rocketed up his forehead, and a look of childish pleasure spread across his wrinkled face. "That's right! Old Shazimar, that's me!"

"From the gardens. How long has it been? Must be more than eighty years," Kemal said, secretly proud that he was again counting time in Mercurian years.

"That's right. You used to play in the gardens, before they sent you away to the academy. Let me look at you, young prince." The old man began to reach for Kemal's shoulders, then hesitated and drew back, as if he dared not touch a member of the royal family.

Kemal also noticed that Shazimar studiously avoided calling him by name; his rank forbad that familiarity.

Purposefully, Kemal grasped the man's arms, pulling him forward into a hug. "Shazimar, my old friend, it's good to see you again. I'm glad you came to visit me."

Shazimar stepped back from the embrace, his eyes moist. "You've grown into a fine man, haven't you," he said, smiling.

"Thank you. Now, what can I do for you?"

Some of the childish innocence left the man's eyes, as if a mask suddenly dropped away. He leaned forward and whispered, "Is this room safe?"

Safe? Kemal wondered. Shaz could only mean safe from listening devices. The abrupt change from the harmless, doddering gardener to a man concerned about electronic surveillance seemed out of character. Kemal stepped back, suspicion forming like a knot in his stomach.

"Yes," he said slowly, watching the old man. "The room is clean. I've checked it myself."

"Good," Shazimar said. "I needed to tell someone, and I didn't know who else to turn to."

"Tell me what?" Kemal asked.

"They killed him, young sir."

"Killed who?"

"Your uncle."

Kemal stepped closer and grabbed the gardener by the shoulders. "Gordon is dead?"

"Not Gordon . . . your uncle Garrick."

Kemal felt his jaw drop open. Garrick! He had met his uncle only once, years before, when Garrick had come to the Ulyanov Military Academy on Mars to invite Kemal back to Mercury at Gordon's request. That was the beginning of Kemal's entanglement with Gavilan intrigues—and the end of Garrick's involvement with the family. After that visit to Mars, Garrick had simply disappeared. No one seemed to miss him, and Kemal had a feeling Gordon was pleased his brother was gone.

Kemal sat heavily on a chair near his desk. "Who did it?"

"Three gennies it was, sir," Shazimar said. "Desert Runners, I think. They strangled him."

"Why haven't you gone to Gordon with this information?"

"It's not my place to go to the Sun King," he said. "Besides," Shazimar shuffled his feet nervously and looked away from Kemal's gaze as if trying to avoid what he had to say. "There was another . . ." he said hesitantly.

"Who else?" Kemal demanded.

The old man frowned and looked around the room nervously. Finally he said, "Dalton was there, too."

Kemal slumped back in his chair. "Dalton murdered Garrick?"

Shazimar nodded. "They chased me off," he said quickly. Having opened the floodgates, he wanted to tell his story as fast as possible. "But I know that greenhouse. I know where to hide and listen and watch. I saw them do terrible things," he said, forcing the words out. "And Dalton watched, too."

Kemal closed his eyes and rubbed the bridge of his nose. "Garrick left Mercury years ago. Why would Dalton have him killed?"

"I'm sure I don't know, young sir."

Abruptly Kemal stood up. "Can you take me to where it happened?"

"If that's what you want."

"I do. Let's go!"

❍ ❍ ❍ ❍ ❍

The garden was much as Kemal remembered it: green. He didn't know much about plants, but the rarity of colors on Mercury—and especially green—made the lush growth of the greenhouse stand out vividly in his childhood memories.

The garden was enclosed in a huge, transparent dome on the outer edge of Mercury Prime. Although the verdant park was no secret, most of Hielo's inhabitants preferred the more sophisticated pleasures available in the palace to the quiet peace of the garden.

Yet Kemal could remember his father bringing him here, to run across the soft grass and to splash in the small pond fed by a stream, which should be somewhere close by, he thought. Kemal craned his neck, looking around, but could find no sign of either stream or pond.

The old man led Kemal through the garden at an infuriatingly slow pace. Kemal bridled at the wasted time, but he also knew Shazimar couldn't match his own anxious excitement, so he swallowed his impatience and followed quietly.

Finally Shazimar stopped at a rough patch of dirt near a small wooden building and said, "Here's where they brought your uncle."

Kemal kneeled at the edge of the bare land and inspected the area. Something violent definitely had happened here recently; the plants were badly mangled, their leaves crushed, their stems broken. The earth had been scuffed and smoothed over carelessly. Long gashes that looked like claw marks crisscrossed the dirt, and a very clumsy hand had tried to cover the imprint of a body outlined in the soil.

Kemal looked up at Shazimar. "Have you disturbed this area? Did you rake here?"

Shazimar recoiled with a look of horror. "Sir! Do you think I would leave the ground looking like this?

A raking smooths, heals the land. These gouges have hurt the—"

"Yes, yes, of course," Kemal quickly interjected. "I should have known. I was just wondering if this is how they left the area. I don't see any signs of blood."

"No, young sir, there wouldn't be any blood. As I said, he was strangled."

"And you saw that?"

The old man took a deep breath and frowned. "Yes, I saw it," he said bitterly.

Kemal stood and faced him. "Shazimar, this is important. Would you tell the full council what you just told me?"

The gardener's eyes grew wide with fear. "Oh, sir, it's not my place to talk to the council, or to accuse a prince."

"I'll do the talking," Kemal said, "but I need you to verify what I say."

Shazimar stepped back, fidgeting. "I don't know . . ." he stammered. "I couldn't . . . face all those . . . I just want to live my remaining time among my plants, without trouble."

"Listen to me," Kemal insisted. "You knew my father."

"He was a good man." Shazimar nodded. "And a good king."

"You know Gordon, too."

Shazimar's face creased in concentration, his eyebrows bending into a frown. He shook his head but said nothing.

"And after him will come Dalton," Kemal continued relentlessly.

The old man's frown deepened.

"Are these the kind of men you want to see ruling Mercury? Shazimar, you can stop them!"

The old man slumped under the weight of his duty. Finally he shook his head. "I'm sorry, young sir," he said weakly. "I'm old and afraid. I just want to live out my life quietly."

Anger swelled into a flood within Kemal. His fists balled at his sides, he took a step toward Shazimar. The old gardener flinched and turned aside, his hands quavering before his face in an effort to ward off the coming blow.

Kemal watched Shaz shaking in terror and wondered if he was really capable of inspiring such fear in a harmless attendant. What kind of treatment were the servants accustomed to from Gavilans?

Gently Kemal reached out to the old man and patted his arm. "If you don't want to tell anyone about this, you don't have to, Shaz. I won't make you."

Shazimar looked up at him gratefully. "I don't have to?"

"Of course not."

"I'm sorry, truly sorry, young sir. Forgive an old man's weakness," he said.

"Don't worry about it," Kemal said. "You told me, and I know something I didn't before." He bent down to inspect the patch of disturbed dirt. "And now that I know, I'll find a way to prove Dalton killed his uncle. Do you know where they took the body?"

"No, I didn't see that, young—" He stopped himself, then added quietly, "Kemal."

Surprised to hear his name pass the old man's lips, Kemal glanced up at him, a smile playing across his face. "Thank you, Shazimar. Does that mean we're friends?"

The gardener blushed furiously beneath his dark complexion and stammered, "Well, if that's not . . . presumptuous."

Kemal laughed and went back to scouring the scene of the murder. Shazimar watched for a long time, then sighed.

"I'm afraid this garden hasn't been good for your

family," he said.

"Hmm?" Kemal answered, but his concentration was centered on the patch of ground.

Kemal finished his inspection and sat down beside the wooden shed, facing the old man. "You liked my father, didn't you? As a person, I mean."

Shazimar smiled broadly. "Oh, yes! He used to come here often to wander by the old creek that fed the—"

"The pond!" Kemal finished, delighted. "I remember that pond! What happened to it?"

Shazimar's face darkened. "Oh, they filled it in after . . . you know."

"No, I don't know. What happened?" Kemal asked with a sinking feeling in his stomach.

Shazimar looked at him, puzzled. "Your father died in that pond."

Kemal bolted upright. "No one ever told me! Are you saying my father drowned here?"

"That's what they say."

"Did you see it?" Kemal shouted, grabbing the gardener by the shoulders. "Were you here?"

"N-no, I was sent away by Gordon."

"He was here? Gordon was with my father when he died?"

Kemal's eyes blazed as he stared at the old man. Shazimar backed away a step, frightened.

"Don't even think like that, young sir! Thoughts like that lead to trouble and death!"

"If Ossip was killed by Gor—"

Shazimar howled. "No!" he cried. "Don't say it! Things happen . . . It was long ago . . . Let the dead rest," he gibbered.

Kemal shook him. "Stop it, Shaz!" he said through clenched teeth. "He was my father! I've got to know what happened to him! If Gordon murdered him, I'm going to prove it!"

"Please, sir," Shazimar wailed. "You're hurting me!"

Kemal blinked and looked at his thumbs digging into the gardener's shoulders. He quickly released his grip and stepped back.

"I'm sorry, Shaz. I lost my head," he said. "This has been eating at me for a long time."

Shazimar shrugged, wincing slightly with the movement. "It's all right, young sir," he said. He looked at Kemal with concern. "I didn't realize you didn't know about Ossip."

"No one ever said anything to me about his death," Kemal replied bitterly. "It's been a mystery to me since I was a child."

"Well, I'm sorry it had to be me who told you."

Kemal smiled wanly. "At least the news came from a friend." His face turned grim. "Shaz, I *am* going to bring my father's killer to justice. You can help me. You've *got* to tell the council what you know about Ossip's death—and Garrick's."

"Oh, sir." Shazimar recoiled in fear. "Don't ask me that! You said I didn't have to!"

"You don't *have* to, but I'm asking you as a friend," Kemal said. "If not for me, then for the sake of my father's memory."

Shazimar hesitated, his face a battleground of conflicting emotions. Slowly he said, "Would it do any good? The word of a gardener?"

"We've got to try, Shaz!"

"Well, if you think it's the right thing."

"It *is* the right thing to do!"

Shazimar shuffled his feet uncertainly. "Young sir, I'm afraid . . ."

Kemal held his hand up, stopping the gardener. "Shaz, I'm going to bring this information to the council myself, whether you speak to them or not. But I *do* need your help."

Shazimar only looked at him bleakly; he closed his eyes and shook his head in the affirmative.

❍ ❍ ❍ ❍ ❍

Back in his quarters, Kemal quickly sat at his computer and activated the screen. He started to type in his mother's access code, eager to share the first real information he had learned about his father's death. Despite the Sun King's universal disinterest and apathy over Ossip, surely she would want to know what happened to her husband.

He finished the code and paused before entering it, wondering if she would indeed be interested. He had few childhood memories of his mother; she was a lively, beautiful woman who had hovered at the edges of his life, always dressing for a formal state function or exhausted after attending one. She cared for him, certainly, but in a distant, preoccupied way, just as she had cared for her husband. Kemal couldn't remember ever seeing her touch Ossip.

Kemal had visited her just after he returned to Hielo, and found her much as he remembered her—as beautiful and delicate as a carefully made doll. She had been born and reared in the upper strata of Mercury Prime's aristocracy, trained to be a gracious hostess and dazzling decoration.

Their conversation had been stilted, at best. After Ossip's death, she had retreated to the women's quarter of the Palace, taking on her role as Royal Widow, with all the respect and duties that the position brought. She knew very little about Ossip's death; in fact, Kemal discovered, she remembered very little about him at all. The royal physician, Catiff, had "treated" her for grief with an extensive hypno-drug therapy that removed her memories of Ossip, and most of her life to that point. She had only her role left, and lived in it completely.

No, he finally decided, she wouldn't be interested in his discovery. Her old life had no meaning for her, and he could do nothing but stir old embers that had no fire. He canceled her code and called up *Council Procedures* instead.

Any authorized delegate had the right to present petitions and speak to the assembly. Usually a representative simply stood up during a session and said what he or she had to say, but Kemal wanted to make absolutely certain he would be heard; he carefully typed in a request to address the next session of the council.

The computer digested his petition to speak for a few minutes, then assigned him a time: just after lunch the next day. However, the computer screen went on to say, due to a "recent disruption," the council would meet in the royal audience hall.

Kemal switched off the computer and sat back in his chair, watching his reflection in the dark screen. The image didn't seem so repulsive to him now. Yet there was one other thing—foolish, perhaps, but necessary—that he needed to do.

He opened a communication channel to the Sun King, with the highest priority code.

Within minutes Gordon Gavilan's image flashed on the screen. He looked tired and worn; his face was puffy, and an ugly red scar snaked along his cheek.

"This better be very important, Kemal," Gordon said, his voice a mixture of exhaustion and anger.

"It is, Majesty."

"Does this concern your request to address the council tomorrow?"

Kemal raised his eyebrow, surprised by the speed and thoroughness of the king's electronic spy network. "Yes."

Gordon winced at some ache and looked away. "Tell

me now," he said. "I've just gone through a miserable morning with Doctor Catiff and I don't feel like receiving guests."

"This isn't something to discuss over an open comm link," Kemal said.

Gordon paused, his eyes narrowing as he studied Kemal's face on the viewing screen. Despite the Sun King's pain, there was something in Kemal's grim determination that arrested him. "Very well," Gordon said at length. "Come to my quarters in an hour." He broke the connection.

❍ ❍ ❍ ❍ ❍

The twisted, byzantine palace always irritated Kemal. He was accustomed to the clean, straight-line efficiency of a rocketjock's world; the contorted corridors of Hielo confused him, made him uneasy.

The architecture was a dizzying mishmash of too many styles. Generations of Gavilan kings had added their own touches until the royal grounds looked as chaotic as an old Earth city.

The predominant style was derived from the ancient Muslim culture. The walls were constructed of long, alternating bands of red and white stone that gave the palace the appearance of a huge peppermint candy. At frequent intervals niches had been cut into the walls, with stone benches covered with pillows.

Gordon's own taste ran to the baroque. As Kemal neared the king's quarters, he noticed a change in the decorations; doors became more heavily ornamented, carved with interlocking knots and flowers. Columns twisted their way to the ceiling under a busy welter of vines and vegetation. Kemal got the feeling that Gordon couldn't stand a flat, bare surface.

A vast army of courtiers, guardsmen, ministers, officials, and court hangers-on added to the decorative confusion of the hallways. Kemal had begun working his way through the crowd politely, but by the time he reached Gordon's personal suites he was impatiently elbowing through the mass of humanity.

As he approached his uncle's royal apartments, Kemal saw Dalton step out of the king's quarters.

"I'm glad you're feeling better, Father," Dalton called into the room, a shallow smile playing on his lips. "I'll look in on you later."

As Dalton stepped away from the door, his politic smile dropped away, replaced by a vicious scowl that stopped Kemal.

Dalton looked up and locked eyes with him.

"You!" Dalton hissed through clenched teeth. "What are you doing here?"

Kemal put on his best look of innocence. "Just visiting a relative who has been hurt. The same as you, I'm sure." He couldn't resist adding a small barb.

"Yes." Dalton sneered. "How very caring of you."

"This is a time when family is important to a person," Kemal said as casually as he could. He knew he shouldn't goad his cousin—whose frustration over his failed assassination attempt would be nearly boiling over—but something else inside him wanted to push a little further. "Have you tried to contact Garrick?"

Dalton's eyes suddenly blazed, then just as quickly darkened. "What do you know about Garrick?"

"Nothing at all," Kemal replied innocently. "Just that he is Gordon's brother and should be told of the attempt on his life."

Dalton studied him under hooded eyes that still smoldered. "I know what you're trying to do, Cousin," he spat. "You replaced me on the Rising Sun project, but I won't let you usurp my throne!"

Kemal took a step back and raised a hand to his chest theatrically. "Why, Cousin," he said with mock surprise. "You wound me!"

A deep guttural sound broke from Dalton's throat and his hand made a quick move toward his belt. Suddenly both men were holding mono knives, the lasers along the edges of their blades shimmering with rainbow colors.

Someone in the crowd screamed, and a small space instantly cleared around them. Several guardsmen reached for their weapons but couldn't decide how to restrain royal princes.

Kemal knew Dalton had the advantage in size and strength, but he was slow and not as battle-trained. Kemal felt adrenaline energy surge in his body as his muscles tensed for combat.

A small voice of reason awoke inside him then. He almost hungered for the fight, but knew it shouldn't be here. "Dalton!" he shouted. "This isn't the time or place for this! Remember where you are!"

Dalton glared at him, then looked around at the crowd of people staring at them. Slowly he lowered his knife, watching Kemal warily until he sheathed his own blade.

Dalton stepped forward and roughly shouldered past Kemal. "This isn't over," he whispered.

"No, it isn't," Kemal told his retreating back.

Scowling, Kemal stepped between the confused guards and knocked at Gordon's door. After the briefest hesitation for the cameras to verify his identification, the door silently opened and he entered the royal presence.

Gordon was having his hair cut when Kemal came in. Actually the king was having his beard trimmed to even it up after Doctor Catiff had hacked half of it away treating a cut on his cheek.

The ancient Doctor Catiff hovered close by, wringing his thin hands in a comic gesture of stylized worry. The old physician had served the Gavilan family for three generations, and his skin looked like yellow parchment stretched over bones that jutted out at awkward angles.

"For someone with such an important matter to discuss, you took your own time in coming here," Gordon snapped peevishly.

"I ran into a problem in the hall," Kemal replied.

"Well, what is it that you can't tell me over the comm lines?"

Kemal glanced at Catiff and the barber. "I think this is something we should discuss in private."

"Oh, very well," Gordon said and made a short gesture of dismissal. "Leave me, both of you."

Doctor Catiff stepped forward obsequiously. "Shall we come back later, Your Majesty?"

"No, you've tortured me enough. Get out!"

The two servants left, shuffling out under Kemal's impatient gaze.

After they'd gone, Gordon turned on him. "Now will you tell me what this is all about, Kemal?"

"Did you know your brother Garrick is dead?"

Gordon winced slightly. "Yes," he said softly. "His body was just found in Caloris. How did you know?"

"He didn't die in Caloris. He was killed here on Hielo. In the greenhouse."

The king's eyes narrowed as he watched Kemal. "Is this what you are going to tell the council tomorrow?" he asked slowly.

"Yes."

"Why are you telling me this?"

"Because . . ." Kemal hesitated, unsure of what to say. No matter what he felt about Gordon, he was about to tell him his son was a murderer who was planning to assassinate him. "Because Dalton had him killed. He was there."

Gordon closed his eyes, a look of profound pain spreading across his features. After a very long silence, he whispered, "How do you know this? Was there a witness?"

Kemal looked at him a moment, not sure whether to reveal the truth or not. He didn't trust his uncle enough to tell him about Shazimar, yet Gordon had guessed more than Kemal wanted to tell him. A vague fear began to gnaw at the back of his mind.

Gordon slumped back in his chair. Suddenly he seemed very old as he raised his hand to his face and rubbed his eyes. Finally he looked up at Kemal, his cheeks drained of color. "Why would he do that?"

Kemal frowned. "Can't you guess, Your Majesty? Your brother is murdered. You are the object of an assassination attempt!"

Gordon turned away, his eyes hardening again. Kemal could almost hear him weighing options, making plans.

"You haven't told me why you are telling me this."

Kemal looked at him, puzzled. "I'm going to present evidence that your son has committed treason. I felt you should know before you heard it in session," he said.

Gordon raised his eyebrows. "An honorable man?" he said with a faint trace of irony. "How rare."

Kemal didn't answer. "That's all I wanted to say. If there's nothing else . . ."

"Yes, of course," Gordon said, already deep in thought. "You may go."

"Thank you, Your Majesty." Kemal backed to the door, but he paused before leaving. "I'll see you tomorrow at the council meeting."

Gordon was no longer aware of him. He sat for a long time after Kemal left, staring at his computer screen. Finally he activated the machine and typed in Dalton's personal communication code.

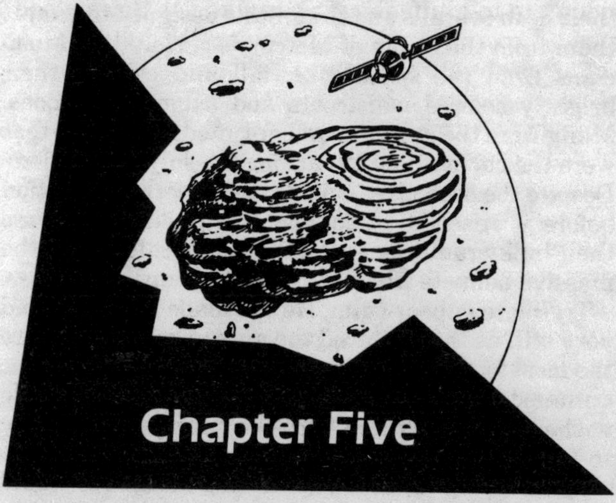

Chapter Five

Kemal paced before the great doors of the audience hall, nervously chewing his lower lip.

He had been waiting all morning for Shazimar, but there was no sign of the old gardener, not even a message. When the council broke for lunch an hour ago, he had sent a guardsman to fetch the old man from his greenhouse. The guard hadn't returned yet, although the delegates themselves were beginning to filter back.

Kemal suddenly realized he was walking at a breakneck speed up and down the hall, his head down. With a conscious effort he stopped and took three deep breaths.

It didn't help. He was about to begin pacing again when a group of delegates turned the corner, laughing among themselves. Kemal recognized them by their costumes and body types: the short, squat Miners with their drab overalls and thick boots designed to protect them from the rigors of Mercury's surface; the Musicians from the spacedocks, tall and thin in their brightly colored waistcoats and baggy pantaloons. Many wore the rose-and amber-tinted eyeglasses that were the current fashion among the surface dwellers. Despite the protective shields that absorbed radiation before it reached Hielo, the Mariposans still wore their bulky radiation suits, though most forewent the massive helmets when on Mercury Prime.

Trying to appear calm, Kemal made himself stand very still as they entered the audience hall. He wore the most formal suit he could find, a vivid yellow robe trimmed in black and gold—the Gavilan colors. He wished to be identified with the ruling family today so his words would carry more weight, but he felt very uncomfortable in the flowing robes. He would have much preferred a functional rocketjock suit or the colorful sashes and scarves of the Desert Dancers.

The delegates entered the hall, barely acknowledging his presence with polite nods. Kemal peered past them down the long corridor but saw no sign of Shazimar or the guard he had sent.

More delegates approached. Lunch was over and the afternoon session of the council would soon convene. If Shazimar didn't arrive in time, Kemal would just have to present his accusations and hope the gardener would testify for the investigation that would follow.

Squaring his shoulders, Kemal stood before the great doors of the hall and drew another deep breath, then gripped the ornately carved handles.

"Preparing yourself for the session, Cousin?" he heard Dalton call.

Kemal turned to him, a little too quickly. "Yes," he said, trying to keep his voice calm.

"Any hints for us about what you're going to say?" Dalton said with a sneering smile as he approached. "You've got us all wondering what's so important. You didn't list any subject matter in your request to address the council."

"I didn't know it was necessary."

"It isn't, of course," Dalton continued, smoothing his own saffron robe. "But as a courtesy . . ."

"Since when have you been concerned with courtesy?" Kemal snapped.

"Tut-tut," Dalton said. "You won't make any friends in the council with that surly attitude."

"Are you attending the session?" Kemal asked, waving a casual hand at Dalton's formal attire.

"Yes, I believe I shall. It's time to learn the duties of a Sun King. A sort of apprenticeship, if you will."

Kemal's eyes narrowed and a muscle jumped out along his jaw. "You will never have the throne!" he said between clenched teeth. "I'll see to that myself, Dalton!"

"You can't stop me, Little Cousin," Dalton whispered, leaning close. An ugly humor played across his face, mixed with hatred and certainty. He pushed his way past Kemal to enter the audience hall.

Kemal shook himself to clear the knot of tension in his head as he prepared to follow Dalton into the session, but before he could enter he heard the steady footsteps of a guardsman.

He spun around as the guard he had sent to the greenhouse approached—alone—and snapped to attention.

"Where's Shazimar?" Kemal nearly shouted.

The guard frowned and pursed his lips as if to

squelch his message. "The gardener is dead, my lord."

Kemal felt his jaw drop. "What?"

The guard stood ramrod straight. "I said, the . . ."

"I heard you!" Kemal exploded.

"Yes, Sire." The guard winced slightly but didn't waver in his stiff stance. He was obviously prepared for Kemal's anger.

"How did he die?"

"Natural causes, Sire."

Kemal rubbed his forehead, trying to think clearly. "Did you see the body? Are you sure he's dead?"

"I'm sure, Your Highness. I saw the body."

"And there were no marks?"

The guard's eyes flickered to Kemal's face quizzically. "Marks?"

"Signs of violence, man! Think!"

The guard's eyes snapped forward again. "No, Sire. No violence. Doctor Catiff showed . . ."

"Catiff was there?" Kemal interrupted. "What was the royal physician doing in the greenhouse?"

"I don't know, my lord."

Kemal stood for a moment, his mind spinning. Without Shazimar, there was no link between Dalton and Garrick, or Gordon and Ossip. He could make accusations, but they would be hollow, unsubstantiated.

"Will that be all, Sire?" the guard asked.

Kemal looked up, jolted from his thoughts by the man's voice. "Eh? Oh, yes, you may go. And thank you. I'm sorry I shouted at you."

The guard looked at him uncertainly. "Yes, Sire," he said and paused, confused by Kemal's apology. No one of royal rank had ever apologized to him before. "If you need anything else . . ."

Kemal nodded to him absently. "I'll call you. Thanks."

As the guard backed away, Kemal turned to the great doors, unsure of what to do. He couldn't walk away, but neither could he speak to the council.

He heard the sergeant-at-arms call for order and rap his Staff of State to open the afternoon session of the council. Reluctantly Kemal pushed the doors open and stepped into the audience hall as though he were walking to his execution.

"And here is our first speaker," he heard Gordon call out to the assembly. "Prince Kemal Gavilan. Come up to the dais and tell us your business."

Unlike the council chamber amphitheater, the audience hall was a long, rectangular room that led to a raised platform where Gordon sat. Dalton stood smirking at his side. Chairs had been placed along the walls for the delegates, creating an infinitely long aisle down which Kemal marched. His feet dragged as though gravity had been increased ten times normal.

As he neared the speaker's dais, he stared at Dalton, seeing the smug assurance of his smile. He knows, Kemal realized with a sinking feeling. He glanced at Gordon, but the king's face was a mask of ice. And Gordon told him, he thought.

Kemal forced himself up to the raised stand and turned to face the delegates.

"What is it you wish to bring to the attention of the council?" Gordon said in a monotone voice.

Kemal opened his mouth but found he couldn't make a sound. His tongue felt swollen and dry while his palms were slippery with sweat.

The moment stretched into a minute of agonizing silence.

"Come, come, Cousin," Dalton said beside the king. "Surely you have something to tell the assembly. We're waiting to hear it."

Kemal looked at the delegates watching him. The

long silence was making them restless; several of them began whispering to each other.

"Come on, man," one Miner shouted. "Get on with it!"

Kemal's hand twitched. He tried desperately to think of something—anything—to say, but his mind refused to work.

"Kemal," he heard Gordon call softly.

He spun around to face the king, numb with fury. Gordon studied his face, then seemed to wilt. Weakly he waved in dismissal and looked away.

Kemal turned to the delegates. "I have nothing to say," he told them slowly and stepped off the dais.

The assembly fell silent as Kemal strode down the aisle between them.

"Nothing at all, Cousin?" Dalton called after him. Kemal could hear the supercilious air in his voice. He paused for a split second, then continued walking stiffly.

"You petition to address the council," Dalton went on, goading him, "and when the moment to speak arrives, we get nothing? What's wrong, Kemal? Stage fright?"

A titter of laughter swept through the delegates. Kemal stopped dead and slowly turned. He felt his face burning. An uneasy stillness fell over the assembly as Kemal faced Dalton, raising his hand to point accusingly.

"Dalton," he said hoarsely, his voice like rusted iron, "do not mock me . . . murderer!"

Dalton's face went white with rage. He bolted forward, fumbling at his belt for his weapon.

"Dalton!" Gordon barked and reached out a hand to restrain his son. "Come back and sit *down!*" The last word exploded from the king with enough force to startle Dalton.

The prince stopped and glared at Kemal, hatred

flashing from his eyes. He jerked his arm free of Gordon's grasp and returned slowly to his place beside the throne, staring steadily at Kemal.

"And you," Gordon said, turning his attention to Kemal. "I want to see you in my quarters after this session. Both of you," he swung around angrily to Dalton. "In my chambers! Do you hear me? As soon as the session . . . no, right now!" Gordon rose from his seat, his anger building into a fury. "This council is adjourned!"

The delegates gaped at him in a shocked silence. One Musician scrambled to his feet and quickly raised his arm like a schoolboy. "Your Majesty, surely you don't mean to cancel the afternoon session? We have business . . ."

Gordon took a reckless step toward the man. "Yes, I do!" he shouted. "I told you, the assembly is dismissed! Budgets and trade squabbles! I'm tired of your petty concerns! Get out, all of you!"

The delegates began to rise, a wave of muted anger running through them like the flow of molten metal during the sun time of Mercury's surface.

Kemal walked to the door with deliberate care to mask his feelings. To tell the truth, Kemal wasn't sure what he felt: shock, rage, numbness, fear, or grief. Shazimar was dead because of him. Kemal concentrated very hard on putting one foot in front of the other. That was easier than thinking.

Two guards met him at the door and fell in step with him, one on each side. They didn't touch him and never spoke a word but directed him firmly down the corridor to the royal suite.

○ ○ ○ ○ ○

"I don't understand you, Dalton!" Gordon shouted, slamming his brandy snifter on the table. "Brawling in the corridors of Hielo . . . a shouting match in the audience hall, like some Miner hooligan!"

Dalton sat unconcerned before the vanity mirror, studying his face. He rubbed his upper lip thoughtfully. "You know, I've been thinking of shaving off my mustache," he said casually. "It gives my face a melodramatic look. Don't you think?"

Gordon sputtered, his face turning a deep red. A small artery throbbed in his temple as he swayed above Dalton. Without a word, he turned to a cabinet and snatched out a bottle of rare Terran brandy. He splashed another generous dollop into his snifter and tossed it down.

"You really should learn to relax, Father," Dalton said, leaning back in his chair. "You very nearly lost control in the council yourself today. That can only hurt our position in the government."

Gordon recognized his own admonition in his son's words and heard the mockery in his tone.

"Dammit, Dalton!" Gordon began.

"Uncle," Kemal said as he stepped across the room. "If you're going to argue with your son, I don't see why you called me here."

Gordon turned to his nephew. "Sit down, Kemal."

Kemal remained standing stiffly. "I'd prefer to stand."

"Oh, don't posture in front of me," Gordon cut in. "Sit!"

Kemal didn't move.

Gordon watched him for a long moment, noting the firm set of his jaw, his defiant stance, facing whatever came unafraid—or at least showing no fear.

The Sun King sighed. "There's much of your father in you, boy."

Kemal looked at him quizzically for an instant, then his face hardened again. "Why?" he said, nodding toward Dalton. "Why did you warn him?"

Gordon glanced down, frowning. "He's . . . my son," he said feebly. "I had to know."

"It cost Shazimar his life."

Gordon's eyes snapped up, his face puzzled. "Who?"

"The gardener," Dalton said, obviously bored with the detail.

Gordon shook his head as if he couldn't understand why the old man's life concerned a royal prince.

"The price has been paid," Kemal said fiercely. "Are you satisfied now? Do you know?"

Gordon hesitated, unwilling to face the knowledge. "I know . . ." he began, but couldn't finish the thought.

"Do you know now," Kemal insisted relentlessly, "that your son killed your own brother to clear his way to the throne?"

"The Dancers are responsible for Garrick's death," Dalton interrupted. "The investigation will prove he died in Caloris with a Dancer scarf around his neck!"

Gordon winced visibly as if some pain gnawed at him, but he said nothing.

"Your Majesty," Kemal said desperately. "You can't believe that!"

Gordon remained silent, his head bowed with a look of defeat and acceptance on his face.

"Perhaps not," Dalton said, clearly in control now. "But it is a convenient reason to move against the Dancers."

"So you can take their crystals," Kemal reasoned.

"Politics is a game of appearances," Gordon said faintly. He winced again as his stomach muscles convulsed beneath his tunic.

"If you accept that, you've signed your own death warrant," Kemal said. "You know the bombing was—"

"The work of the Dancers!" Gordon exploded. Despite his uncle's vehemence, Kemal thought his voice sounded hollow, as if he were trying to convince himself with volume.

"The Dancers had nothing to do with it," Kemal said softly.

Gordon rose stiffly to his feet. "Kemal," he started to say, but another spasm of pain gripped him and he gasped, leaning heavily on a table for support.

Kemal hurried to him. "Are you ill, Your Majesty?"

Gordon waved him away. "It's nothing." He paused for a moment until the pain passed, then straightened himself and looked at Kemal. "You did me a favor as an honorable man," he said. "I would like to return that gesture. It might be for the best if you left Hielo. Mercury Prime could become very dangerous for you."

Kemal stood still for an instant, digesting the words. "Thank you for the warning, Your Majesty," he said finally, "but I began something here and I will finish it."

"Bravo, Cousin." Dalton clapped. "I approve of your stiff-necked honor! There may even be a way I can use your self-righteous principles."

"What are you talking about?" Gordon asked wearily. "Another of your plots?"

"Of course, Father," Dalton replied with an easy grin.

Gordon reached for the brandy bottle and poured himself another drink. "What are you planning now?"

"I think things have advanced far enough that matters will take care of themselves of their own weight," Dalton said. "I believe I'd like some brandy as well."

Gordon handed him the bottle. "You're being very mysterious. What matters?"

Dalton waved the brandy away. "Not that bottle. One of the unopened ones."

Gordon looked at him curiously, then winced as another spasm of pain crossed his face. "Why? What's the matter with this bottle?"

"Oh," Dalton said lightly. "It's poisoned."

Gordon and Kemal froze in shock as the words stabbed into their brains. Gordon's mouth fell open and the snifter he held dropped from his nerveless fingers.

Gordon's mouth moved soundlessly, then he croaked, "Dalton, . . . why?"

Gordon lurched forward to his computer and stabbed the comm link. "Catiff!" he shouted, then doubled over in pain. "Come here, quickly!"

"Ah, Catiff, certainly," Dalton smiled, drawing a small vial from his pocket. "I'll leave a sample of the potion for him. It's one of those nasty things they find in the lowland bogs of Venus. There's no antidote, I'm afraid, but Catiff might be curious about it."

Kemal watched in horror as Gordon's legs folded beneath him and he sank to the floor.

"Now, as for you, Cousin," Dalton said, crossing his arms over his chest thoughtfully. "This was originally intended to add to the evidence of the Dancers' hatred for the house of Gavilan, but now I think it would be helpful if you were implicated and eliminated from the scene. Yes—" He ran a finger along his jaw—"tell me. How does it feel to commit regicide?"

Something in Kemal snapped. With an animal snarl, he leaped toward Dalton blindly and ran into the rock-hard battering ram of his cousin's fist.

The blow knocked Kemal across the room, leaving him sprawled beside Gordon. The room spun as Kemal shook his head, trying to clear his vision.

The king weakly reached over and grabbed his arm. "Get out," he gasped. "Leave Hielo, now!"

Dalton ambled to Kemal's side, rubbing his skinned knuckles. "He's right, Kemal. You should run now, while you have the chance. Run—and prove your guilt! Or stay here and be tried for high treason. It will all come out the same."

Kemal reached for his mono knife, but the weapon had been taken by the guards at the door. With a casual gesture, Dalton drew his own knife and flicked on the multicolored laser along its edge. "I get to keep my weapon in the presence of the king," Dalton drawled. "Special privilege of rank."

Gordon's fingers dug into Kemal's arm with surprising strength. "Run . . . escape . . ." The king's face twisted with agony as his hand fell away.

Kemal scrambled to his feet. With an almost courteous flourish, Dalton backed away from him and swept his arm toward the door, smiling.

A bitter taste of gall rose in Kemal's throat as he looked at the door. Keeping his eyes on Dalton and his mono knife, he began edging toward the exit.

Dalton's mocking smile broadened. A deep laugh rumbled from him and grew with each of Kemal's steps. Unable to bear the sound, Kemal broke into a run and crashed through the door.

Chapter Six

Kemal watched the approach to Mercury's surface on the view screen aboard the *Sun Spot,* the cruiser he had been given months earlier for his trip to the Rising Sun Station, where Gordon had built his laser.

Kemal spent the trip from Mercury Prime in silence. The crew tried to talk to him, but he ignored them until they stopped trying to draw him out.

Kemal relived his last moments on Hielo over and over, like some terrible tape loop that kept repeating in his mind: Gordon dying in front of him, Dalton's jarring blow, and his cousin's laugh following him down the halls. He had run until he was well away from the king's chambers . . . and still he heard Dalton's psychotic laughter echoing in his ears.

"We're approaching Caloris, Your Highness," the first mate, Kal Hawker, said.

"I think we can dispense with the title from now on, Mister Hawker," Kemal said.

"Yes, sir."

Hawker had come with the ship, like a piece of the cruiser's furniture. He looked anything but hawk-like, with short, silver-gray hair and beard, rounded features, and a silver stud punched through one ear. He was an experienced veteran and longtime spacer, so the two of them got along well enough, but Kemal wasn't sure where Hawker's loyalties lay or how far he could trust the mate. Best to say as little as possible, he decided.

Kemal turned his attention to the screen again. Caloris was the largest Class A spaceport on Mercury, but it didn't look like much from space. The most prominent feature of the port was the huge double doors of the spacedock that could slide apart to accommodate the most massive cargo freighters in the solar system. Kemal could see construction crews beginning work on two more similar doors at the other end of the Caloris Basin. Smaller spacedocks that handled lighter cruisers dotted the surface like artificial craters. A dozen small craft circled overhead in holding patterns, waiting their turn to land at the busy port.

The *Sun Spot*'s communications officer looked up from his console. "Caloris Central has acknowledged our request to land and assigned us pattern coordinates. ETA twenty minutes."

"Very good," Hawker said.

"There will be a change of plans, gentlemen," Kemal said abruptly. "Take us out of the holding pattern and plot a new course for . . . Mozart."

"Sir?" Hawker asked.

"Just do it," Kemal snapped.

"Right away," Hawker replied and turned to the pilot.

Kemal wasn't sure what kind of reception was waiting for him on the surface, but he knew something was happening. The escape from Hielo had been too easy. He had met no resistance in the corridors on the way to the shipyard; he'd seen guards, but no one had attempted to stop him. Apparently Dalton intended to let him "escape" and capture him while fleeing.

The obvious place to go was Caloris, but it was also the most obvious trap; the tightly monitored checkpoints and customs searches would be impossible to slip through.

So, Kemal decided, let the Caloris authorities know he was coming, then go somewhere else.

The communications officer looked at Kemal nervously, then made a covert gesture to Hawker. The mate went to the officer and bent over as he whispered something. Hawker glanced at Kemal over his shoulder, then nodded and patted the man on his shoulder.

Kemal felt his stomach muscles tighten. Something was up on his ship as well, and he was on one end of whatever it was.

Hawker ambled to his side casually. "Speak to you, sir? In private?"

"I'd like to stay on the bridge," Kemal said, leading Hawker to the rear of the command station. "In case something goes wrong."

"No one is going to turn the ship around without your order, sir," Hawker said with a grin.

Kemal smiled at him, grateful for the understanding. "That's good to hear. What did you want to see me about?"

Hawker's grin faded and he studied Kemal with a stern face, lined and scarred from years of service. "Mozart's a bit wild," he said finally. "Not much in the way of authority there."

Kemal nodded. "Just the kind of place I'm looking for."

Hawker's lips tightened into a thin smile as he examined his young commander. Kemal felt he was being judged by standards that didn't exist in the court at Hielo.

The pause dragged into an uncomfortable silence. Finally Kemal said, "Is that all you—"

"We just got a message about you," Hawker said curtly.

Here it comes, Kemal thought. "Yes?"

"Prince Dalton has offered a ten-thousand-credit reward for your head. Dead or alive."

Kemal watched him, trying to read his face. "What are you going to do about it?" he asked.

Hawker snorted and chuckled softly. "Well, Kemal, I guess I'll go to Mozart."

The mate's hard face relaxed into a genuine smile, and Kemal knew he could trust him. For the second time since he had returned to Hielo, a "subject" had dropped his royal title and called him by name; Kemal found he liked that acceptance of himself.

"All right, Kal. Take us in."

❍ ❍ ❍ ❍ ❍

Debarkation procedures on Mozart were simple, as Kemal had hoped.

Dressed in a familiar rocketjock's suit, he had followed Hawker and the other crewmen to a bored official at the end of a long corridor. Hawker flashed his papers briefly, and the man brushed them through without checking the other men's identification.

"If news from Hielo has reached Mozart, nobody seems to care very much," Kemal remarked.

"The Musicians are a pretty independent lot," Hawker said. "They have their warrens, and what goes on among the Gavilans doesn't concern them much."

That was an odd discovery for Kemal. His own involvement with the royal family had created the impression that the solar system revolved around the Gavilans. Yet Mercury was a planet of some two million people who had little contact with the Sun King, except for his portrait on their coins. And, given the Miners' and Dancers' preference for barter, even that link was thin.

As they left the area of the spacedock, they found that the Mozart warren became seedy. Many of the overhead lights were missing or damaged, leaving the halls dark and gloomy. The Musicians' shops and living quarters were packed and stacked haphazardly along the sides of the long tunnel, tilting into each other. In many places, the ceramic tiles that lined the tunnel walls had peeled away, leaving the insulation visible.

"Well, this is Mozart," Hawker said.

Kemal found it hard to reconcile the elegant, ethereal music of the ancient composer Mozart with the run-down, decrepit warren that bore his name. Perhaps it was a touch of Musician irony to name their roughest warrens after the most elegant artists of old Earth.

"I know a spacer bar just down the way," Hawker said, pointing to a side tunnel. "If you have time for a drink."

"No, I've got to get to . . ." Kemal stopped himself. There was no point to telling the men he was going to Caloris—not that he didn't trust them, but, if Dalton's guards caught up with them, the less they knew the better. ". . . some business," he finished.

"How long will your 'business' take?" Hawker asked.

Kemal stopped. "Just a minute," he said as the others halted. "I don't think it's safe for you to know me anymore. There's been some trouble on Hielo, and I don't want you to get hurt because of me."

The men looked at each other, puzzled. "We heard about the reward Dalton offered for you," one of them said.

"It's more than that," Kemal said. "I'm not coming back. It would probably be best if you men took the ship and left."

"We don't need to be so hasty," Hawker said. "News takes time to travel on the surface. Dalton's men won't find their way here for a few days, and we've been cooped up on the *Sun Spot* for a long time. Two days of shore leave would feel good now. If you're not back by then . . . well, I understand there are plenty of opportunities in the asteroid belt for men with a fast ship."

Kemal smiled at the scarred veteran. "It sounds like the pirate population is about to increase."

Hawker grinned back. "I wouldn't deny that possibility. Two days, Kemal."

"Okay," Kemal agreed and started heading for the trains. "Good luck!"

○ ○ ○ ○ ○

Caloris radiated outward from its central hub like an enormous wheel, with hundreds of tunnels like spokes that stretched out, converged, diverged again, twisted around themselves, and riddled the planet. The tunnels all connected at some point eventually, so a person could start at Caloris and walk to every warren on the planet—though it would take decades, or even centuries, to cover the entire maze.

The train system made travel through the labyrinth considerably faster. The trains hung from the roof by a single rail, gliding noiselessly above the busy bustle of the warrens. The narrow, cylindrical cars reminded Kemal of the safe, closed-in feeling of a rocket, though the throng of people quickly dispelled the illusion of quiet privacy he felt in space. He had purposefully chosen a crowded car close to the front of the train to lose himself in the mass of humanity. The three-hour trip to Caloris had cured him of his desire for crowds.

After the decay of Mozart, Caloris seemed like a pristine jewel. From the train windows Kemal watched the magnificent shops that curved along the tunnel walls and the palatial living quarters—some of which even had artificial lawns—sprawling along the tunnel floors.

The elegance of the warren reminded Kemal of Hielo, but the buildings had none of Mercury Prime's jumbled mix of art and architecture. Musicians admired functional design rather than ornate decoration. Surfaces were flat and clean, well lighted by hidden lamps.

As the train approached the central hub, Kemal noticed a change in the warren; the inner area was obviously older and less elegant. Repairs to the buildings and tunnel walls were common and not skillfully executed. But the repairs had been made, and if the inner warren lacked the dignified luxury of the outer rim, it was clear the inhabitants were still proud of their buildings and shops. Kemal felt himself relax in the unpretentious atmosphere.

He wasn't sure what he was going to do when he arrived in Caloris, but he knew he had to get to the Dancers and warn them about Dalton's plan to blame them for his own murders and seize the crystal fields.

Then, too, he desperately wanted to see Duernie again.

As the train pulled up to its stop, Kemal noticed too many of his fellow passengers craning their necks to look out the window. He slid over to the next seat and looked out.

The passenger platform was in pandemonium. The Musicians outside were scrambling toward the exits or pressed themselves against the walls as a dozen guardsmen in heavy armor herded a group of Dancers through their midst.

Kemal lunged against the window, his fists beating at the heavy plastic panes. The guards were wearing Hielo uniforms, reflective black body armor trimmed in yellow and gold. Their helmets were on full opaque, giving them an anonymous, inhuman appearance. One of the Dancers stumbled, and when his companion paused to help him up, the guard smashed them both with the butt of his laser rifle.

Kemal bolted from his seat, but the aisle was already full of passengers crowding around the doors. Kemal pushed his way through them and began beating on the sealed exit.

"What's going on here?" Kemal demanded from a woman Musician standing beside him.

"Everyone return to your seats," a metallic voice grated out of the public address system. "There has been a security breach, but the situation is under control. Guardsmen will check your identification papers, so please cooperate."

The message began to repeat. With the doors still sealed, there was nothing to do but sit, and the passengers started drifting back to their seats.

"What are Hielo guards doing in Caloris?" one Musician asked loudly.

"What they always do," another answered from across the car. "Cause trouble!"

"Hielans have no business here," someone else grumbled. "We have our own security."

The doors abruptly slid apart and two armored guardsmen pushed their way into the car. "Remain seated and prepare your idents," one of the guards said. It was impossible to tell which guard spoke, since they both wore identical armor and opaque helmets; the voice came from a suit radio set on broadcast.

Muttering but compliant, the Musicians began digging out their identity cards for the guards as they passed.

Kemal knew he was trapped. He couldn't fight two armored guardsmen in the middle of a crowded train car. His identity card would result in his immediate arrest; he should have gotten a false card as soon as he had landed. Even better, he should have left Mercury altogether.

A lot of good should-have-dones, Kemal told himself, but what was he *going* to do? He couldn't fight two guards, but one—maybe. How to separate them, though . . .

Kemal quietly slipped out of his seat and worked his way to the rear of the car. He glanced at the guards, who were still occupied with the passengers' IDs, and ducked into the washroom.

An agonized minute passed as Kemal waited. For a moment, he almost hoped the guards had passed by the rest room, but the heavy knock inevitably came.

"Someone in there?" the guard demanded.

"Yes, just a moment," Kemal answered, trying to make his voice sound high and weak.

"You got five minutes to get this door open or I'll break it in!"

"Please," Kemal added in a begging whine, "I've been ill."

He heard an indistinct voice outside the door but

could make out no words. Then the guard said, "No, I've got this. You go ahead and start the next car. I'll be along in a minute."

The pounding on the door began again after a few seconds.

"Yes, I'm ready," Kemal said, opening the door. He held his ident card close to his chest. When the guard impatiently reached for it, Kemal grabbed his hand and yanked.

The guard flew across the small washroom and crashed heavily into the sink. Kemal twisted the man's arm over his head, exposing the gap where the torso armor ended and the arm sheath began. Kemal had his mono knife out and pressed against the guard's bare skin.

"One move and I'll put this knife through you," Kemal hissed. "You understand?"

The guard nodded.

"Good! Now use your other hand to snap open the helmet seals." Kemal tightened his grip and pressed the blade into the man's flesh until a drop of blood welled around the point. "And do it very slowly!"

The guard reached awkwardly over his helmet and unfastened the four seals at its base. With one swift movement, Kemal ripped the helmet away and brought it down heavily on the man's head.

❍ ❍ ❍ ❍ ❍

Kemal found he hated wearing body armor.

The guardsman's protective suit chafed his elbows and knees, the extra weight threw his balance off, and even walking felt awkward. Kemal wondered how long guards had to train just to march in the bulky armor; the idea of fighting while encumbered in such a suit seemed impossible.

Plus, it made him itch.

Kemal clanked along the side tunnels of the train station, trying to find a dark corner to throw off the armor and get away from the area. He fervently hoped he wouldn't run into any other guards who would know he wasn't where he was supposed to be.

In fact, he had no idea where he was. The endless tunnels and shafts of the warren turned and twisted until Kemal was hopelessly lost.

He turned a corner and ran into a group of Musicians. They balked when they saw his armor, then quickly hurried by with resentment smoldering in their eyes. Kemal stared after them, trying to decide whether to follow them or take the tunnel they had come from. He shrugged and took a step . . .

. . . and was hit by what felt like a fully loaded ore carrier. The force sent Kemal tumbling across the tunnel floor. As he rolled into the wall, a whirl of brightly colored scarves threw itself on his chest and wrenched at his hand. He felt his arm suddenly twisted over his head, exposing the same vulnerable gap in the armor that Kemal had aimed for when he attacked the guard at the train.

He twisted his head around as a knife arced toward his armpit, and caught a glimpse of the face. He recognized not only the woman's long, dark hair and compact, bronze features, but the panther-hilted dagger that was her trademark.

"Duernie!"

At the sound of her name, the Dancer paused and checked the path of her knife. "Who . . . ?"

"Duernie, you're breaking my arm!"

She bent closer, trying to see through the black faceplate of the helmet. "Kemal?" she asked tentatively.

"Yes, it's me," he said. "Now let go of my arm!"

She released his wrist and twisted open the helmet seals but remained firmly planted on his chest. Kemal jerked the helmet off.

"It *is* you!" she cried and flung herself on his neck in a hug that almost choked him. Kemal wrapped his arms around her and buried his face in her hair.

When she finally drew back, her cheeks were damp with tears. Kemal found his own eyes moist.

"What are you doing here?" she asked, rolling off him. "It's dangerous for you to be on Mercury. You know Hielo is offering a reward for your capture?"

"Yes, I know," Kemal said, struggling to his feet. "Help me get this armor off, and I'll explain. Why are you in Caloris? I thought you'd be with the Dancers."

"I'm trying to get to a track city," she said, unfastening the side clasps of his torso plates. "Since I left you on Hielo, I've been track-hopping, hitching rides on different track cities in exchange for doing odd jobs, trying to sort out my thoughts about you."

Kemal shucked off the chest armor and began peeling away his arm shields. "What have you decided?" he asked quietly.

She paused a moment. "I'm not sure," she said. "I don't know what I *think,* but I *feel* you didn't betray us to Gordon."

Kemal stopped and looked at her. "Is that enough for you?"

She smiled and kissed him on the cheek. "Yes," she said. "More than enough."

Kemal reached gently for her face and brushed a strand of hair from her forehead. "So you're just waiting for a track city now?"

"I was," her face became grim. "Now I've *got* to get to the Dancers. Guardsmen have started arresting Dancers in all the warrens. They're not giving any reason, and I'm afraid Gordon is going to do something to the track cities. I've got to warn the Dancers."

"Gordon isn't doing anything," Kemal said. "He's dead."

"Dead?"

Kemal nodded. "Dalton killed him, and Gordon's brother, Garrick, too. He's trying to blame the Dancers—and me—for the murders, so he can move against you and take the crystal field."

Duernie slumped against the wall. "Dalton is king?" she asked, sounding sick.

"Yes. The council hasn't confirmed him yet, but that's just a formality. He is the Sun King now."

"I *have* to warn the Dancers," Duernie said.

"Do you have a radio?"

"No, I don't usually carry one. Do you?"

Kemal frowned and started to shake his head. "Wait . . . the guard's suit has a radio." Kemal stooped to the pile of armor and scooped up the helmet. He glanced inside, then started to slide it over his head.

Duernie put her hand on his arm, stopping him. "You better let me talk to them," she said. "The Dancers don't exactly trust you."

"I know," Kemal paused, then handed her the helmet. "I met Corianne on Hielo and she . . ." He let the sentence die.

Duernie took the helmet and reached inside to the radio. "How do you adjust the frequency?"

"I don't think you can. These are single-channel communicators. Do you think the track cities will monitor all bands? The guards certainly are."

"Let's hope the Dancers are listening," Duernie said, settling the bulky helmet over her head. "This is Duernie calling any track city in range. Please respond. This is Dancer Duernie calling any track city. Please respond. Urgent!"

There was a moment's silence, then the radio crackled. "Duernie? This is track city *Renaissance*

Gold. Do you copy?"

"I hear you, *Renaissance Gold,*" Duernie said. She reached over and squeezed Kemal's hand in victory. "I know your city. I've ridden with you."

"Yeah, I remember you, Duernie," the voice on the radio replied. "This is a Hielo frequency you're broadcasting on. Are you in trouble?"

"We're all in trouble. There are mass arrests of Dancers throughout all the warrens. Dalton is Sun King and he's moving against the Dancers!"

"We know. Hielo contacted all the track cities and ordered them to report to the Hand of Ra mountains in seventy-two hours."

Duernie looked at Kemal fearfully. "What is your current heading, *Renaissance Gold?*"

"As far away from the Hand as possible. Do you want to hitch a ride?"

Kemal smiled and raised a fist in silent salute to the rebellious spirit of the Dancers.

"Yes, we'd like a ride," Duernie said. "Where can we find . . . No, don't broadcast that, this channel is being monitored."

"You can't hide a track city," the *Renaissance Gold* voice said. "We're going to the Eye of Phidias. Hielo knows where we are and where we're heading. If they come for us, we'll be ready."

"That sounds like a declaration of war," Duernie said.

"If that's what Hielo wants. Take care of yourself, Duernie."

"You, too, *Renaissance Gold.* See you at the Eye." She pulled the helmet off and tossed it away.

Kemal looked down the long tunnel in front of them. "So how do we get out of here?"

Duernie grinned at him. "This way . . . I think."

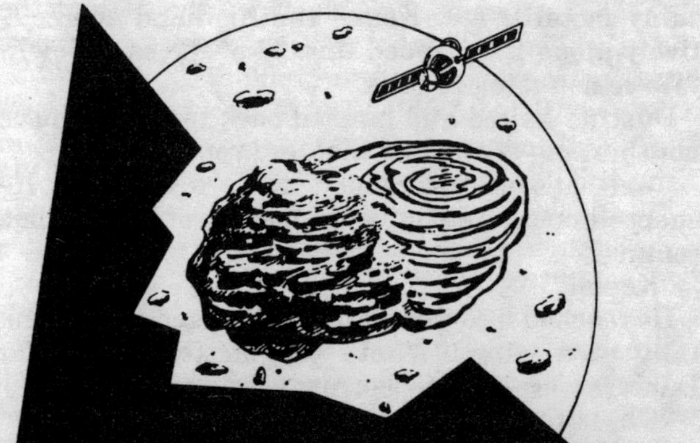

Chapter Seven

Kemal and Duernie edged along the shadowed rim of Caloris's main tunnel, dodging past the bright shops and knots of Musicians parading on the promenade. The warren was easily a quarter of a mile in diameter, with stores and offices lining the walls; the central thoroughfare was crowded with jetcars and skimmers hovering at all levels.

"All right," Duernie said, "what are we going to do once we get to the surface?"

Kemal shrugged. "Get to the track city. Where did you say it was going?"

"The Eye of Phidias," she answered. "It's a hundred miles southeast of here. What are we going to do, walk there?"

Kemal slowed as they passed a parked skimmer, one of the new compact models only eight feet long—all smooth curves and upswept wings. And red . . . a shiny metallic red. Kemal ran his hand appreciatively along its rounded fins. "No," he said slowly. "We're not going to walk."

Duernie halted and hurried back to him. "You're not thinking of stealing that, are you?"

"Well, it's an emergency, and we need it." He snapped open the engine compartment. "Is anyone coming?"

"Kemal!"

He reached into the engine and tugged experimentally at a wire. "What's the matter? I thought Dancers were used to 'borrowing' things."

"Oh, is that what you think?" she demanded angrily, hands on her hips. Her eyes became chips of flint. "All Dancers are thieves! 'Here come the Dancers! Hide the liquor!' "

"Duernie, I didn't mean it that way," Kemal said desperately. "I just . . . just watch for people, will you?"

She folded her arms across her chest and slumped back against the skimmer. "I get tired of hearing that kind of talk," she said. "We're not all thieves, you know."

"I know," Kemal's muffled voice came from the back. "I'm sorry. I don't like stealing either, but this is necessary."

"Then get on with it!"

Duernie glanced nervously up and down the warren, smiling amiably if a Musician looked their way. One passer-by came close enough to look curiously at Kemal's activities, then at Duernie.

"Won't start," she said, smiling. The Musician shrugged and continued walking.

"Hurry up, will you! Do you know what you're doing in there?"

Kemal looked at the bewildering confusion of wires and tubes, belts and fans, strange cylinders and circuit boxes. "Um . . . sure. I've worked on rocket engines all my life."

"That's a skimmer, not a deep-space cruiser."

"Yeah, well, engines are engines," he said. "Where are the blasted Sammler coils on this thing?"

Duernie stomped over to the motor. "Here," she said, reaching in and snapping off two wires from a cylinder. "Just short these. Better yet, get in and press the ignition."

"I can . . ." Kemal started, his face flushing.

"Just do it! We don't have time to argue."

Kemal climbed in the skimmer and looked at the unfamiliar control panel for a moment.

"You got it?" she called.

"Um . . . just a minute," he said, then saw a red button embossed with the letters *Ig.* He pushed the button firmly and held it. "Go!"

The engine sparked to life. The skimmer bucked wildly for a few feet, then died.

"Kemal!" Duernie snapped. "Don't hold the ignition down after the motor's going!"

"Right," he said. "I know, I was just . . ."

She reached back into the engine compartment. "Ready?"

"Go!"

The motor hummed and Kemal quickly released the button. Thankfully the skimmer stayed in place. Duernie came to the driver's side and leaned against the door.

"You know how to fly one of these?" she asked, raising an eyebrow.

"Um . . . sure," he said. "I've been flying rockets . . ."

". . . all your life, yeah, I know," she said, then nodded toward the passenger seat. "Better let me drive."

Kemal hesitated, then slid reluctantly across to the passenger seat. "Know-it-all," he muttered.

"Big time rocketjock," she answered.

They looked at each other, trying to be grim, but a smile was already spreading across Kemal's face. They both burst into laughter as the skimmer rose into the air.

○ ○ ○ ○ ○

The deep Mercurian night enclosed them and blotted everything out, like a smothering blanket. Without an atmosphere, light could not diffuse and spread, so the faint glow of Caloris was soon a thin crack of yellow that outlined the great sliding doors of the spacedock.

For Kemal, the darkness seemed like home; floating above the surface of the planet in the jet blackness, he felt as though he were in space again.

"Do the stars look like this when you're out there?" Duernie asked.

The sound of her voice almost startled him. He'd nearly forgotten her in the silence and darkness. "Huh? Oh, yes, they do," he said, looking through the skimmer's bubble top at the expanse of tiny dots of light overhead. "They seem so cold and still, don't they?"

"It's hard to believe each star is a huge sun," she said, leaning back in her seat to gaze up. The skimmer was on automatic pilot, and the car's radar would warn them of any objects in the path big enough to scrape the bottom. "When I was a little girl, I'd go to the upper levels of the track city and find a window so I could watch the stars. I used to wonder what they looked like on other planets or deep in space."

"Pretty much like this—small, hard dots of light," Kemal said, then realized with a pang of guilt that he might be shattering fond dreams. "They look different on Earth. The thick atmosphere gives them a kind of glimmer, like jewels heated until they shimmer."

"So you've become a poet, too, Kemal?"

He smirked at her and shook his head. "No, I'm a rocketjock. That's how I think of myself."

"You're also a Gavilan," Duernie said, suddenly grim.

"I'm not sure anymore," he answered. "I used to have a secret dream that maybe I would be Sun King someday and repair the damage Gordon and Dalton have done to Mercury. But lately I find I don't like being a prince. I don't like the barriers it puts between me and other people. I like being Kemal, Duernie. It doesn't feel right to be 'Your Highness.' I'd rather have a deep spacer clap me on the back and call me by my name than live with the intrigues and backstabbing of the Hielo palace."

She studied him for a minute, trying to read his face in the dim glow of the skimmer's control panel. "You've changed, Kemal. Or are those just words?"

He smiled and patted her knee. "That sounds like an old Terran saying: You talk the talk, but can you walk the walk?"

She laughed softly. "What does that mean?"

Kemal shrugged. "It's just an old saying. They can mean anything. I guess the point is that words don't mean much, it's what you *do* that counts."

A soft beep from the radar drew Duernie's attention. "It's only a big rock," she said and adjusted the skimmer's path to go around it. "Well, we'll get to *Renaissance Gold* in an hour or so. I'm curious about what everyone will *do* then." She looked at him and tried to smile reassuringly.

○ ○ ○ ○ ○

"I don't understand. I've got *Renaissance Gold* on the radar screen," Duernie said, tapping at the monitor. "We're in visual range, but I can't see anything."

Kemal stared into the impenetrable darkness. "What should we see?"

"There's always light around a track city," she said. "Windows, floodlights for the Miners, sidecars and carts. They're beautiful, but I can't see anything and we're only fifteen minutes away."

The radar screen beeped again. Kemal looked to see half a dozen blips intrude from the north.

"Duernie . . ." Kemal began.

"I see them," she said, her mouth set in a tight scowl. She grabbed for the radio and raised it quickly to her mouth. "*Renaissance Gold, Renaissance Gold,* this is Dancer Duernie approaching from the south! Respond!"

Nothing.

"*Renaissance Gold!*" Duernie shouted into the transmitter. "Please respond!"

Kemal watched the radar blips from the north swing to a course that would take them to the track city. "They're not going to answer," he told her. "They blacked out the city and are maintaining radio silence. I'd bet my oxygen tank those blips are guardsmen closing in."

The radio crackled to life. "Duernie, this is *Renaissance Gold.* We have you on our radar. Turn around and go back! Hostiles are approaching and we expect to be under attack in a half-hour. Turn back!"

"Negative, *Renaissance Gold,*" she said. "We're coming in!"

"You can't help us, Duernie! Get out of here before they sight you!" The radio went dead.

Duernie held the transmitter and stared at it

numbly long after the track city had cut the line. She turned to Kemal, her gaze hardening. "I know those people. We can't leave!"

"Of course we won't leave," he said. "We have to figure out what to do."

She stared at the radar monitor, watching the large blip of the track city directly in front of them.

"Do you think they can see us? The guardsmen, I mean."

Kemal tilted his head and frowned. "Certainly they know about us. They've got radar, too."

"Yes, but look at the screen," she said. "We can see *Renaissance Gold,* but not the guards. We're in the track city's shadow now."

Kemal looked through the observation bubble as the hulking mobile city began to take form in the darkness, a deeper black in the inky night. The track city was a hodgepodge of additions and improvised compartments that had grown over the generations until the vehicle was a complex network of interconnected quarters, offices, corridors, and maintenance stations. Somewhere in the middle was the original central control deck, designed to crawl along the night side of Mercury. As with all track cities, perhaps a Miner attached his tool cart to the back and added a living bubble; someone else built a laboratory on top of the control deck and added living quarters for a family. The process had continued for generations until the mobile arcology had become a lumbering behemoth wandering across the surface of the planet, like a restless beehive teeming with life.

Duernie flew the skimmer to a knot of men scurrying around the northern side of the city and landed the car beside the vehicle's huge treads.

Kemal finished sealing the last seams of the smart suit he had found in the skimmer as Duernie popped the door and jumped out quickly. He climbed out with less enthusiasm.

She rushed to a bear of a man helping to set up a barricade. "Shak!" she shouted.

"Duernie?" The man turned to her. "What are you doing here?"

"Didn't Central tell you I was coming?"

"I thought they told you to leave before the guardsmen arrived."

"Did you think I would?"

Shak hefted a heavy box onto the makeshift wall. "No, not really. Who's this?" he said as Kemal slowly approached the two. Shak froze as he recognized him as the man who'd betrayed the crystal field. "You!" he spat. "What are you doing here? Leading the guards?"

Kemal stopped a few feet from the large Dancer and stared at him. "I'm here to help."

"We don't want your help."

"You're going to need every hand you can get."

"Not yours!"

Duernie came to Shak's side and put her hand on his arm. "He's a friend, Shak. I trust him."

He looked at her, his face hard. "After what he did to us?"

"That was a misunderstanding," Duernie said. "I don't think—"

"I do!" Shak cut her off.

"Look, do you want to stand here arguing or do you want to build that barricade?" Kemal asked, reaching down to pick up a sandbag.

"Get away from here!" Shak shouted and shoved Kemal's shoulder, knocking him off balance. Kemal sprawled in the dirt, then jumped to his feet with his fists clenched. A group of Dancers gathered around the two men.

Duernie quickly stepped between them. "Stop it, both of you! Guardsmen are approaching, and you are wasting time squabbling!"

Shak glared at Kemal with eyes that seemed a little too close together, then turned quickly and strode to the barricade. The other Dancers drifted back to their jobs as Kemal stood silently, his face stony and immobile. Without a word he turned and walked beyond the barricade to the north. As he passed a forward observer, Kemal grabbed the man's macroglasses and glared at him until he backed away.

Duernie watched him for a moment, then joined the flurry of activity around the arcology's treads.

She found Shak standing by the city's door, speaking into a radio transmitter.

"What kind of weapons do we have?" she asked.

Shak turned away from her. ". . . and move the people away from the outer layers. Put as many as you can in the central core, and send everybody else to the southern perimeter."

"Shak," Duernie said, grasping his shoulder.

He jerked his arm away from her. "Put the drilling laser as high as you can. In the observatory bubble if you can get it up there. Anywhere you can get some elevation so we're shooting down on them." He switched the radio off and dropped the transmitter.

"Shak," she started again. "What are—"

"Did you join them, Duernie?" he asked bitterly. "Are you a Gavilan now?"

"What are you talking about?"

"How did he buy you? With a kiss and a hug?"

She stared at him in shock for a moment, her face turning red. Then she flung herself on him in sudden fury. The force of her attack knocked him over, and she leaped on his chest. Before he could react, her knife was out and pressed against his throat.

Chapter Eight

Duernie!"

She leaned back slowly, drawing the panther-hilted knife from Shak's throat, and glanced behind her.

Corianne stepped down from the track city's door in a flurry of colored scarves. "Do we fight among ourselves before we face a battle?" she demanded.

Duernie stood and sheathed her blade. "No, Corianne. It was a misunderstanding."

"She brought *him* to us again," Shak said as he scrambled to his feet. "The Gavilan traitor!"

"Kemal?" Corianne asked. Her eyes became chips of flint. "You dare bring him here when we face attack by his own people?"

"He's not one of them," Duernie said, returning the older woman's gaze.

"But maybe she is," Shak said.

"Duernie! Shak!" Corianne shouted. Duernie pulled up short and stood glaring at Shak, her hands resting on the hilt of her knife. "This is no time to quarrel! You've both got jobs to do!"

Without a word, Duernie turned and strode away from the barricade.

"Just keep *him* away from me!" Shak shouted.

Duernie found Kemal crouching behind a small mound of dirt, staring intently through a set of macroglasses. "See anything?" she asked, carefully controlling the anger in her voice.

"They're here," he said. "Three jetcars, a troop carrier and two transport vehicles I don't recognize."

"How many men?"

"I saw five guards on the forward perimeter, but there is some kind of activity by the transporters I can't see well enough." Kemal watched the guardsmen for a minute in silence, then asked, "How are your friends? Glad to see you?"

She looked at him quickly, but he continued to gaze through the macroglasses. "They're less friendly than I thought," she finally said.

He lowered the macroglasses and looked at her. "Because of me?"

"Because of them," she nodded furiously back toward the track city. "Small minded . . ."

"Duernie." He put his hand on her arm to stop her tirade. "I'm sorry."

She looked down for a moment, then shook her head. "How are the guards outfitted? Can they attack us?"

Kemal smiled and patted her arm. "They're wearing their ceremonial armor. It's good for maybe an hour on the surface. Guardsmen were never trained to fight a surface battle. If we can just keep them away, we can wait them out. Besides, there can't be too many. There aren't more than a thousand guards on Hielo, and Dalton probably left half of them home. How many track cities are there—twenty-eight? That leaves maybe ten or twelve men assigned to each city. I don't think we're in any real danger."

A sharp red line from one of the guardsmen's laser rifles shot out and struck the barricade. Kemal heard someone on his radio scream, then a babble of voices.

"What kind of weapons do we . . . do the Dancers have?" he asked.

She glanced up at him, hearing the alienation in his voice. "Nothing to speak of," she said. "Some drilling lasers and a couple of laser rifles. Some Dancers have pistols, but most just carry knives."

The thick crimson beam of a drilling laser darted from the track city but faded into a weak pink and dissipated before it reached halfway to the guards. In answer, five crisp laser shots followed the drill's beam to its source and focused on an upper observation deck. Kemal heard a muffled *whump* from the track city and saw a brief flare within.

He felt a thin film of sweat break out across his forehead. "Maybe a dozen guards *can* take the city."

Duernie gasped and clamped a hand to the ear of her smart suit helmet. "Kemal! I think the Dancers are planning to rush the . . ."

Kemal turned to look as ten men suddenly jumped the barricade around *Renaissance Gold* and spread out as they ran toward the guards.

Simultaneously, five of the guardsmen's lasers stabbed out, each aimed at a different attacker. Obviously the guards were prepared for a rush and had already assigned targets. Kemal winced as the first screams came in on his radio. Four Dancers went down in the first volley, three more in the second. The remaining Dancers hesitated for a split second; they had lost seven men and hadn't even gone a hundred yards. Another laser beam shot out and cut down the eighth man. The last two Dancers dove for cover and began scrambling back to the track city.

Several small streams of ruby light flashed from the Dancers' short-range laser pistols. Kemal raised the macroglasses to his eyes but couldn't see if the weak streams of light were striking their targets.

"Don't they have anything bigger than hand weapons?" Kemal asked.

"No, not really . . . Kemal! What was that flash?"

"Where?"

"Behind the guardsmen! Can you see anything?"

Kemal snapped the viewer up just as another crack of lightning threw a brief illumination over the guardsmen gathered around a double barrel projecting out of the cargo transport.

"Duernie!" he cried. "They've got a cannon!"

They both turned toward the track city as the first shell struck. The bulky city shivered as the explosion tore through its outer chambers. Moments later, the second rocket hit closer to the massive treads that carried the mobile arcology; a lethal hail of metal and plastic fragments exploded over the Dancers behind the barricade. Kemal couldn't shut off his radio before the agonized chorus of screams and cries reached him.

"They're going to destroy the whole city!" Duernie shouted.

Through the macroglasses Kemal could see the forward rank of guardsmen advancing toward them. There were only six of them, but after a few more rocket rounds, six would be enough to mop up the whole Dancer colony.

"Kemal, we've got to stop them!" Duernie gripped his arm desperately.

"How? We're not even close enough to throw stones at them!"

Duernie opened her mouth but closed it again without saying anything. She looked at the advancing guards, then at the track city rolling along with two jagged holes torn into its hull. Out of the corner of his eye Kemal saw another flash of light from the guards' cannon.

"Another round coming!" he shouted, hoping the Dancers would hear him.

An ominous stillness fell over the track city, as though the Dancers were holding their breath. Then the rocket struck.

Kemal could see a blaze of fire flash through the compartments around the ragged hold left by the shell; the fire lasted only as long as the tiny pocket of air in the track city supported it. The airless environment of Mercury's surface quickly smothered the explosion, but enough damage had been done. The *Renaissance Gold* teetered for a moment but regained its ground firmly and continued slowly crawling forward. The next round might knock it over or damage its treads enough to immobilize the city; then, when the sun rose and the surface temperature climbed to over eight hundred degrees, the city would turn into a boiling puddle of molten metal.

"We've got to get behind them," Kemal said, his mind racing. "The skimmer!" he shouted and jumped to his feet.

Duernie was up and beside him as he started running toward the skimmer they had left beside the track city.

"What about it?" she asked as they dodged debris from the rocket blasts.

"I'm going to ram the cannon," Kemal said.

"I'm coming with you," Duernie said as they reached the car.

"No," Kemal ripped the door open and jumped in. "Stay here and tell the Dancers what I'm doing. When the car hits the cannon, that should cause a diversion. Have them rush the guards!" He slammed the door and reached for the ignition, but there was no key.

"You're not leaving me here!" she insisted, tugging open the passenger door.

"Duernie, I can't start the car. Would you short the engine again?"

"Only if I'm coming."

"All right, do it!"

She pulled the engine compartment open and reached in. "Go!" she shouted and Kemal pressed the ignition button. The skimmer hummed to life.

He thought about bolting away without her but realized she had the right to make her own choices.

"It really would be better if you were here to tell them what to do," he said.

She hesitated a moment, then another rocket round struck the city, ripping open an ugly gash along the wall. Glowing fragments of metal showered the skimmer as Duernie ducked her head.

"I'll stay," she gasped and slammed the door. "Just be careful!"

"You, too! Don't get too close to the treads—that's what the guards are aiming at."

The skimmer rose a few feet and Kemal pushed it ahead as fast as it could go. He glanced back, but Duernie was already beside the *Renaissance Gold,* pounding on the door.

He headed south, trying to stay in the radar shadow of the track city to avoid detection by the guards. After two miles, he came to the foothills of the Phidian Mountains, and eased the car up to the shallow crest of the hills. He aimed back north, hoping the ridges would shield his car from radar, and punched the speed to maximum.

Within five minutes he had turned the jetcar onto a knoll overlooking the guardsmen's position and opened the door. The cannon was just inside the car's radar range; he took a position reading on the weapon and fed the vectors into the skimmer's automatic pilot, then checked the fuel level—low, but adequate. On impulse, he looked into the cargo box and found two fresh canisters of fuel, just enough to make a grand explosion if there was enough oxygen in the rocket transport to support combustion.

We'll see in a minute, he told himself and swung out of the car. He set the speed on fifty miles per hour and bent into the car to engage the engine. The skimmer lurched away, banging his side as it tore down the foothill, aiming straight for the cannon.

Kemal dropped to the ground and raised the macroglasses to his eyes. The skimmer stayed on course, coming up on the transport from behind. From his vantage point he could see three men darting between the cannon transport and the second vehicle, each man carrying an unwieldy rocket in his arms.

He shifted his gaze forward. The front line of guards continued to advance on the track city, more slowly now that they were within range of the Dancers' weapons. Quick stabs of fiery red light crossed in the darkness.

Anxiously, Kemal glanced back at the skimmer. It was close to the transport now . . . close enough to be seen if anyone turned around. But the guardsmen were so intent on their duties that no one noticed it.

Another few seconds. Kemal gripped the viewer tighter in his sweaty hands. Don't turn around . . . eyes front like good soldiers.

The skimmer struck.

The transport carrying the rocket launcher rolled a few yards with the impact, then ripped apart in a violent orange burst. The explosion was short-lived on the airless surface, but there had been enough atmosphere within the vehicle to ignite the rockets and fuel canisters.

Kemal felt an eerie sensation watching the silent explosion; ragged sheets of metal tore free from the vehicle and scattered across the ground. Two men caught by the force of the blast hurtled through the blackness and landed like broken dolls against the treads of the second transport.

Kemal turned to the advancing guards again. The explosion had caught them by surprise, and they stopped to stare. Whatever messages were being sent over their radios, the men clearly didn't know what to do next.

A wave of Dancers suddenly poured over the barricade along the side of the *Renaissance Gold.* Beams from half a dozen lasers shot haphazardly at the guards, reflecting harmlessly off their armor. Kemal could tell that the Dancers had made no effort to pick their targets or aim for vulnerable chinks in the guards' protective suits; their attack was a chaotic rush that even the moderately trained guardsmen could repulse.

But the loss of the cannon and the ensuing confusion panicked the soldiers. They broke ranks and fled to the central camp as the Dancers charged them.

Kemal ran down the hill toward the transport just as the Hielans reached it. The Dancers were close behind, shooting their lasers and swinging their knives over their heads. Kemal grinned at the babble of shouting, laughing, screaming, and cursing that poured into his receiver.

The guards packed into the troop carrier and quickly pulled away from the Dancers swarming around the abandoned jetcars and cargo vehicle. Several desert nomads followed the transport a few yards, but dodged away when a rear-mounted missile launcher swung on them.

Kemal searched the Dancers for Duernie but couldn't find her in the crowd. He hurried back toward the *Renaissance Gold,* trying not to look for her among the bodies sprawled on the ground.

"Kemal!" he heard her over his radio.

"Duernie! Where are you?"

"Here, behind you," she said.

Kemal turned as Duernie came running toward him from the now deserted guardsmen's position. She jumped into his arms as he hurried to her.

"Are you all right?" they both asked at the same time, then started to laugh together.

She snaked her arm around his waist and gently led him back toward the track city. "It took so long for the explosion, I thought something had happened to you."

Kemal swung his arms across her shoulders and he hugged her. "They're gone, Duernie!"

"Yes, we did it! We drove them off!" she cried. "They'll be back, of course, but we know we can beat them!"

As they neared the city, Kemal sighed and let his shoulders slump. "I didn't realize how tired I am, Duernie. I haven't slept for . . . a long time."

"Then let's get into the city and find some quarters," she said as they approached the door.

Shak stood by the opening, helping a wounded Dancer into the vehicle. Duernie stepped beside him and climbed into the city, then offered her hand to Kemal.

Shak roughly grabbed his shoulder and spun him around. "Not you!" he snapped. "You're not coming in our city!"

"Shak!" Duernie shouted. "Leave him alone! He helped us!"

"His people attacked us! They killed fifteen Dancers, and now he wants to come in and eat our food, drink our water," Shak's gritty voice proclaimed.

"Stop acting like this." Duernie grabbed Shak's sleeve. "He's not—"

"He's not a Gavilan?" Shak sneered. He jerked Kemal away from the door and pushed him away.

Kemal stumbled but this time managed to roll as he fell. "I don't want a quarrel between us," he said, raising himself on his elbow.

"Good," Shak said. "In another three hours, the sun will rise and you won't have a quarrel with anybody. Duernie, are you coming?"

She looked back at Kemal. "I'll talk to them," she said. "Will you be all right here?"

Kemal sat up. "Go ahead," he said. "But this smart suit isn't going to last three hours—talk fast." He smiled weakly at her.

She nodded and disappeared into the track city. Kemal watched the last stragglers climb into the arcology. Finally the door closed.

Then there was nothing.

Kemal watched the *Renaissance Gold* continue rolling along in silence. The debris of battle lay scattered around him, but he couldn't bring himself to move. It felt good just to sit.

He checked the temperature gauge on his suit; the external temperature was minus two hundred thirty-three degrees. He felt comfortable enough, but his feet were starting to get cold. Was the suit giving out already, he wondered, or was he just tired?

It didn't really matter much either way, he decided; this was a fine place to rest. He lay down . . . just for a moment.

The *Renaissance Gold* lumbered on at a steady ten miles per hour, a few feet per minute. Kemal watched the mobile city pass in front of his eyes, and then even that was gone.

The blackness of Mercury's night closed around him. It was as though he was in space again at zero gravity—nothing to see, nothing to feel. It was like the first time he rode a rocket, going to the military academy on Mars when he was four, and he shut off the lights in his quarters. In the morning, the steward had brought steaming cereal to the breakfast table . . .

Suddenly Kemal became aware of a bright light stabbing into his eyes and a rough hand shaking his arm. "Kemal!" someone far away shouted.

"Please, Enash, let me sleep a few more minutes. I'm not hungry yet," Kemal responded deliriously.

"Kemal, *please!*"

He blinked his eyes and tried to focus. "Duernie?"

"Get up, Kemal! Come on," she tugged at his arm. "You're coming into the city!"

She pulled him into a sitting position, then several hands grabbed him and hauled him to his feet. A ground vehicle waited a few feet away.

Corianne stood inside. She watched Kemal as he half-crawled into the car, her face a tight mask. "Are you well?" she asked flatly.

"I'm alive," he answered.

"I understand you walk some kind of walk," she said, glancing at Duernie. "I'm not sure what that means, but I wish to talk with you, and I can't speak with a dead man."

"Oh . . . yeah . . ." he mumbled as the car began to spin around him. "I don't think . . . I can walk at all . . ."

Chapter Nine

Kane leaned across his console and adjusted the focus on the *Rogue's* stern monitor; the picture flickered slightly, then resolved into a sharp image of the RAM cargo ship he had been hired to escort. The ship was huge, and somewhere along its outside hull Parsonawitz had packed the laser they were going to test.

The monitor flickered again and a crackling white line of ragged static formed along the left edge of the screen. Kane frowned and made a mental note to have the whole monitor assembly replaced when he returned to Mars. The repair was not really critical, but he was obsessive about keeping the *Rogue's* equipment in perfect working order. That obsession cost him dearly, but given the fortune he spent outfitting his private ship with the most elaborate weapons systems and monitoring devices, it was worth it. Then, too, in his line of work, any flaw in the equipment could cost him his life.

A radar blip appeared on the upper left of his screen—a very small ship, very far away.

Kane opened the communication link to the cargo scow. "*Rogue* to *Stellar Queen,*" he said, wondering why the most mundane working ships always bore such pretentious names—possibly to make those who worked on them feel they were something more than menial drudges. "Come in, *Stellar Queen.*"

"Yes, Kane." The image of Parsonawitz sprang to life on Kane's comm screen. "What's the matter?"

"Intruder in quadrant four," he said curtly. "I'm going to investigate." He had already begun feeding the course change into the ship's navigation computer.

Parsonawitz raised his eyebrows and looked away, giving Kane a good view of the small, discolored scratch Ardala had left on his cheek. "I don't see anything."

"You will," Kane said and abruptly veered off.

He set the ship's speed to three-quarters full and smiled to himself, smugly pleased that his own radar was better than the RAM ship's. Radar that powerful had cost him, but it had also saved his life.

As he neared the intruder, Kane saw it was a single ship, too small to be a pirate vessel . . . possibly a lure, however. They were deep in the asteroid belt, and a larger raiding ship might be lurking behind any of a hundred rocks floating nearby.

Kane activated the audio comm link, carefully leaving the visual broadcast channel off. "Come in, unidentified vessel," he said.

"You talkin' to me?" a prospector's hard, deeply

wrinkled face appeared on the comm screen. Kane could see the cockpit of the ship, a small, cramped cubbyhole of dangling wires and makeshift repairs that had seen more deep space than it should have.

"Yes, I'm talking to you," Kane said. "Who are you and what are you doing here?"

"The name's Keever," the prospector said. "My partner's had an accident and I'm trying to get some help."

"This is a forbidden area," Kane cut him off.

"Forbidden? By who?"

"By me!" Kane growled.

"Who the hell are you to shut down free space?" Keever demanded. "You're . . ."

"I am the man who's goin' to blow your ship past Jupiter if you don't turn that scrap bucket out of this quadrant in ten seconds!"

The miner scowled and started to argue, then bit back his words. "Look, I'm not trying to start a fight. I'm not working for pirates. Me and half a dozen guys are mining one of these rocks, and we had an accident. If I don't get my buddy to a doctor soon, he's gonna die!"

"There are no mining operations authorized in this area."

"Well, it's not exactly an authorized mine. We're just prospecting. Now, will you help us?" He reached over and swung the camera over so Kane could see his wounded comrade.

Kane looked at the injured miner; his head was poorly wrapped in a crude field dressing, and his arm was bound to his chest tightly with bloody bandages. It looked real, and Keever's voice had a genuine sense of emergency to it. He was more than likely exactly what he claimed to be. Still, Kane thought, I'm not paid to nursemaid miners.

"Keever, you have two seconds left to turn your

ship around and go back the way you came!"

"That's the opposite direction from Mars!" Keever said desperately. "My partner'll die!"

"Then go to the asteroid station at Ceres," Kane said and fired three short bursts from his laser in front of the prospector's bow.

"You son of a—!"

"That was a warning," Kane said calmly. "My laser is already locked on your hull. It's your move."

Cursing incoherently, Keever swerved aside and began a slow crawl away from the *Rogue.* It's probably as fast as that bucket can go, Kane thought with a thin smile. He watched the miner's course long enough to determine that he was indeed leaving the quadrant, then turned his ship back toward the *Stellar Queen.*

As soon as he entered communication range, Parsonawitz was on the line.

"Was it a pirate?" he asked.

"No, I don't think so," Kane replied. "Just some free-lance miners from one of these rocks. He won't bother us."

"Well, I'm glad you're back. We're about to set up the laser for the test. Do you want to come aboard and watch?"

"I'll stay here. That miner said something about an unauthorized operation out here, and I want to scan for it, just to make sure we don't have pirates in the wings."

"Oh, yes," Parsonawitz said. "That's your—"

"That's my job," Kane finished and cut the link.

He veered away from the cargo ship and made a show of sweeping the area. Then he eased his cruiser into a path that matched the *Stellar Queen*'s speed and direction. He set his scanners on maximum and settled back to watch.

The mammoth hull of the *Queen* slowly peeled

back, exposing the hold containing most of the laser. As Kane watched, the components detached themselves from the cargo deck and floated gently into space. Four extravehicular pods with long, snaking arms met the parts and guided them into position.

The whole assembly stretched about twenty feet in length. The work pods settled a large shiny black sphere in the middle of the components; from studying Ardala's plans, Kane knew it held the laser's guidance system and the capacitors that stored and released the energy to power the laser. Inside the black globe, the capacitors were arranged in a circle that rotated to bring each store of energy into firing position.

Two solar panels jutted from the sides of the sphere like enormous silver wings measuring fifteen by ten feet. Although the panels were connected to the capacitor assembly, they had nothing to do with the laser's destructive powers; the solar energy powered the systems that ran its internal mechanisms.

The weapon's energy came from a receiving dish on the stern; it was designed to draw energy directly from a Mercurian Mariposa station. Kane was sure Parsonawitz had already charged the capacitors for this test, but it was clear the laser was built for use close to Mercury.

The work pods attached another dish to the front of the laser. This was the heart of the weapon, where the energy from the capacitors was focused and directed at the target. Kane adjusted the zoom of his camera for a closeup inspection of the dish. Something was missing, he immediately noticed. The dish itself was complete, but three sets of brackets that were obviously designed to hold something were empty.

A beep from Kane's infrared detector drew his attention. A faint trace of heat energy showed on his screen in approximately the same area he had chased off the miner's ship. Kane opened a comm link to the *Queen.*

Parsonawitz appeared on the screen looking distracted. "Yes, *Rogue,* what is it?"

"I've got some infrared activity," Kane began. "It could be pirates."

"Well, check into it, man!" Parsonawitz snapped. "We're in a very delicate phase of assembly now and I don't want to be disturbed."

"Just thought you'd like to know, in case we have trouble," Kane said. "*Rogue* out."

Kane turned his ship toward the speck he had detected and accelerated. It wasn't far from their present location, since they had drifted farther into the asteroid belt.

His detectors remained quiet as Kane approached; no ion disturbance, no heavy combustion exhaust, nothing but infrared specks on a medium-sized asteroid. Kane matched the rock's speed and drift, holding his ship in a steady orbit at the outer range of his scanners. His visual image was dim, but he could see mining equipment clearly; no weapons other than an excavation laser, no ships larger than personal craft. Nothing to worry about.

He thought of buzzing the operation, just to let the miners know someone was watching them, but decided it wasn't worth the effort—not that Kane had anything against showing off, but he was more curious about the laser than intimidating prospectors.

As he headed back to the *Queen,* he saw the laser was complete and moving away from the cargo ship. Kane swung around to get a look at the front dish.

Yes, he mused with a smile, that's where the sun crystals fit. He zoomed his scanner up as tightly as he could on the forward dish; the three brackets he'd seen each held three of the Mercurian crystals angling upward to carry and focus the charge of energy from the capacitors.

Kane had seen sun crystals on Mercury when he raided the Dancers' crystal farm at the Eye of Phidias. The coordinates Ardala had given him were inaccurate, but he did manage to find the farm and commandeer a dozen crystals to sell later. In the process, he had unknowingly blown up Gordon Gavilan's own laser aboard one of the orbiting Mariposa stations, believing it was a security satellite. Even Ardala didn't know he had taken the crystals.

These crystals looked different than Kane expected. While his crystals stood about six feet tall, straight and clear, the crystals Kane now saw in Parsonawitz's laser were not so perfect; they had a milky color that threw off a dull rainbow shimmer. The crystals Kane got on Mercury shined with brilliant colors that dazzled the eye.

The laser suddenly flickered to life. A broad, ruby-colored beam of light shot out from the dish toward a small asteroid fifty miles away. The red light washed over the rock and then winked out.

Kane opened a line to Parsonawitz.

"*Rogue* calling *Queen*," he said. "Come in."

The monitor brightened on a scene of white-jacketed technicians dancing and hugging one another with howls of laughter.

"Kane, did you see it?" Parsonawitz came on the screen, his face breaking into a beatific smile.

"I saw it," Kane replied, putting just a touch of boredom in his voice. "Let's see what you did to the asteroid." He swung his forward cameras around to the rock and relayed the image through his comm link.

The asteroid was still whole—the laser hadn't fragmented it—but its surface had . . . melted. Kane looked for the rough, jagged rocks and outcroppings characteristic of asteroids but saw nothing but a smooth, glassy sheen.

"Lord," Parsonawitz whispered, awed. "The whole surface has fused, even at fifty miles! Geelin, Holsher, come here and look at this!"

"Parsonawitz, I don't want to get in the way of your celebration, but what's wrong with your crystals?" Kane asked.

"What do you mean? What do you know about crystals?" Parsonawitz turned to the monitor, a haughty disdain in his voice.

"I saw some on Mercury, and they looked much better than the ones you have."

"Oh," Parsonawitz sounded deflated. "You've been to the crystal farm, then? Unfortunately, we don't have access to top-quality crystals. For the purposes of this test, we have had to adapt crystals from the sculpture the Dancers of Mercury sell. Not the best grade, but good enough to conduct initial tests. By the way, what was that infrared blip you went off to investigate?"

"Just some prospectors. I ran one of their ships off earlier."

"Yes, I remember. Where are they?" Parsonawitz asked, an ugly gleam in his eye.

Kane looked at him sharply, then smiled a crooked grin. "They're about a hundred miles away in"—He glanced at his infrared scope—"quadrant three."

"Ah, I have them. They're at the outer range of the laser—at least, the theoretical range. No one has tested the device that far." Parsonawitz's voice was excited.

"I admire a man who tests the limits," Kane said, forcing a laugh.

"Do they know we're here?" Parsonawitz asked.

"At this range, no. I doubt they have any deep-space scanners. They probably spent their last credits just to get here."

Parsonawitz nodded and chuckled. Kane saw him reach down to the console beside him and shift a joystick. On another monitor, Kane saw the laser begin to turn toward quadrant three.

Kane flicked the comm link off and let his face relax into a scowl. Parsonawitz turned his stomach; not for killing in cold blood, but for making sure the miners were blind and helpless before turning his laser on them.

Well, he sighed, the people you have to work with for fifty thousand credits. . . .

The laser oriented itself. Kane drew a deep breath and let it out slowly. He knew what was coming and engaged the visual block on his communication channel.

Within moments, Parsonawitz's voice crackled over the audio. "*Rogue*? Come in, *Rogue*. I can't get a visual from you."

"Yeah, I know," Kane said wearily. "My circuits are getting touchy."

"Better have it looked at," Parsonawitz said, and Kane could almost see the Martian's supercilious sneer.

"What do you want?"

"Get out to that asteroid and confirm the coordinates," Parsonawitz said. "At this distance . . ."

"Your scanners are accurate enough," Kane cut him off.

"Then get out there anyway," the Martian insisted. "I want to see what the laser can do at this distance."

Kane scowled and fed the course into his navigation system. "*Rogue* signing off," he growled and sheered away.

"And make sure your external camera circuits don't get touchy," Parsonawitz called.

As the *Rogue* followed its course, he saw the deep

red laser beam streak past. But it wasn't quite as strong now; there was almost a waver along its edges, and maybe even a little pink in it.

Yes, definitely a faded pink, Kane noticed. He quickly activated his forward scanners as the beam raked across the asteroid. The beam was so pale that Kane could hardly see it as it touched the asteroid.

"Are we on target?" Parsonawitz asked over the radio.

"As far as I can tell," Kane said. "The beam is pretty weak."

"The capacitors are discharging at full power. It must be the crystals. They're not concentrating the energy properly."

Suddenly the beam disappeared.

"Damn!" Parsonawitz shouted. "The crystals cracked! We knew they were fragile, but I didn't think they'd give out after two firings! Get to that rock, Kane! I want to see what the laser did at that distance."

"I'm coming up on it now," Kane said, swinging the *Rogue* into a tight orbit around the asteroid.

The beam had eroded half the surface, including the heart of the miners' operation. Kane ran his camera feed directly into the comm link.

"There!" Parsonawitz said, excitedly. "Get close to that edge!"

Kane zoomed in on the swath of destruction. Again he saw the molten, glassy fusion he'd seen on the first asteroid, but this time half the rock had not been touched by the beam.

"Do you see that line separating the melted surface from the rest of the rock?" Parsonawitz enthused. "See how fuzzy the line of separation is? If I'd had prime-quality crystals, that line would be as crisp as a knife blade even at a hundred miles! Check for traces of the miners or their equipment."

Kane wasn't squeamish about death, but Parsonawitz's ghoulish excitement made him uncomfortable. He swept his cameras across the melted area until he found a large discolored blotch.

"That looks like the remains of some heavy equipment," Kane reported. "Maybe a drill assembly."

"Are there any . . . bodies?" Parsonawitz asked, his voice quivering with excitement.

Kane frowned and fidgeted uneasily. "Those dark smears around the big blotch are probably the miners," he said coldly.

"Get in closer," Parsonawitz almost panted. "It's for . . . scientific curiosity, you understand. The laser's effects on a person have never been properly documented."

"You've got these transmissions on tape!" Kane exploded. "You can slaver over them all you want later. I've had enough! *Rogue* out!"

"Kane!" Parsonawitz shouted. "You're being paid—"

"I'm being paid to head security, not run errands for you!" He smashed his fist on the console, cutting the comm link.

❍ ❍ ❍ ❍ ❍

The *Rogue* hovered at the extreme range of the *Stellar Queen*'s monitors—close enough that Parsonawitz knew he was still on the job, but far enough away that Kane didn't have to listen to the Martian. After all, there were always problems with communication links.

He studied the cargo ship for a long time as it hung in space. The work pods were disassembling the laser and packing it back in the hold as Kane watched.

The ship really was unwieldy, he thought. A huge transport with a six-man crew, fourteen science technicians for the laser, and four of Kane's own men for internal security. If he wanted it, the *Queen* was a ripe fruit ready to be plucked. He could have it without a fight. Well, maybe there'd be one casualty, he thought with a smile.

Since Gordon Gavilan of Mercury was unwilling to sell any of his sun crystals, Kane's cache became immensely valuable. If he could offer a client both the laser *and* a supply of crystals, he could name his own price—and get it.

Anyone with that kind of money and ambition would be in the upper levels of the solar system's power structure. You don't just walk up to a Gavilan or Holzerhein and say, Hello, wanna buy a laser that can destroy a quarter of a planet in fifteen seconds?

No, Kane realized, he needed a broker who moved in such circles. And the only person he knew in that rarified realm was . . .

Ardala's image formed on his personal communication line. "Come in, Kane," she said. "Are you there?"

"Why, Ardala," he said with a trace of irony. "I was just thinking about you! What a pleasant coincidence."

"Yes, we fill each other's thoughts constantly," she said with a seductive smile. Then her face hardened—time for business, Kane knew. "Is this line safe?"

"Yes, but if it would make you feel better, punch in scrambler code eight-seven-four-slash-zero-zero-two." As he told her the numbers, Kane entered them himself. The screen went dark as the ship's computer switched to the security code. Like everything else on the *Rogue,* the scrambler codes were expensive, and he changed them often.

After a moment, Ardala's face appeared once more. "There," Kane said. "We're as safe as RAM's security can make us. What's on your mind?"

"You're not thinking about stealing the laser, are you?" she asked bluntly.

Kane balked. Even with the best scrambler money could buy he didn't want to talk about the laser over a comm link. "No, of course not," he said with just the right amount of righteous indignation. "I've been hired to guard it. To even think about stealing it wouldn't be ethical."

"I'm relieved to know you are so . . . ethical," she said, emphasizing the last word.

She has to know better than to discuss something like this on a line, Kane thought; she *wants* me to say no. "I am, however, thinking of selling a very big product. Very big indeed. Do you think you can help?"

She paused a moment, studying his face on the monitor. "Yes," she said slowly. "But I am engaged in several projects just now."

"Oh, Ardala, where's your sense of adventure? Are you getting cautious in your old age?"

"It's not a matter of caution," Ardala bristled. The reference to age rankled her, as Kane knew it would. "But I think we're being manipulated."

"Manipulated? By whom?"

She hesitated. "It doesn't matter. Someone who wants to control everything just for the sake of controlling. Kane, don't you think it's odd that you were hired to head security for the laser test? I mean, your reputation is—"

"My reputation is my concern," he interrupted.

"Yes, but hiring you to guard the laser is like hiring a cat to protect a bird. You're being invited to steal the laser."

"Why? Why would someone do that?"

"I don't know! It's just part of some twisted plan."

"Ardala, you see plots behind every sunrise. And

even if it's true, does it really make a difference as long as I—or we, rather—make a profit?"

"I just don't like feeling that somebody can make me dance to a tune I didn't choose. Besides, we can do better than the laser. Kane, we can have a planet! The laser itself is useless without sun crystals, and the only place to get them is Mercury."

"I have some crystals," Kane interrupted her gush of words.

Ardala stopped in midsentence. "You have—"

"Yes, after that fiasco you sent me to on Mercury, I picked up some as compensation. I've got crystals, and the laser is mine for the taking. How much do you think a package like that is worth?"

She didn't say anything for a long moment, her mind racing furiously. "Where are they?" she finally asked.

"Ah, my dear, I think that information is better left in my care."

"Kane don't do anything until we can talk."

"You *have* become cautious. We both know hesitancy can cost an opportunity."

"Damn you, Kane!" Ardala burst, then regained control over herself. "Listen. I'll be at the Juniper Tree Restaurant tomorrow evening. You'll be back by then. Let's talk, Kane." There was an edge of urgency in her voice.

Kane leaned back in the cockpit and smiled. "All right, Ardala. We'll talk. At the very least, we'll talk."

"Kane, I'm telling you, don't do anything rash."

"My dear, I wouldn't dream of it."

Chapter Ten

"How did you choose me, Miss . . ." Dak Melinov glanced at the plastic card lying amid the clutter of his desk, "Miss Sharr?"

"Please, my name is Toyana."

Melinov leaned back in his battered chair and set his feet on the corner of his desk. The ancient chair groaned under the weight of his portly physique. If not for his stubbly jaw and crow's-feet, the detective's freckled face and reddish hair would have made him seem young. He was nevertheless motivated. No doubt about it, he decided, this Toyana Sharr has that special *oomph*. She had a fine nose that swept up just right and coal-black hair with a shimmer of colors in the highlights; her suit looked as if it had been sculpted out of maroon candy and stuck to her voluptuous curves.

"You didn't say why you came to me," Melinov said again.

"Well," she looked down, slightly embarrassed. "I have a friend who employed you in a . . . domestic matter."

Melinov heaved a deep sigh and slipped his thumbs beneath the suspender straps that circumscribed his girth. "Naturally," he said wearily. "It seems ninety percent of a private detective's cases are divorces." He snapped forward to his computer and flicked it on. "What's the problem? Got a straying husband you want followed?"

Her head snapped up, a tinge of blush coloring her cheeks. "Nothing like that, Mister Melinov," she said, shocked. "We've already gone through the legal proceedings. But, you see—" She leaned forward, her eyes wide with concern—"he has something of mine, some gems I'm very attached to."

"That's something you'll have to take up with the court," Melinov said.

"I already have," she pouted. "The judge gave my husband the jewels on some technicality."

Melinov shut his computer off and swept a clear space on his filthy desk for his elbows. "Are you asking me to steal something, Miss Sharr? Because if you are you can just—"

"On, no!" She recoiled, her mouth forming a cute little "o." "I just want you to find where Kathgo is keeping my property. Kathgo is, or rather was, my husband."

Melinov scratched the side of his nose. "Just what is it you want me to do, Miss Sharr?"

"Toyana, please."

"All right, Toyana!" Melinov snapped, getting

exasperated with the woman's coyness. "Why are you here?"

"I just want you to follow my husband and find out where he's hiding my jewels." She opened her eyes wide with a look of vulnerability and . . . promise? Melinov wondered. He felt his heart go out to her.

"Okay, Toyana, what does he look like and what are the jewels like?"

"They're crystals, really." She smiled and fluttered her eyelashes. "Very long, about six feet. They're part of a very valuable piece of sculpture."

"I get the idea," Melinov cut her off. "Now, how do I know this guy when I see him?"

"He'll be at the Juniper Tree this evening at eighteen hundred hours. Here's a picture." She passed him a high-resolution computer printout with a five-hundred-credit note clipped to it.

Melinov raised his reddish eyebrows at the sight of the bill. His usual fee was seventy-five credits plus expenses. Five hundred credits was more than he earned in a month. He sat up at his desk like a man who suddenly found a reason to live.

"Yes, well." He quickly slipped the money into his pocket in a smooth, sweeping motion. "Nice-looking guy," he said, glancing at the picture. Kathgo—if that was his name, and for five hundred credits Melinov was willing to believe it—was handsome. He had dark hair, a straight nose skirted by a thin mustache, and green eyes.

"Shall we draw up a contract then?" Melinov asked.

She leaned forward intently, gripping the edge of his desk. "Do we really need such legal formalities? I mean, locating my jewels is just the first step. Other steps need to be taken, and I'm sure we don't need to involve you in what may happen later." She let the implication hang.

Melinov coughed gently. "I see. Yes, I don't want any records, either. How do you want me to let you know where your merchandise is?"

"You don't have to contact me at all," she said, handing him a small cylinder with a transmitter antenna. "Just activate this marker when you find them and leave it with them. I will take care of everything else."

"Where can I get in touch with you?" Melinov asked, a wolfish smile spreading across his face. "I never get personally involved with a client, but after the case, we could maybe have a drink."

"I don't think so, Mister Melinov." She stood up and turned to the door, then glanced back with a seductive smile that made the detective's heart skip a few beats. "But if I ever have need for your . . . services, I shall certainly look you up." She opened the door and wriggled out of his office.

Melinov whistled softly and sniffed the lingering scent of her perfume—very expensive perfume. She was somebody he wanted to know better.

Well, he sighed, after all, he was a detective and she shouldn't be hard to find. He'd keep his ear to the ground. If he heard of a big jewel theft, it wouldn't hurt to know where she was; his silence could be worth a lot more than five hundred credits.

Outside the shabby office building, Ardala let her face relax into a distasteful scowl. She hated this part of Coprates, with its dirty streets and cutthroat denizens waiting around every corner; she had more hidden armaments on her than even Kane normally carried.

Come to think of it, she reflected, life here wasn't that much different from her own business. It was just that the people here got less money for what they did than she received. And they dressed badly, she mused.

○ ○ ○ ○ ○

Melinov felt uncomfortable and took a long sip of his second drink to still the feeling. He had his best suit on—or rather, his least dirty and wrinkled suit—and was still getting sneers from the stunning fashion plates who came into the bar.

After all, he told himself, this is just another bar, even if it is in the most expensive part of Coprates. These ultra-uppers are such a pain, he thought, and glanced across the street to the entrance of the Juniper Tree Restaurant. Still no sign of Kathgo, or whatever his name was.

Melinov had spent the rest of the afternoon chasing down information about the man his client called Kathgo. Or rather, trying to find information. Nothing was in any computer network file under the name she had given him or his picture. And there was nothing about Toyana Sharr, either. Something was wrong, but for five hundred credits he could at least check the story out.

Melinov took another sip and almost choked. There he was! Dark hair, mustache—it had to be him! Melinov jumped from his stool and headed for the door as the man entered the Juniper Tree. He just reached the street as Kathgo stomped out of the restaurant, his face dark with anger.

Melinov dodged behind an elegant skimmer and watched as Kathgo stormed down the street, staring at the ground. He fell in step a few yards behind and waddled along, trying to keep up with Kathgo's furious pace. Whatever had happened in the restaurant, this guy was *mad*! Melinov followed him for a while, but it was clear he wasn't really going anywhere, just walking off anger. Well, eventually he'll have to go somewhere, the detective thought.

Where he ended up was the rough side of Coprates.

In fact, Kathgo turned into a bar just across the street from Melinov's office. What the hell would a classy guy like Kathgo want in a dive like this? Something to do with the jewels? Melinov knew he had to get closer.

He looked around the street and saw three familiar figures shuffling in an alley.

"Match!" he called. "Lump! Kashka! Commere, I got a job for you!"

O O O O O

Kane was furious. He boiled with anger and frustration.

Three days of listening to Parsonawitz's bragging and superior sneers, his sick tastes . . . and Kane had to walk away, leaving him untouched. He could have had that laser in his hands, made sure Parsonawitz had an accident, and been several million—a billion—credits richer. Now the laser was locked in a RAM lab, where he couldn't get at it.

All because Ardala had to open her mouth and tell him to wait. And he did! "Let's talk at the Juniper Tree," she had said, but when he arrived at the restaurant there was a note saying: "Things are happening—can't explain but will see you here at midnight."

Kane crumpled the note in his pocket and looked up. He had been walking blind for the last hour, just blowing off steam, and found himself in an area he didn't recognize. Dark streets, cracked sidewalks, battered skimmer cars, suspicious figures watching him from alleys. Just the part of town he wanted now.

Kane went into the bar on impulse and found probably the worst dive he'd been in on Mars—cracked tables held together with cargo staples, stools that had been patched together with other discarded stools, naked fluorescent lights flickering from the peeling ceiling. The whole place reminded Kane of the countless bars he had grown up in on Earth. The bartender even had an eye-patch—too broke to have the simplest corrective surgery.

This will do just fine, Kane thought with a grin.

The bartender looked up as Kane came to the bar, then gave him a cold once-over. "Nice suit," he said in a rough whisper. He had a throat injury, too, it seemed.

"Should be," Kane said. "It cost me enough." The rest of the patrons stopped their conversations and stared at him. Kane could almost feel them counting the money he had.

"We don't get many of your kind in here," the bartender said.

"Yeah? What happens when you do?" Kane asked with an arrogant sneer.

"Trouble," the barkeeper said. "Whaddya want to drink?"

Kane pulled a roll of money from his pocket and peeled off a fifty-credit note. He could feel every eye in the place following the bill as he let it drop on the bar. "Give me a Lambro Swirl with a twist," he said, naming the most ridiculously fancy drink he could think of.

The bartender scowled in disgust and reached under the bar. He banged a cheap bottle of Wodkar in front of Kane and folded his arms as if daring him to protest.

Kane took the bottle of liquor and nodded. "Just what I had in mind," he said, and turned to face the barflies, wondering which of them would make the first move.

A middle-aged Martian starting to get a paunch sidled up to the bar next to Kane. "Sleeve," he called to the bartender. "Give me some of what you gave my friend here." He nodded toward Kane.

"Get it from him, Melinov," Sleeve growled. "Your tab's big enough already."

The newcomer turned to Kane as three shabby men entered the dive. "Hey!" one shouted. "You serving ultra-uppers in here now?"

"He's got the credits," the bartender said. "That's more than I can say for most of you scum!"

The three men sauntered over to Kane. The first was tall and thin, almost emaciated; the man behind him had a broken nose and only one ear.

The shortest of them stepped close. "So you've got credits, huh?" He leered. He wore a big, bulky radiation jacket—perfect for hiding weapons. He's the first one to take out, Kane decided, measuring the man; a quick kick to the kneecap to break his leg . . .

"Come on, boys," the paunchy red-headed man next to him said. "He's a stranger here, and we don't want to seem unfriendly."

Kane glared at him, baring his teeth in a snarl. Before he could tell the Martian to shut up, one of the three men grabbed at him.

In one movement, Kane caught his wrist and slammed his palm against the man's elbow. There was a satisfying snap, and the man screamed. The small guy reached into his coat, and Kane slammed into him with his shoulder. He staggered back, his arms flailing; a laser pistol flew from his jacket and clattered across the floor.

Yes! Kane thought, a wave of exhilaration washing over him; this is just what I need to get this day out of my guts!

He turned to the third man, shifting his weight for a quick kick. The man was already winding up for a punch.

Melinov abruptly jumped off his stool and stepped

between Kane and the last man. "Stop it, Match!"

Melinov's interference fouled Kane's kick, leaving him off balance. The thin man's fist shot past Melinov and connected with Kane's chin. His head snapped back, and dark swirls clouded his vision. Melinov threw his arms around Match as Kane grabbed him roughly by the shoulder and ripped him away.

"Get out of my way," he hissed, reaching for the man's neck.

Match knocked Kane's hands aside and grabbed him in a bear hug, pinning Kane's arms to his side. He knew he didn't have the strength to hurt Kane, but he needed a moment to collect his thoughts. He hadn't expected so much fight from the ultra-upper; in seconds, both Kaska and Lump had been taken down and he knew if he didn't do something soon, he would be on the floor, too.

But Kane wasn't giving him time to think. Snapping his leg up, Kane kneed him in the groin. Match screamed in agony and reeled backward. Kane followed him, driving his fist into the man's stomach. With a strangled grunt, Match crumbled to the floor.

Kane watched him for an instant, then turned to the others in the bar; before he even raised his head, someone smashed a stool across his back. The flimsy seat flew apart without doing any harm, but Kane rolled with the blow. He somersaulted across the floor, rolling into a crouch as he searched for the small man's laser pistol.

Melinov held the weapon, staring down at Kane for a paralyzing moment. He smiled, then turned to the men gathering around.

"That's enough, boys," he said. "I think the man has had enough excitement for one night."

A dozen men glared at him and his laser, then slowly went back to the bar to finish their drinks.

Melinov extended his hand to Kane. He brushed it away roughly.

"What did you do that for?" Kane scowled, getting to his feet. "It was just getting fun!"

Melinov raised his eyebrows slightly. "The odds were getting a little too rough and I figured you needed some help."

"You'll get a sunburn on Pluto before I'll need help against trash like that," Kane nodded toward the patrons.

Melinov set the pistol on the bar and nodded to himself; having seen the man's lightning reflexes and strength, he knew he wasn't just boasting.

"Well, sorry to spoil your fun," Melinov said. "I was just trying to lend a hand."

"Yeah, thanks," Kane said sarcastically. Despite his snarl, Kane felt good inside. The fight was just what he needed to get rid of the past few days' tensions, and he felt himself starting to relax. He even found that he was starting to like the pudgy Martian.

"Let me buy you a drink," Kane said, pushing the bottle of Wodkar to him.

"Thanks, I appreciate that," Melinov said, pouring himself a shot. "My name's Melinov."

"Kane."

Melinov looked sharply at him when he mentioned his name, but Kane didn't notice. Without the cloud of anger and frustration, he could see through the tangle of words and schemes Ardala was weaving around the laser. What did she say—something about a great controller manipulating their lives? She was either getting paranoid, or just trying to keep *him* from stealing the laser she wanted.

The laser really could have been his for the taking; well, he could find out where it was easily enough. Combined with his crystals, he had a package that could make anybody a king.

Of course, why should someone else have that power? Kane thought.

Everything hinged on his crystals, and Kane realized with a start that Ardala knew he had them now. The first thing he had to do was move them off Mars to a secure orbit Ardala couldn't find.

"Listen, Melinov, you said before that you wanted to help me. Are you still feeling benevolent?"

Melinov shrugged. "For a few credits, I can be real helpful. Watcha got in mind?"

"I need to move some merchandise. Fifty credits?"

"Make it seventy-five."

Kane nodded, smiling. "Got a smart suit?"

"Sure. We going Outside?"

"Yeah. Get your suit and I'll meet you here in twenty minutes."

○ ○ ○ ○ ○

"So, what are you going to do with these jewels?" Melinov asked again.

Kane scowled and made an impatient noise deep in his throat. For the last two hours, Melinov had been chattering about the "jewels" and asking what they were for. Even beyond the prying—which was irritating enough—he kept referring to the crystals as "jewels," and that was getting on Kane's nerves.

"Look, there's another twenty-five credits for you if you can keep your mouth shut until we get these loaded at the spaceport," Kane said through clenched teeth.

"Anything you say, pal," Melinov said.

Pal. Kane grimaced and jerked the jetcar into the cargo loading lane of the Pavonis port. Melinov slid awkwardly across the seat and banged into the door painfully.

Kane grinned at him as he pulled into the loading

bay beside a small cargo ship.

"End of the line," he said as he shut the engine off and popped open the storage compartment. Before Melinov could get out, Kane was gently lifting one of the long crystals out of the car.

Kane opened his mouth, but Melinov cut in quickly. "Yeah, I know—be careful!" he said. "I heard that enough tonight."

"Good," Kane said shortly. "Remember it. If you break one of these . . ." The threat hung in the air.

One at a time, the two men loaded the crystals into the cargo ship. Melinov glanced at the cockpit to see if there was any sign of a pilot. "You gonna fly this yourself?" he asked as he loaded the last "jewel."

"What do you want, another fifty credits?" Kane sneered. "This is as far as you go. The ship's a radio-controlled model and I'm going to get my cruiser to take her as far from here as I can." He pulled a wallet from his coat and took out a hundred-credit note. He gave it to Melinov. "Your services are no longer required." Kane started to walk away.

"How am I supposed to get back?" he asked.

Kane turned back, extracting another bill. "Here's a twenty," he said, stuffing the credit note into Melinov's coat pocket. "Take a cab. And secure that hatch." He disappeared into a corridor.

Melinov sighed, relieved that Kane was finally gone. He'd been waiting for an opportunity to plant the transmitter Toyana Sharr had given him, but Kane—or Kathgo—had been watching every move he made since they reached the jewels, hidden at the edge of the Forest of Pavonis. Melinov took the small marker device out of his pocket and hid it in a corner of the small ship's hold, then switched the transmitter on. . . .

The explosion ripped apart the loading dock with enough force to knock Kane against the wall of the hallway. A cacophony of alarms and emergency bells began instantly.

Kane bolted down the corridor the way he had come, but he knew what had happened even before he reached the gaping hole that had been the dock of his cargo ship.

He knew very well.

○ ○ ○ ○ ○

"Ardala, my dear!" Kane said, rising from his chair. "You look wonderful!"

She swept around the table and brushed his cheek with her lips. She did indeed look wonderful in a vermillion gown with broad shoulder platforms that curved into her waist and billowed down to the floor.

"And you're looking your usual dashing self, darling," she answered. "Am I terribly late?"

"No more than is your habit," he replied, smiling. "I believe the Juniper Tree customarily adds a half-hour to your reservation time as a matter of policy."

She laughed lightly as she sat opposite him. "How was your day?"

"Oh, busy and exciting," he said casually. "And it's been an explosive evening."

"Has it?" Ardala asked absently as she glanced over the menu. "I don't recall if I've ever had the Soya-Prot Pavonis here before. Do you know how it is?"

"Before we get too deeply into the small talk," Kane began with a feral grin, "I should tell you I have a small, discreet laser locked on that organ you laughingly call a heart. There is only a slim chance you will survive the main course."

Ardala continued studying the menu. "Are you upset about something, my love?"

"I don't like having my plans ruined!" Kane said in

a low whisper that had a dangerous overtone.

Ardala brushed back a strand of hair, her sleeve slipping back to reveal an ornate bracelet of small cylinders, each with a flashing LED display.

Kane recognized the bracelet as an explosive device linked to a life sign monitor; if her vital functions fluctuated, it would detonate with the force of a heavy cannon shell.

"I don't like my plans interfered with either," she said, her face now deadly serious. "We don't want to do anything messy in this restaurant, do we?"

Slowly Kane brought his pencil laser up and set it on the table. Ardala unsnapped her bracelet and laid it beside his laser. She knew he had other weapons on him, but he knew just as well that she did, too.

"Shall we talk?" he said.

Ardala leaned over the table, looking steadily into his green eyes. "The laser is *small,*" she said, emphasizing the last word.

Kane started to laugh. "That's odd coming from you. You've done nothing but rant and rave about your stolen laser for weeks!"

"Maybe I've been too caught up in old habits and patterns," she answered. "Maybe we've both become too predictable. When you get predictable, you can be manipulated."

"Is this that paranoid fantasy you told me about on the radio?" Kane sneered.

Ardala pursed her lips grimly. "It isn't a fantasy, but that doesn't matter. Kane, the laser is just money. We can have a planet!"

Kane leaned back, studying her face thoughtfully. "You've never been hungry for an empire before. Something has changed in you, Ardala."

"I just think it's time to do something unpredictable. A planet, Kane! Think of it!"

"With that laser and my crystals, I could have had

a planet!" he whispered fiercely. "I could have *taken* a world!"

"But how long could you have held it against RAM?" she interrupted.

Kane paused. "I could have held it with the laser," he said stubbornly.

"What if RAM *gives* us a planet?"

"Why would RAM do that?"

"Kane, think for a minute! RAM has the laser, but it's useless without . . ."

"Mercurian crystals. I know. I *had* some."

"And if RAM got its hands on them, it wouldn't need us anymore."

"Then it'll just go to Sun King Gavilan and buy some."

"That's something we'll have to work on," she said. "Or rather, I will. You need to get back to Parsonawitz—" Kane snorted with disgust—"and get RAM to begin making invasion plans for Mercury."

"Anything else, General?" Kane asked sarcastically.

Ardala reached across the table and took his hand. "Oh, did I hurt your ego?" she asked solicitously. "Did I usurp your precious male prerogatives?" Her face hardened. "Swallow your pride this once, Kane. It'll be worth it. I promise you."

Kane flicked her hand away, but continued to watch her with narrowed eyes. He could go along for a while; it wouldn't cost anything. It sounded good, and if things started to go bad, he could always get out. Besides, new opportunities always came along.

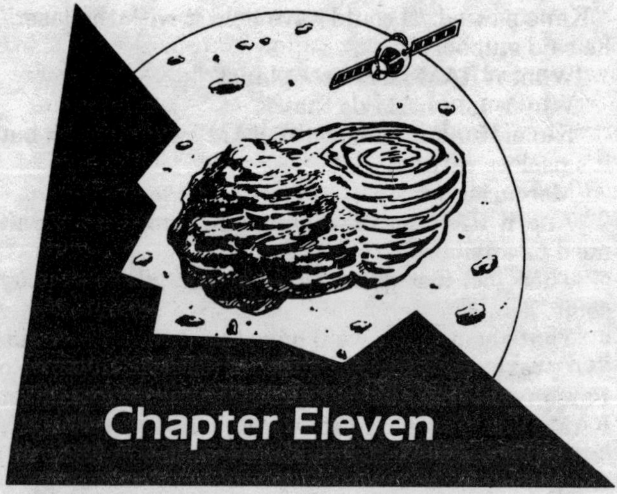

Chapter Eleven

The procession stretched endlessly. A double rank of guardsmen dressed in the gold, black, and yellow Gavilan colors stood at attention in an unwavering line from the halls of the palace complex through the courtyard and disappeared down the streets of Mercury Prime.

An army of courtiers and high-ranking citizens accompanied the royal coffin as it slowly progressed along the route. Custom dictated the king's funeral procession should wind through the major thoroughfares of Hielo so every citizen could pay final respects in his or her own way. But that custom came from a time when the people actually cared for their Sun

Kings. Most of Hielo's citizens came out for the procession, but there were no displays of grief, just stone-faced silence as the coffin was wheeled along its path.

The Gavilan colors were everywhere—a virtual flood of gold, black, and yellow. Banners with the royal tricolor hung from every building; clothes for the courtiers were made in the color scheme, uniforms, arm bands . . . it was enough to make Dalton sick.

He stood with the ministers of state on a raised platform at the end of the courtyard, watching the glass coffin inch its way past them. Dalton tapped his foot impatiently, wishing the body would wend its way out of sight so he could get on with being Sun King. Sun King. Dalton liked that. His Royal Majesty Dalton Gavilan, Sun King. He rolled the syllables around in his mouth silently, savoring them.

A gentle cough beside him broke Dalton's reverie. He glanced irritably at the minister of state as he delicately touched a gold-colored handkerchief to his lips. They were all there—the seneschal, minister of war, secretary of trade, the whole lot of them, wearing appropriately dour faces that were supposed to represent grief.

And Tix was on the platform, too. He was perhaps the most irritating of all, Dalton thought, because his face seemed marred by genuine sorrow. The little hypocrite.

Tix looked down at the glass coffin as it slowly passed them. The last few days had been so filled with work and taking care of details that he hadn't really had time to think or feel. Or maybe, he thought, I haven't allowed myself to think. Now, with the stately procession filing past, he had no tasks to focus on, no last-minute crises to fix; there was nothing to do but stare at his father's body.

He had never been close to Gordon. He was always a disappointment to the king—always a younger son without the forceful personality of Dalton, never involved with the important matters of state, never able to earn the respect of the people who made worlds move. That realm made Tix uncomfortable, left him feeling off center, unbalanced. Only when he was drawing or sculpting did he feel at home with himself. Kemal had been the first to give him enough faith in himself to trust his art.

Tix caught himself looking around the crowd for Kemal's face. Of course he wouldn't be present. Dalton had accused him of killing Gordon and put a price on his head. That puzzled Tix; he knew Kemal wasn't a killer. Certainly Kemal was a soldier who had killed in war, but he wasn't the kind of man who poisoned.

Tix shook his head and rubbed his eyes, trying to shake the image of Kemal out of his mind. He turned his attention to the funeral. The glass coffin had advanced to the end of the platform they stood on. The transparent casket was his idea. Tix had volunteered to oversee the "arrangements" for Gordon's funeral; if he couldn't please his father in life, at least he could do something for him in death.

Not that there was really much Tix could do as far as the funeral went. Custom dictated most of the events, from the three-hour eulogy to the formal vigil kept by the highest ranking members of the government and family, culminating in the long parade through Mercury Prime to the spacedock, where a ceremonial rocket would carry the body into the sun.

But Tix managed to add a few touches. He arranged the Gavilan colors to be displayed with different proportions of yellow, black, and gold in various places along the route, so the colors wouldn't become monotonous. The design of the glass coffin was his;

four sheets of glass held by baroque pillars under a dome of marble in the shape of an old Earth mosque.

Every step of the program was sniffed at by Ral Terens, the court arbiter of taste, an irritatingly fastidious man who always had an answer for every question of etiquette based on age-old custom. Tix suspected he made up most of his "customs."

Dalton snorted impatiently as the casket cleared the end of the platform and continued through the courtyard. His foot began tapping an erratic rhythm. Arbiter Terens leaned close and whispered in his ear; Dalton scowled and shook his head.

"It's far enough out of sight for *my* custom," Dalton growled and abruptly walked to the rear stairs.

Terens gaped after him, his thin eyebrows dancing a jig of disbelief across his forehead. He *harrumph*ed indignantly and clutched at the minister of state's shoulder as if to emphasize the horrendous breach of protocol.

The others on the platform watched in shock as Dalton stomped down the stairs; after a moment, they started to follow him back to the palace. Tix remained on the platform, torn between watching the coffin and joining the others. As the last official left, he suddenly felt very vulnerable and foolish standing alone, staring after his father. With a sigh, he turned slowly and climbed down.

The palace staff was apparently not expecting Dalton and the others back so soon. Guardsmen lounged in the throne room, chatting with servants when Dalton burst in through the doorway. Everyone made a mad scramble to their places, but he just waved absently at them.

"Get out, all of you!" Dalton said irritably.

The guards and servants looked at each other.

"Leave me, I said!" Dalton bellowed.

The underlings jumped toward the doors as the officials and courtiers glanced at one another, wondering if he meant them as well.

"Prince Dalton—" Terens came forward, all smiles and tactful conciliation—"that was a very moving ceremony this morning. Please allow me to express my deepest sympathies for you in this time of sorrow and transition."

Dalton stared at him until the arbiter's smile wilted. Finally Dalton shook his head and said, "Thank you, Terens. But the title is wrong. I'm surprised at you. I'm no longer a prince, but the Sun King."

Terens stammered and cleared his throat. "Well, of course, in essence you are, naturally. But the official coronation ceremony has yet to be conducted, and the customary—"

"Damn you and your quibbling!" Dalton suddenly exploded. "I *am* the Sun King! The son of a Sun King, from a long line of Sun Kings! Do you dispute my right to the title?"

"Certainly not, certainly not," Terens said quickly. "It's just that the council has a traditional role in confirming your succession and bestowing the Chain of State."

"The council?" Dalton echoed. "You can blast the council into the heart of the sun along with my father's body! I don't need the council to confirm anything! Where is that chain you're so proud of?" He glanced around the room and saw the chain hanging on the throne.

The Chain of State was the symbol of the Sun King's power; it consisted of a heavy gold chain with a pendant depicting a stylized image of the sun. Bulky and unwieldy, it was rarely worn except for coronations and funerals. The chain had draped Gordon's body while it had lain in state, then had been hung carelessly over the arm of the throne.

Dalton picked up the chain and swung it over his head. It wrapped itself awkwardly around his shoulders. "Now," he said, turning to Terens. "I've got the chain on. That makes me king, right?"

Terens's mouth flapped open, but he made only a short, choking sound. The ministers and officials of court stood back motionless as Dalton descended on the hapless arbiter.

"If . . . if you do this," Terens finally managed to stammer, "the council will see it as a challenge to its authority."

"Good!" Dalton snapped. "That's exactly how I want it to see it! I will not have the council 'grant' me my title! They have no authority over me." He grabbed Terens by the front of his shirt and pulled a mono knife to his throat. "Do you dispute my title?"

Cartonah, the minister of war, hurried to Dalton. "Your Lordship!" he said urgently. "What are you doing?" He had been captain of the guardsmen thirty years ago and still fancied himself a soldier, though the position had been only ceremonial.

Dalton ignored him, keeping his knife firmly against Terens's throat. "Do you accept my authority?" he repeated grimly.

Terens's eyes bulged in terror. "Yes, yes, Your Majesty," he babbled. "My liege lord, you are king!"

Cartonah put his hand on Dalton's shoulder. "All right, he said it," he began, but Dalton turned on him with his knife still humming.

"How about you, Minister?" he said threateningly. "Do you recognize my right to the throne?"

The old guardsman stepped back, flustered by the weapon. "I . . . acknowledge your title," he said slowly, a gleam of anger burning in his eyes.

Dalton grinned at him, then turned to the others in the room. "And the rest of you?" he shouted. "Anyone question my sovereignty?"

The courtiers glanced at each other, their faces uncertain.

Dalton swept his eyes around the room. "I asked you all a question!" he shouted. "Now answer me!"

A low murmur began among the ministers. Dalton took a step toward the seneschal, who cowered away from him.

"You're the king!" he said quickly. "Hail to the Sun King! Hail to the Sun King!" The seneschal looked around the room, seeking support from the other courtiers. "Hail to the Sun King!" he repeated, a note of desperation in his voice.

Another voice joined him weakly. "Hail to the Sun King."

Another man took up the chant, then another.

Dalton glanced at them, his grin widening into a smile of triumph as the entire room began chanting.

"There is a new custom I wish to institute," Dalton said. "Or rather, a very old custom from Earth—you will appreciate this, Terens! I want you to bow to your king."

Terens looked up at Dalton, his eyes wide with a mixture of horror and rebellion. Obeisance to the king had never been a tradition on Mercury; the stiff-necked miners and gamblers who forged a living from the inhospitable planet had no patience for humbling themselves before anyone. Even after generations of court life, there was still a seed of independence and pride in Mercurians that balked at bowing to a king.

"My lord," Terens said, raising a hand to protest.

Dalton's arm shot out, his fingers clamping around the arbiter's hand. He began to squeeze.

Terens's face twisted in agony as Dalton exerted more force. Slowly his knees buckled and he sank into a grotesque crouch. The minister of war stepped forward, his fists clenched at his side.

Dalton spun around on him, glaring. He flung Terens's mangled hand from his grip and stepped toward Cartonah. "I said bow to your king!"

Cartonah stepped back and stared at Dalton, blinking furiously. Slowly he sank to his knees and lowered his head—more from shame than in honor of his sovereign.

"Terens, make a note of this in your book of traditions." Dalton sneered. "The proper obeisance is on one's knees with the head down. Do you all understand that?"

The others grudgingly knelt, hanging their heads. Dalton looked around with satisfaction, until he saw Tix still standing.

"What's this?" Dalton said, walking toward him. "No respect for your king?"

Tix stared at him, his eyes hard. "You are m-m-my brother," he said with a cold voice.

Dalton nodded as he approached him. "Very well. Terens, add this to the tradition: Those of royal blood needn't bow."

"Yes, my liege," Terens said softly.

Dalton wrapped his arm around Tix's shoulder and leaned close. "Well, little brother," he whispered. "It's been a rough morning, eh? But at least we've got their attention." He chuckled quietly. "Help me with this, Tix. Smooth things over for me. Use some of your artistic tact. Get these fools out of here, but do it gracefully." He gave Tix's shoulder an affectionate squeeze and smiled. "Do that for me?"

Tix shook himself free of his brother's grip. "Yes, Y-y-your Majesty," he said, his face a frozen mask.

Dalton looked at him, still smiling. "Good. Remember, tactful!" He turned and walked to the throne, pulling the chain over his head.

Tix stepped over to Terens, who was still on his knees, clutching his hand. "That's enough, Arbiter

Terens," he said gently, touching his shoulder. "I think we've all had enough of this t-t-travesty."

Terens raised his head, a stream of tears rolling down his cheeks. "Tix . . . " he began but couldn't continue.

"I know," Tix said. He helped the arbiter up by his arm. "Let's j-j-just get out of here."

Terens stood and coughed softly. "Gent—" he started, but his voice broke. He cleared his throat and straightened to his full height, carefully facing away from the throne, where Dalton sat. "Gentlemen," he said finally, his voice shaking, "I believe the king's business is concluded for today."

The others began to rise and shuffled sullenly to the door.

"Your Majesty," Terens said coldly, still standing with his back to Dalton, "are there any customs regarding how we are to take our leave of you?"

"You can crawl out on your bellies for all I care," Dalton said. "As long as you get out!"

Terens closed his eyes and pursed his lips but said nothing. The arbiter fell in line with the other officials as they left the throne room, walking with stiff dignity.

"Is there some kind of comm link in here?" Dalton asked as the last man left.

"I don't know," Tix said.

"What about the computer that records the dreary details of state affairs?" He rose from the throne and went to the console beside the secretary's station. "Ah, here we are," he said, activating the comm line.

Tix started toward the door but paused, curious about who Dalton was in such a hurry to call.

Dalton was spending more time than usual opening the link; his fingers moved across the keyboard slowly, with painstaking concentration, as if he were struggling to make sure a very long code was absolutely perfect. Tix wandered to his side as the monitor screen lit up.

The image on the screen was of a very tall, pale man with inhumanly beautiful features. He was speaking, but no sound came through the line. Tix recognized the man's general morphotype. "He's a Martian," he whispered to his brother.

Dalton shrugged Tix away and adjusted a knob on the console.

". . . to whom am I speaking?" the Martian asked as the sound came up.

Dalton cleared his throat and leaned closer to the receiver. "You are Joachim Parsonawitz?"

"Yes, that is correct. Who . . . ?"

"Ah, good. I am Dalton Gavilan, Sun King of Mercury." He paused for a moment, as if to allow the significance of his identity to awe the man.

Parsonawitz tilted his head slightly, studying him. "I offer you my condolences on the death of your father," he said with cold formality.

"Yes, yes, thank you." Dalton waved the subject away impatiently. "We need to talk."

"Before we get to that," Parsonawitz interrupted, "I would like to ask how you got my personal communication code."

"You are head of RAM's munitions division, Warhead," Dalton said pompously. "As such, you are a very important man in the solar system. Your comm code is—"

"Highly classified," Parsonawitz finished.

"But available," Dalton added with a smile. "Now, let us talk about the laser. The laser my father had built before you—yes, I believe it would be accurate to say you—stole the design."

Parsonawitz raised his eyebrow a fraction of an inch. "Well, first I'd like to congratulate you on your spy network. It's sometimes hard to remember that even a backwater like Mercury can take an interest in matters beyond its scope."

Dalton's face reddened at the insult. "That depends on the ambition of the man in charge," he said, a note of anger beneath his words.

"Yes," Parsonawitz said slowly, appraising him. "I can see that you do have ambitions." His voice was calm, but there was a disturbing undercurrent, almost a threat. "Well, what is it you wanted to ask me about the laser?"

Dalton blinked. Somehow he had lost control of the interview and felt an unnerving sense of uncertainty. "The laser was designed for use by Mercury, and there are certain features that make this world indispensable to its operation."

"Yes," Parsonawitz said, his voice bored. "The energy receiving dish, the sun crystals. We are well aware of the design flaws." He emphasized the last words. "What is the point of this call?"

Dalton swallowed hard enough for Tix to hear him. "The point is that the weapon is useless to you without Mercury. You need me."

"Useless?" Parsonawitz repeated. "Perhaps you would be interested in seeing a tape we recently made." He reached for a button, and the comm screen suddenly darkened.

Tix leaned closer and saw the dim image of the laser take shape. A vivid red beam shot out from the end of the weapon and swept across a tiny asteroid; the screen dissolved in a white scatter of static, then focused on the melted rock. After a moment, the screen showed the laser again, facing a different direction; again the ruby-colored light shot forth, but this time no target was visible.

"The test tapes you are viewing now were made under my personal supervision," Parsonawitz said, off the screen. The image zoomed in on a larger asteroid, its features fused and glassy. Several dark stains spread across the ruined surface of the rock. "This is a closeup view of a mining operation that—unfortunately—got in the way of a test firing. You'll understand if I don't give you the details of the weapon's range at this point, but you can see its destructive power is impressive."

Dalton gaped at the image on the monitor. "How did you get crystals?"

"Oh, they're available," Parsonawitz said casually. "Crystal sculptures have been sold throughout the solar system for years. They may not be prime quality, but they are adequate for our purposes."

"I have top-quality crystals," Dalton said desperately. "If you bring the laser into Mercury's orbit, we could—"

"Is that what this call is about?" Parsonawitz was incredulous. "You want RAM to *give* you the laser?"

"Not give—it would be a mutually beneficial agreement."

Parsonawitz laughed. "Mercury is very far from Earth and the NEO forces. What would be the point of parking our weapon in your territory, for your use? You offer a trade agreement?" he scoffed. "There are other ways for RAM to get what it needs without trading with a pompous little tyrant—"

"Pompous little . . ." Dalton sputtered, his eyes bulging with fury. "How dare you address me . . ."

"If there is nothing more you have to say, I believe this discussion has taken enough of my time," Parsonawitz said. The monitor abruptly went black.

Dalton backed away from the computer, his gaze fixed on the screen. Impulsively he grabbed the first thing at hand—a technician's cup—and flung it at the screen. The machine exploded in a shower of colored sparks and flame. The smell of burning electrical insulation spread into the room.

"That insignificant pup!" he shouted. He turned on Tix murderously. "Who does he think he is to speak to me that way?"

"He thinks he's the head of RAM's weapons division," a cool, feminine voice said behind them. "And that makes him one of the most powerful men on Mars."

Tix turned to look at the woman as she stepped into the room from an adjacent door. He gaped at her for a second; she was the most beautiful woman he had ever seen—tall and slender with raven-black hair that cascaded onto her elegant shoulders. She wore a candy-striped jacket that looked as though it had been chosen to match the striped design of Hielo's palace. Her dress was split to the hip, revealing a long, flawless leg when she walked.

"That means nothing on Mercury, Ardala," Dalton raged, pacing furiously across the throne room. "I am king here!"

"He is just a servant who has risen above his station," the woman said. "You must impress upon him your position and not allow him to dictate terms."

"Your advice was less than helpful," Dalton snarled.

She smiled with some secret satisfaction, Tix noticed. From the way they spoke, it was clear she had been on Hielo for some time, plotting with Dalton. Tix glanced at the shattered monitor. Not a very successful plot, he thought, then remembered her smile. He gently coughed to gain her attention.

She turned to him. "Who is this, dear?" she asked of Dalton.

The king glanced up. "Oh, that's just Tix, my younger brother."

Tix drew himself up to his full height. "Tacitus Orrin G-G-Gavilan," he said, trying to sound as dignified as possible for her. "Miss . . . ?"

"Ardala Valmar," she replied, her voice as smooth as honey. "Pleased to meet you." She smiled at him and Tix felt his heart jump.

"You're from M-M-Mars, aren't you?" he asked, flustered by her attention.

She laughed, a soft musical sound. "Yes, that's right."

"A-a-and you know that m-m-man, the one Dalton w-w-was talking to?"

"Joachim? Naturally I know him," she purred. "He is a very high-ranking member of the RAM board of directors, and so I know him well. RAM felt the new sovereign of Mercury should be greeted and welcomed to the realm of interplanetary politics—" She glanced at Dalton to make sure he was listening—"and power."

Dalton slowed his pacing at her words and nodded slightly; his chin came up an inch and he smiled with an air of royal dignity.

She's flattering him, Tix realized; she's playing on his pride and ego to make him . . . do what?

"You really shouldn't let a mental inferior like Parsonawitz spoil your plans," she said. "After all, you are the absolute ruler of one of the most important worlds in the solar system."

"Yes, I am," Dalton said, smoothing his tunic. "I proved that to those fools this morning."

"Dalton, you heard w-w-what the man said. He doesn't n-n-need to trade to get what he wants."

Dalton looked from Tix to Ardala. "You're not trying to say RAM would actually launch an attack on a sovereign world?" Dalton demanded.

"Of course RAM wouldn't," Ardala said quickly. "Besides, Joachim hasn't the authority to start something like that." She faced Tix, her eyes turning hard. "RAM's interests lie in another direction."

"Yes," Tix said. "Earth."

She smiled. "That's right. It's an old conflict that has nothing to do with you." There was the slightest hint of a warning in her voice.

Tix straightened, raising his head imperiously. "RAM's conflicts with Earth *are* of no interest to me. I'm an artist, and your b-b-battles are boring."

Ardala stared at him, her eyes glittering as she tried to read his face. Tix returned her gaze unflinchingly, until she abruptly turned to Dalton.

"Your Majesty," she said, "surely there's been enough business for one day. You did promise to show me the surface of Mercury. Perhaps we could take my cruiser. There are several features you might find interesting." Her voice made Tix shiver with curiosity.

"Of course, my dear," Dalton said, approaching the seductress and extending the crook of his arm. She delicately wrapped her hand around his elbow and followed him out.

As soon as they had left, Tix ran to the computer console. The screen was utterly destroyed, but he managed to activate the voice link and punched in Planet Security.

"Captain Hazid here," a crisp military voice said. "Who is this?"

"Prince T-T-Ta—"

"Oh, Tix," Hazid suddenly sounded bored.

"Dalton asked m-m-me to oversee the s-s-search for Kemal. Do you have a r-r-report on his location?"

"Yes, I believe one of our patrols did monitor a message from Kemal about joining a track city."

Kemal is with the Dancers! Tix rejoiced silently. He made it! "Do you know w-w-which track city?"

"There's been so much disruption because of the funeral, our reports are getting backlogged," the captain said. "Let me check the records."

Chapter Twelve

Kemal! Are you there?" The metallic voice of the intercom startled Kemal out of his half-doze. "Come in, Kemal!"

He jumped out of his bunk and banged his head on the low ceiling. Cursing and rubbing his head, he flipped the intercom switch on the decrepit computer, then fumbled for the light knob. Even at its highest intensity, the light was never more than a dull glow. Like everything else in his quarters, the lights were old and substandard.

"Kemal here," he growled into the receiver. "What is it?" His mood was ugly, to say the least. The Dancers had taken him into their city, but they obviously didn't like him; they'd given him the oldest and smallest room in the arcology, he was shunned by everyone except Duernie, and anytime a Dancer did have to speak to him, he knew he was being tolerated—just barely. After two days of such treatment, Kemal was almost ready to take his chances on the surface.

"There's a Gavilan ship approaching us," the intercom reported. "We don't know who it is, but they're calling for you."

"For me? Who knows I'm here?"

There was a pause. "I don't know," the voice answered impatiently. "But if you've led the Gavilans to us again . . ."

"All right, I'm coming!" Kemal snapped. He turned to the door and banged his head on the jamb.

He stormed into the corridor, rubbing his forehead. As near as Kemal could tell, he had been put in the front of the *Renaissance Gold*; the Dancers had no jail cells, but his quarters were as close to the concept as the nomads could get. The halls of the track city were almost as dim as his room, but then again there wasn't really anything to see. The walls were dull metal plates riveted together; the Dancers, with their innate desire for ornamentation, had draped colorfully printed clothes and woven tapestries over the iron walls. Most of them had ragged patches.

Kemal frowned at the shabby decoration but couldn't quite bring the scowl to his lips. The colored rags had a warm feel that made the metal monster at least bearable if not comfortable. There were no mistakes in a track city, no treachery, no sense of watching over his shoulder for a poisoned drink or a knife. Something to face and defeat, or be beaten—it didn't really matter as long as he was away from the intrigues of Hielo.

And now Hielo was following him here. He heaved a deep sigh as he approached the entrance to the track city's central control.

Control was a wide, low-ceilinged room, suffused with a bright yellow light. Individual work stations glowed with different colors, depending on the computer console or scanning screen at the station. There was a friendly smell of food and hot drinks drifting from the stalls; Kemal smiled to himself, imagining what his former commanders would say about such laxity. All in all, the room had a human feeling missing from the more efficient—and severe—military life.

As soon as Kemal stepped in, two Dancers grabbed his arm and led him quickly to the communication station.

"Where have you been?" Vamir, the control ace, demanded. The track city was commanded by an "ace" for eight-hour shifts; Kemal had met the current chief the day before and was impressed by his straightforward manner. Whatever the short, portly Vamir felt about Kemal personally, he didn't let that interfere with his business or how he treated Kemal.

"I've been finding my way through these halls," Kemal said curtly. "Now what about this ship?"

Vamir turned to the console. "He's been staying out of visual range, but we have voice contact. He wants to talk to you."

"Who is it?"

"We don't know, but the ship is Gavilan registry." Vamir punched a button and handed Kemal the microphone. "You tell us who's up there."

Kemal took the transmitter. "This is Kemal, aboard the *Renaissance Gold,*" he said. "Will the Gavilan craft please identify itself."

The radio spat static for a second, then: "K-K-Kemal, is that really you?"

"Tix!" Kemal cried. "What are you doing up there?"

"Trying to f-f-find you. Something happened on Hielo."

"What?"

"I d-d-don't want to say on the radio. Can I land?"

"Just a minute." Kemal turned to Vamir, but the man's stony face froze the words in his throat.

The ace stood with his feet planted like a stone, his arms folded over his chest. "No," he said shortly. "I'm not letting another Gavilan in my city."

"I know this man," Kemal said. "He's not like Gordon or Dalton. You can trust him."

"I'm supposed to take *your* word on that?" Vamir snorted. "Man, I'm not sure I trust you yet."

"Vamir, something happened on Hielo. I don't know what, but it's important enough to make Tix leave Mercury Prime to come looking for me. Now . . ."

"Look, Kemal," Vamir interrupted, "I'm responsible for the lives of more than two hundred Dancers in this city. During my shift as ace my decision is final. If you want to appeal to the tribe, go ahead, but until I hear from them, my word is no."

"Let him land," a low, feminine voice as hard as iron called from behind.

Kemal and Vamir turned together.

"Corianne!" Vamir exclaimed as the small woman came to his side. Kemal stepped back a pace as she stared at him.

"I don't believe there is any treachery in this man," she said quietly.

Vamir looked at her, confused. Although she was high in the Dancers' loose hierarchy, she was not a resident of *Renaissance Gold* and had no real authority, other than the universal respect she earned in a lifetime of devotion to Dancer goals.

"I beg your pardon, ma'am," Vamir said hesitantly, "but I'm ace right now, and that decision is mine."

She smiled and put her hand on Vamir's arm. "Of course you're right. I didn't mean to interfere," she said. "But I would like to add the weight of my words to whatever decision you make."

Vamir stared at her for a moment, then looked to Kemal. He glanced back at Corianne, then shook his head. "All right," he said. "There's a small platform on the port side . . . oh, here, I'll give him the coordinates." He took the microphone.

"Bring him to the common room when he lands," Kemal said. "I'll talk to him there. Oh, and have Duernie meet me there, too, would you?"

Vamir was already on the radio. He nodded to Kemal absently, waving him away.

Smiling, Kemal turned to leave. Corianne stepped in front of him.

"May I come with you, Kemal Gavilan?"

"Certainly," he said. "I'd like to thank you for helping me."

She smiled at him, looking directly into his eyes. "Did I help you, or the Dancers?"

O O O O O

The common room was the largest chamber in the track city. It had probably been designed originally for storage or cargo transport, but now it served as a combination tavern, restaurant, exercise room, meeting hall, art gallery, and home to any of a thousand other activities the Dancers came up with.

Like virtually every Dancer structure, its ceiling just barely cleared Kemal's head. Tables and chairs scattered over part of the floor while other areas were clear. Some parts of the room were furnished with very elegant couches and carpeting, while other areas had a run-down appearance. It was almost as though the common room was a microcosm of the planet itself and its inhabitants—everyone from manual laborers to administrators crammed into one huge cavern.

Kemal and Corianne walked over a section of the floor covered with sand, picking their way through tables where Miners sat nursing cheap drinks, to a space paved with polished stone slabs. Hanging lamps with colored lights reminded Kemal of the garish spacer bars he'd seen in some free ports of the asteroid belt. After the dull, colorless environment of Mercury's surface, the bright lights and colors provided a much-needed diversion for the senses.

Corianne sat on a sofa and made a motion for Kemal to join her. He glanced longingly at a simple stool near the counter, but sat beside her instead.

"So tell me," Corianne began, "how do you like life among the Dancers?"

"I've always liked it," Kemal replied, trying to emphasize the point that he was familiar with Dancer ways. "But I don't think they like me much. Or at least they don't trust me."

"I think they're uncertain about you," she said. "If they didn't trust you to some degree, your body would have been vaporized by the sun already."

He looked away with an uncomfortable feeling of just how thin his link with the Dancers was.

"Kemal!" he heard Duernie call, and looked up as she waved at him from across the room.

He returned her wave and watched as she hurried through the tangle of tables. She hugged him fiercely, then slid down on the couch next to him, leaving her arm across his shoulders.

Kemal turned to Corianne. "Why do you suddenly trust me?" he asked bluntly. "When I saw you in the council chamber on Hielo, you hated me."

"Since then I've seen you risk your life to save this track city. Then, too," she added, "there is the testimony of the heart. Words can lie, and actions can be other than they seem, but it's hard to deceive with the heart."

"How can you see into my heart?" Kemal asked.

"I can't," she said simply, then glanced slyly at Duernie with her arm around Kemal. "But there are other signs, tracks a heart makes in its journey. I trust those tracks."

Duernie became self-conscious under Corianne's gaze and shyly snaked her arm back to her lap. Kemal smiled at her and put his hand over hers.

Two Dancers approached the group, leading a third figure between them. One of them stepped forward. "This is . . ."

Kemal leaped from his seat. "Tix!" he cried, embracing his cousin. "What are you doing here? This is very dangerous for you!"

"I had t-t-to tell you," Tix began. "Dalton is p-p-planning something. I overheard him on the radio."

"Sit down." Kemal gestured to the couch. He waved to Corianne and introduced her.

Tix stopped in midstep and looked at her. "Corianne of the D-D-Dancer council?"

She nodded slightly. "I'm surprised you know me."

"All of Mercury knows C-C-Corianne the Dancer," he said, awed. "You're almost a l-l-legend."

She studied his face dispassionately, trying to decide if his words were genuine or simple flattery.

Kemal waved to Duernie. "And this is Duernie."

Tix stepped closer to her, smiling broadly. "So this is who K-K-Kemal has been talking about for so long."

"He's told me all about you, too, Tix," she said, laughing. "He says you're an artist."

Tix blushed and turned his face away, obviously

pleased at the recognition.

"What about Dalton?" Kemal interrupted.

Tix turned to him, his eyes suddenly urgent. "I heard him t-t-talking to a Martian—Parsonawitz," he began. "Dalton was trying to g-g-get RAM to let him use the laser in exchange for crystals. Parsonawitz wouldn't agree."

"Thank the stars!" Duernie breathed. "Without crystals the laser is useless."

"The laser is operational," Tix said. "I s-s-saw tapes of the test! It *melted* half an asteroid—a big asteroid! There were p-p-people on it, too, I think."

"Where did they get crystals?" Kemal asked, feeling a knot form in his stomach.

"They used D-D-Dancer sculptures. Kemal, I think Parsonawitz is going to attack Earth with the laser. Maybe Mercury, too. Ardala said—"

"Ardala?" Kemal broke in. "Dalton talked to her?"

"She was there, on Hielo."

Kemal's face drained of color. He turned to Corianne. "If RAM doesn't want to trade for crystals, it means they're going to attack Mercury! We've got to do something to prepare! Can the Dancers . . ."

"The Dancers have been arrested," Duernie said bitterly. "We watched the guards rounding them up."

"Not all of them," Tix said. "Only a few hundred. M-m-most escaped into the desert or the w-w-warren tunnels."

"Can you collect the Dancers?" Kemal asked Corianne. "Organize some kind of defense? Maybe get the Miners to help, and the Musicians."

"I don't believe the Dancers will die to help the Gavilans," she said coldly.

"This is greater than the Gavilans, or the Dancers," Kemal leaned forward. "If RAM comes here for the crystals, Mercury will become a colony of Mars! Ardala is utterly ruthless. She'll stop at nothing to get those crystals for RAM."

"You know her?" Duernie asked.

Kemal ducked his head. "I met her once, yes," he admitted.

"What did she want?" Duernie demanded.

"She offered to make me Sun King if I'd share the crystals."

"Sun King? How could she do that? The royal family . . ." She paused as Kemal looked up at her, and the meaning in his eyes sank in. "You mean invasion?"

He nodded. "Mercury is facing a very real threat. Corianne, can the Dancers put aside their distrust of the Gavilans to face this? Could all the factions of Mercury work together for the planet as a whole?"

Corianne shook her head. "I don't know, Kemal Gavilan. There is a long history of division and distrust here. Any unity would depend on the leader, and I assure you, the Mercurians will not rally behind Dalton."

Kemal licked his lips thoughtfully. "We've got to try." He turned to Tix. "You said Parsonawitz told Dalton something about using the laser on Earth? Does NEO know?"

"I don't think so," Tix replied.

"We've got to warn Doctor Huer, then."

"Is there a comm satellite nearby that we can bounce off to the solar lines?" Duernie asked. "I'm not sure the computer system in this city can link to NEO."

"It doesn't matter," Kemal said quickly. "Huer gave me a portable uplink." He held up his arm, showing them a small band around his wrist. He removed the bracelet and punched in a short code, then placed it on the table. A small LED display glowed a dull red, then blossomed into a rainbow of colors that slowly projected into the room. The swirl of colored flecks coalesced into the computer-generated image of Doctor Huer.

Although he could have taken any form he chose, Huer preferred to appear as he looked to Buck Rogers when the aviator had known him in the twentieth century: an eccentric middle-aged man with a lean body.

Huer removed the ever-present pipe from his mouth and smiled. "Ah, Kemal," he said. "It's good to see you again. And you, Duernie. I'm sure this isn't just a social call, Kemal. What's the matter?"

❍ ❍ ❍ ❍ ❍

A swirl of light-particle confetti suddenly filled the cockpit of the pirate ship *Free Enterprise*. Black Barney's genetically enhanced reflexes did not waste time with surprise or bewilderment. His hand instantly reached for his hand laser and drew it into firing position in the split second before the lights formed into Doctor Huer.

"You," Barney said shortly and returned his gun to its holster as quickly as he had drawn it. The same biological engineering that removed the momentary paralysis of shock also eliminated the period of readjustment after danger had passed. Barney was essentially an emotionless fighting machine. His reactions were simple—a threat meant battle; if there was no threat, he went about his business.

"I'm sorry, I didn't mean to startle you," Huer said unnecessarily. His image formed in the ship's copilot's seat. "There's an emergency and we need your help."

Barney looked up from his console. "Emergency? What else is new?" his deep, rumbling voice said.

"The RAM laser is functional, and I think it's going to be used on Earth."

Barney turned to him. "How do you know?" he demanded.

"Another part of me is talking to Kemal on Mercury right now, and his cousin saw tapes of the test firing. Barney, it looks as if RAM is planning to attack Earth and Mercury!"

A dangerous gleam grew behind Barney's eyes. "What's the problem?" he asked. "We destroy the laser and everything's fine."

Huer drew a deep breath and frowned in frustration. "Barney, it's not that simple. We don't know where the laser is, but RAM is certainly guarding it with its best troops."

Barney nodded enthusiastically. "Then it'll be a good fight!" His seven-foot muscled body tightened with excitement. Barney had been developed as part of a clone project by the RAM subsidiary Dracolysk; the brutal training that killed so many of his clone mates had left Barney with the only genuine emotion Huer had ever seen in him: a deep, obsessive hatred for Dracolysk and its parent corporation. That hatred gave birth to the Oath of Blood and Steel between the surviving clones of the Barney project, an oath that had bound them in loyalty to one another over the years since their liberation.

"Barney, this is too much for you alone," Huer said with exasperation. "Get in touch with the other Barneys and try to find out where the laser is. I'm going to alert the NEO forces. If I find out where the laser is, I'll let you know."

The pirate scowled. "All right," he said begrudgingly. "I'll call the others. Don't know how many are close enough, though."

"Get who you can," Huer said. "We'll meet at the free port Sanctuary in twelve hours." Huer's holographic image abruptly dissolved.

○ ○ ○ ○ ○

Huer's sudden departure left Kemal and the others startled into silence. More accustomed to the computer personality than the rest, Kemal quickly recovered his composure and jumped from his seat.

"Well, Huer can warn the NEO forces and Black Barney," he said, pacing with nervous energy. "That leaves us to worry about Mercury. Corianne, you're the most respected figure on the planet. Can you organize the Dancers, maybe contact the other factions—the Miners and Musicians and—"

"Slow down, Kemal," Duernie said. "We're not even sure—"

"There's no time to slow down!" Kemal burst out. "We don't know when the RAM forces will leave Mars. Any delay gives them the advantage!" Kemal felt better with a clear cut enemy threatening. Even if the odds were against him, at least he knew which way to face.

Corianne stood, smiling indulgently to Duernie. "I suppose I'd better start doing my part," she said.

"Yes," Kemal said, stepping close to her and unconsciously putting his hand on her arm to direct her toward the door. "Now Tix says the funeral is over, so the guards will be coming back to round up more Dancers . . ." His voice faded as they walked away.

Shaking her head with a chuckle, Duernie turned to Tix. "What are you going to do?"

He shrugged. "Go back to Hielo, I g-g-guess."

"You don't seem happy there."

Tix shrugged again, more a gesture of defeat than uncertainty. "It's m-m-my home."

"You could stay here, with the Dancers."

Tix smiled weakly. "They don't seem to like G-G-Gavilans much."

Duernie opened her mouth to protest, but Tix

shook his head. "My uncle Garrick tried to leave Hielo, but Dalton caught up with him. There's n-n-no running. I've got to g-g-go back and face my life. At least I have my art."

Duernie smiled and reached across the couch to pat his shoulder. "You don't even know how strong you are, do you, Tix?"

"M-m-me?"

Duernie laughed gently. "Yes, you. You're welcome to stay, but if you go back, I want to wish you luck, . . . Tacitus."

He returned her gaze, his eyes darting across her features, looking for some trace of mockery. "Thank you, Duernie," he finally said, standing up. "Kemal seems busy, so I'll ask you t-t-to say good-bye for me."

Duernie leaned over to look past him. "No, here he is. You can tell him yourself."

Kemal rushed up, his face a mixture of worry and exultation. "Well, at least that's started. Duernie, we need to visit some other track cities, talk to the Dancers, maybe some Miners if we can find them."

"Kemal," Duernie stopped him. "Tix is leaving."

Kemal spun around to his cousin. "Already? You just got here!"

"It's dangerous for me to be here. I've g-g-got to get back."

"Yes, of course," Kemal said. "Thank you for taking the risk to tell us."

Tix nodded and started to turn away, then he paused. "Oh, I almost forgot. Kemal, I wanted to give you something." He dug into his pocket and handed Kemal a small lump of metal. "It was your father's."

Kemal took the object and examined it. It was badly melted, but he recognized it as a royal signet ring. "Where did you get this?"

"Gordon gave it to me a long time ago, when I was a child. Just after father b-b-became king, he gave

Dalton and me mementos of Ossip, to remind us that we were Gavilans, he said. Dalton got the royal mantle, and I got this. I'm s-s-sorry it's melted, but it was your father's and I thought you might w-w-want it. He was wearing it . . . you know, when he . . ."

Kemal clenched the ring in his fist. "When he died?"

Tix nodded. "Father said he t-t-took it off Ossip's hand himself."

"Why would he wear a melted signet ring?"

"I d-d-don't know. Maybe it happened when he died."

"Tix, my father drowned in the greenhouse. Shazimar told me so." He paused thoughtfully.

"Yes, that's what F-F-Father always told me."

Kemal opened his hand and looked at the ring again. The edges were melted smooth and the design of the Gavilan arms had been partially dissolved and swirled together. It had definitely been exposed to a great deal of energy.

"Tix," Kemal suddenly said, his voice tight, "take me to Hielo with you! Right now!"

"What's the matter?" Duernie asked.

"I don't know," Kemal stammered. "But this ring . . . something's wrong!"

"What about the invasion?" Tix gripped his arm. "You've got to t-t-talk to the Dancers."

"I . . ." Kemal began uncertainly, a war between duties raging in his mind and across his face. "My father . . ."

Tix moved closer to Duernie; he started to say something, but she put her hand on his arm to stop him.

Kemal's eyes darted from the ring to Duernie as his face clouded with a frown. Then his lips pressed together into a thin, hard line. "Tix, I'm going to Hielo," he said firmly.

Chapter Thirteen

Nestled in the asteroid belt, the free port Sanctuary was the worst place in the known universe—or the best, depending on who was describing it.

Absolutely no outside authority existed on the rock. Mercenaries met to form raiding parties; information brokers lounged in the bars, selling their knowledge or picking up new tidbits from all corners of the solar system; pirates carted their booty through the streets without fear of the wrong eyes seeing them.

Black Barney normally had a calming effect on the asteroid's exuberant inhabitants. People tended to give the seven-foot battle clone a wide berth; the presence of two other Barneys with him made the denizens of the Short Circuit tavern positively docile. There had been only two fights in the bar since they had arrived half an hour ago, and nobody had even been hospitalized.

"That's it, then?" Quinto asked. "Three of us against the whole RAM corporation?" Despite the cautious words there was a ferocious gleam in Quinto's eyes, a battle lust that only a Barney—born and modified for war—could understand. Quinto was a near match for Black Barney, though the pirate was slightly taller and more massive in his arms and chest; they both had a similar network of scars crisscrossing their flesh. The only major difference between them was that Quinto wore his hair long instead of like Barney's functionally short hair. Quinto worked as a free-lance courier, a go-between who "handled" matters for his clients, and while his activities were essentially legal, he had no scruples about crossing the boundary of legality if there was reason or profit.

"How many of us does it take to destroy one laser?" Ochoa-Varilla asked, smiling easily.

Ochoa-Varilla was the most respectable-looking of the Barneys present; just over six feet tall, he dressed in Belter gear—a smart suit with heavy boots—but did not share the rambling life of the independent asteroid nomads. He was a scientist and inventor who had amassed enough of a fortune to buy his own asteroid and employ a small army of security men to safeguard his domain. His "projects" sometimes took years to complete, but they were always eagerly sought by the highest corporate and governmental agencies—except for RAM. Ochoa-Varilla steadfastly refused to deal with the Martian conglomerate.

"I would have thought Black Barney himself could

have handled this task. I for one am delighted he asked me along, since I missed our last reunion," said the scientist.

The "reunion" had been a full-scale attack by the Barneys against the Dracolysk Corporation. Dracolysk had developed and trained the Barney line of clones for RAM; the brutality of that training had killed the vast majority of Barneys and earned Dracolysk the survivors' undying hatred. The attack had destroyed Dracolysk and its founder, but the revenge had cost the battle clones dearly; one of the few surviving females of the Barney project, Lilith, had been killed.

"Tabibi said he would come," Barney growled and sipped at his ginger beer. "He'll know where the laser is—he stole it."

"Tabibi!" Ochoa-Varilla spat in disgust.

Of all the clones, Tabibi had been the only one who maintained contact with RAM; there were stories that he worked for the military-industrial company in some mysterious capacity. No one knew what he did for RAM, but as long as his activities didn't interfere with the battle gennies, they respected his privacy. But that didn't prevent the others from harboring resentment for him.

A loud noise from the other end of the bar drew Barney's attention. Two Belters were discussing something, and one was using a stool on his friend's head to demonstrate the logic of his argument. Barney snorted and drank the rest of his ginger beer.

"Huer," he said abruptly. "Maybe he learned something." Barney removed a portable uplink from his wrist and set it on the table. Before he could key in the code, the LED began to glow red and project a whirl of colored light.

The discussion at the bar heated up as a third Belter used a bottle to make his point. Huer's hologram formed as a glass of amber liquid flew through his head and smashed against the wall.

Barney rose to his feet, his huge frame swelling with anger. "*Quiet!*" he bellowed at the Belters.

The men at the bar looked up at him and froze. One had his hands around the other's neck while a third stood above him, raising a broken table leg. Suddenly two of the men rose into the air, their legs kicking helplessly. Sattar Tabibi stepped in, holding the Belters at arm's length by their collars.

"I believe you're disturbing my friends," he said in a smooth, melodious voice. "Now, you can settle your differences or continue arguing at the hospital." He grinned at them.

The two men looked at each other and smiled as big as they could through newly broken teeth. Tabibi dropped them unceremoniously and came toward the other Barneys.

Ochoa-Varilla glanced away. Tabibi looked very little like a battle clone in his carefully tailored clothes, a fitted black smart suit that reflected the current fashion among Mars's ultra-upper class. His face was smoother than the others, without their harsh angles and sharp edges; in fact, he looked almost plump. Although years of living within RAM's hierarchy had softened his appearance, it had not diminished his strength or fighting instincts; rather, it had augmented other facets of his personality. In addition to the standard combat skills hammered into the Barney line, Dracolysk had specially trained Tabibi in the arts of espionage and deceit.

"Well, gentlemen," Tabibi said as he approached their table. "Are we ready to finally put an end to this laser? I've taken it by myself once already, and I don't want to spend my entire life chasing the damned thing down. But an oath is an oath."

The other Barneys leveled steely gazes at their kin,

each yearning for the opportunity to repay Tabibi for his treachery.

Huer also turned to face Tabibi. "NEO troops are standing by, ready to go. I could get only a hundred and fifty on such short notice, but they're ready."

"Now we just need to know where the laser is," Quinto said dryly.

"I think I can help there," Tabibi said smoothly. "That's why I'm late. I was checking with some friends who know somebody who—"

"Talk straight," Barney interrupted. He had little patience for Tabibi's boasting.

Tabibi frowned at having his moment of glory punctured by the pirate. "You have no style, Barney," he said.

"If you're going to tell us, get on with it," Ochoa-Varilla grumbled. "I'm tired of listening to you babble!"

Tabibi snarled, his soft face hardening into the look of a battle clone. He started toward Ochoa-Varilla, but Huer quickly stepped between them.

"I think a fight between two Barneys would be fascinating," he said, "but we have work to do. Do you want to fight RAM or each other?"

"I don't know if he *will* fight RAM," Ochoa-Varilla said, nodding contemptuously toward Tabibi.

"What are you trying to say?" Tabibi whispered between clenched teeth.

Ochoa-Varilla rose to his feet and leaned over the table. "I'm saying you work for RAM, and I don't like the idea of following you to the home planet of the people who pay for your tailored suits."

"I *work* for RAM," Tabibi hissed. "They don't own me! Before I joined them I came from the same clone program all of you did. We share the same chromosomes, dammit!" He drew back, his eyes playing across the stony faces of his brothers. "We all have the same scars left by Dracolysk. And you're telling me you don't trust me?"

Black Barney suddenly smashed his fist on the table, punching a ragged hole through it. "The Oath of Blood and Steel!" he roared at Ochoa-Varilla. "Do you say one of us would betray the Oath?"

There was a moment of tense silence as the clone brothers glared at each other. Then Ochoa-Varilla looked down, his lips compressed. He nodded a short agreement. Tabibi pulled a chair from a nearby table and sat beside him, clapping him roughly on the back. Despite the joviality in his face, Huer thought he saw something else behind Tabibi's eyes, almost a look of triumph.

Huer glanced over at Black Barney; the pirate was staring fixedly at Tabibi, as though seeing something he had never noticed before.

"Tabibi, if you know where the laser is, tell us," Huer said calmly. "We've got to move soon." Before RAM destroys the Earth and the Barneys destroy each other, he finished to himself.

"Parsonawitz had the laser moved from its orbiting station to a secret lab on Mars," Tabibi said. "It seems he didn't trust the man he hired to head security."

"You have the coordinates?" Barney cut in abruptly.

"They're in my ship's computer."

"Then let's go!" Quinto said.

○ ○ ○ ○ ○

Kemal's trip back to Mercury Prime had been even easier than his flight from it. Aboard Tix's private cruiser the two Gavilan princes and Duernie were untroubled by official inspection or curiosity. Tix was largely ignored by the power structure of Hielo.

When he radioed to the spacedock, he was given curt landing coordinates and left alone—totally alone. Not even a baggage helper came to his craft.

Tix seemed unaffected by being ignored so thoroughly, but Duernie noticed the indifference. She nudged Kemal when Tix had gone ahead to find the way to the medical records section.

"Is it always like this for him? I get more of a greeting when I come to a track city I've never seen before than he gets when he comes home."

Kemal shrugged. "He's a younger brother of a crown prince. No one takes him very seriously."

"And he's learned not to take himself seriously either," she said.

Kemal nodded grimly. "If that's what everyone teaches you, you can't help but learn it."

Tix reappeared then, holding a printout of Hielo's medical complex.

○ ○ ○ ○ ○

They reached a small, nondescript, and—most importantly—empty office of the medical section with little difficulty. Tix and Kemal managed to log on to various computer systems, and the three of them sat searching for clues, ignoring even their own hunger and need for sleep. "Kemal, we've been digging through the medical net for twelve—no, fifteen hours!" Duernie said, rubbing her eyes. She slapped at the computer keyboard impatiently. "And we still haven't found anything about Ossip!"

Kemal leaned back in his chair, running his fingers through his hair. He wasn't sure if his headache came from staring at the monitor for so long or from the bright lights and wretched pale blue walls in the medical records room.

"She's right," Tix said, beside him. "We haven't

found anything about your father except the official b-b-biography."

"I know," Kemal said, feeling defeated. "I can't even find dental records." He sat for a minute, staring at the console, then slid his seat back to the monitor. "Maybe the files are cross-referenced under another name."

"What n-n-name?" Tix asked, with the impatience of exhaustion. "We've tried Ossip Carran Gavilan, Garrick, Gordon, and even yours."

"Why did you try my name?" Kemal asked.

"T-t-to see if records went back that far. They d-d-do," Tix said.

Kemal stared at the computer screen for a long time, thinking. "Maybe we're not using the right form of the name," he said finally, remembering his father's computer personality in his personal system. He then typed: "ossip."

Duernie came to his side and watched as the computer digested the name and gave back the usual "No file present."

He looked up at her, and a look of silent understanding passed between them.

She put her hand on his shoulder. "Try it," she whispered.

"Try what?" Tix asked.

"A program my father fed into the net before he died," he said and typed the code: "kemal."

"What k-k-kind of pro—" Tix began but froze as the hologram of Ossip formed beside the console.

"Kemal!" Ossip said happily. "I'm glad to see you're still safe!" The computer ghost turned to Duernie. "And it's good to see you again, Dancer." Ossip glanced at Kemal, then back to her, smiling at some secret satisfaction.

"It's good to see you, too, sir," she said. "Do you know Tix?"

"Of course I know him," he said. "I like the sculpture you do—at least the pieces that find their way in front of an input lens."

Tix stared at the hologram with his mouth open. "You've b-b-been in the net all this t-t-time?"

"Our little secret," Ossip said with a humorous wink. Then he turned to Kemal. "Why did you call me?"

Kemal sighed heavily. "We've been searching the medical records for hours to find any reference to my father's death."

"I've been looking for years," Ossip's image said. "Believe me, there's nothing in medical records or the rest of the network."

"How can that be?" Duernie asked. "There's got to be something!"

"When ancient Earth kings wished to discredit their predecessors, they destroyed all histories that mentioned the old king and frequently even had their names chiseled off monuments," Ossip said sadly. "I think Gordon had that done for me."

"Why would he remove m-m-medical records?" Tix asked.

"If there was something questionable about my death," Ossip answered, "those would be the first to go. The only hope of finding anything would be if someone was fastidious enough to download the records into a private storage disc that I don't have access to."

Kemal, Duernie, and Tix looked at each other for a second, then said simultaneously, "Catiff!"

Kemal bolted from his seat and was out the door before the others could react. By the time Duernie and Tix ran into the hall, Kemal was halfway down the deserted corridor, beating on the elevator doors with manic desperation.

○ ○ ○ ○ ○

Kemal burst into Catiff's quarters, nearly battering the doors apart. Duernie and Tix followed him in, but he was already standing over the startled physician by the time they reached him.

Catiff reached for the *Emergency* button beside his communication link, but Kemal grabbed the call box and ripped it off the assembly before he could touch it. Kemal pushed him back in his seat roughly.

"Where are the records?" Kemal demanded.

The old man's eyes grew wide with confusion. "W-what records?"

Kemal grabbed the doctor's shoulders roughly. "My father's medical history!"

Catiff's face clouded with bewilderment. "Who?"

"Ossip!" Kemal shouted, shaking him. "Think, damn you!"

The old physician quailed. "I don't know! There are no records!"

"There has to be!" Kemal shook him again.

Duernie ran to Kemal and tried to pull him away. "Kemal! He's an old man—don't hurt him!"

"The records!" Kemal shouted again.

"No . . . no records," Catiff wheezed. "Gordon had the computer wiped."

"Why?"

"Gordon ordered . . . I told him . . . all wiped," the doctor babbled in panic.

Kemal lifted the ancient man from his chair and drew his face close. "You tell me how my father died, or I swear I'll snap your neck right now!"

Catiff uttered a hopeless moan and closed his eyes, his lips moving in a soundless mumble. "Drowned . . . drowned . . ." he whispered hoarsely.

Kemal raised his fist to the old man's face, and Duernie stepped forward again, afraid he would hit him.

"Open your eyes, Catiff," he said. "Open them!" The physician blinked uncertainly. Kemal held a damaged ring close to his nose. "Do you recognize this? It was my father's signet. Look at it! It's melted. That didn't happen in the greenhouse pond!"

Catiff tried to focus on the ring, but terror had dulled his mind. "Melted, fused . . . drowned, Gordon said drowning . . ." his voice drifted away.

Kemal threw the doctor back into his seat. "This is useless," he snarled. "He's half-senile." He looked at Duernie, then glanced around the room. "Where's Tix?"

Duernie, too, looked around and started to say something, but Tix's voice came from another room.

"I'm in h-h-here. I f-f-found something."

Kemal turned from the old man and followed Tix's voice into the next room. Catiff's suite was a four-room complex, all of it painted a deep brown that seemed to absorb light. The walls were lined with shelves crammed with the debris of a very long life: old books printed on paper, medical specimens in jars, computer discs stored carelessly in any available space.

He found Tix in the darkest room, seated in front of an old computer console, digging through a box of discs. "These are all r-r-royal family records. You're here, too."

"Are my father's records there?"

"I don't know, I j-j-just found them." Tix thumbed through the chaotic collection. "There's n-n-nothing with Ossip's name, but here are some discs about 'Sun Kings.' "

"Put one in!" Kemal said, leaning over Tix's shoulder.

Tix fed the disc into the console and called the file up. The screen showed a list of a dozen Sun Kings from the last few centuries.

"Try another," Kemal urged.

Tix quickly put another disc in. This one listed Ossip. Tix called up the name and watched as the computer began to roll through the king's biography.

"Can you jump to the last part?" Kemal asked.

Tix hit the *End* button, and the computer blurred ahead to the last page.

". . . died 27,538 Merc. Stan." Kemal read. "There's nothing here!"

Duernie suddenly leaned over the seat to look at the screen. "What are those numbers?"

Tix glanced up at her, puzzled. "Mercury Standard years," he said. "You know that."

"Of course I know," she snapped. "The numbers below that."

Kemal looked at the screen again. Below the death date was a smaller set of figures. "I can't make them out. Tix, can you blow that up?"

"On this old r-r-relic? I'm not sure I know how." He adjusted a knob and pushed some buttons beside the keyboard, but nothing happened. He tried keying in some coordinate digits, and a small box appeared around the figures. The box suddenly expanded, showing clearly the legend: *RFMR 2473.*

"I s-s-saw some discs with RFMR on them," Tix said and started digging through a bin. "Ah," he said triumphantly, holding up a small storage disc labeled RFMR 2116.

"It's not the right number," Duernie said, sorting through a pile of discs beside the computer.

Kemal turned away to another stack as Tix tried the new disc.

"Hey," he called, "these are Royal Family Medical Records. From w-w-way back."

Kemal grunted and rummaged through the stacks closest to him while Duernie dug through a similar collection.

"Catiff must have stored every scrap of medical history in the computer," she said. "And a lot of these discs aren't even about medicine. They're just computer gossip and history."

Kemal left the computer and hurried back to the other room. Catiff sat where they had left him, staring vacantly into space; his lips still moved, but no sound came from them.

Kemal grabbed a handful of storage discs from the shelves on the wall and flipped through them, tossing the useless ones away. He finished and grabbed another stack, then another, until he stood in the middle of a spreading sea of discarded discs: medical records, Mariposa reports, secret police files, dossiers on asteroid pirates. Catiff had stored a flood of information from the main network—though Kemal couldn't guess why the old man wanted the files.

"My . . . my records," Catiff said weakly.

"Where are the medical histories?" Kemal snapped as he grabbed more discs and sorted through them.

"All there, all there," the physician mumbled. "Everything is there."

Kemal paused; he had seen dozens of discs labeled RFMR with the wrong numbers; this one, though . . . "Tix! I've got it!" he yelled and tore back into the computer room.

Tix quickly fed the disc into the machine as Kemal and Duernie huddled behind him. The screen lit up with a directory.

"There, that one!" Duernie pointed at the monitor. " 'Ossip—death cert.' Try it!"

Tix punched in the code, and the screen began scrolling through the ornate Mercurian script used for formal matters of state.

Kemal scanned the document, his excitement growing as he ran down the lines of medical details:

height, weight, color of hair, cause of death.

Kemal's heart sank. He stared at the screen, frozen, his mouth forming around an unspoken word.

"Drowned," Duernie read, her voice flat and emotionless. "Kemal . . ." She touched his arm, but he didn't move.

After a moment that lasted forever, Kemal sighed and sank onto a chair facing away from the monitor. "It's true, then," he whispered.

"That's the official v-v-verdict," Tix said slowly. "Signed by C-C-Catiff himself."

Kemal slumped in the seat. The last few days' tensions and sleeplessness caught up with him then, and he felt his head spin. Duernie came to his side and put her hand on his shoulder wordlessly. He reached up to touch her fingers.

"There's m-m-more on this disc," Tix said, bending over the keyboard. "You w-w-want me to call something else up? There's something called 'Ossip aut.' "

Kemal heard him, but the words didn't register. Duernie squeezed his shoulder.

Tix shrugged and began tapping at the keyboard. A familiar scatter of colored lights swirled in the small room. "Oh, it's an autopsy h-h-hologram."

A hologram of Ossip's body materialized in the room. Tix stared at the console as the code keys began to shift by themselves.

"K-K-Kemal . . ." Tix began nervously as Ossip's computer ghost solidified.

Without a word, Ossip's computer-generated persona walked to his own corpse and gently ran his insubstantial hand over its features, a look of ineffable sorrow on his face. Tix, Duernie, and Kemal watched the strange tableau in silence.

Finally the computer-generated Ossip looked up at Kemal, his eyes burning with a mixture of grief and anger. "Do you see, Kemal?" he asked. "Do you see?"

Kemal leaned forward, then rose slowly and walked to the hologram of his father's body. Seeing it laying still on a stone slab made Kemal falter. He took a deep breath and stepped closer to study the king's features, slack and pale in death. His memories of Ossip's lively vigor had no relation to this empty image lying before him.

The hair especially . . . Kemal bent over; something was wrong with the hair. Instead of the light brown he knew, his father's head was covered with a tightly gnarled mass of dark curls that looked charred. His skin, too, was blistered, particularly on the hands and wrists.

"This isn't the body of a drowned man," Kemal said quietly. "It looks like he was burned."

"Or electrocuted," Ossip said beside him.

"Yes, l-l-look at his hands," Tix said, pointing to the great charred scars running across the king's palms.

Kemal stared as if trying to absorb everything. Then he turned and strode from the room. "Catiff!" he shouted.

The ancient doctor was startled out of his chair at the sound of his name and tried to run, but Kemal grabbed him by the collar.

"I want to know what happened to my father!" he drew the physician closer.

"Drowned . . . drowned," Catiff began to cry, tears streaking his cheeks.

"He didn't drown!" Kemal exclaimed through his teeth. He brought his hands to the old man's throat and began to squeeze.

"Kemal," Duernie began but saw he was beyond hearing her.

"Gordon," Catiff croaked.

"What about Gordon?" Kemal demanded, loosening his grip. "Did he kill Ossip?"

"Gordon told me . . . drowned, I signed the certificate . . . drowned."

Kemal shook him savagely. "He was electrocuted!"

Catiff suddenly stopped shaking and stared at Kemal, his eyes wide. "You saw?"

"I saw the autopsy hologram. Now tell me the truth!"

The physician's lips trembled. "Gordon said he drowned and threatened me. Had to protect . . . Gordon said drowned. Dalton . . ."

"Dalton?" Kemal paused. "What about Dalton? He was a child when my father died."

"Playing in the generating plant," Catiff mumbled. "I told him . . . I told him . . . Ossip found him."

Kemal released the old man and stepped back in shock. "Dalton killed my father?" he said, bewildered.

"We protected him. Gordon sent him to school and told me . . ." The doctor shook. "I had to lie. I *had* to!" He gripped Kemal's arm as if begging him to believe him.

Kemal shook him off and turned away, almost bumping into Duernie. He looked at her with numb confusion. "It was Dalton," he said hesitantly. "I thought . . . I thought Gordon killed him. I was afraid he would die before I found out. Now . . ."

"It was probably an accident," Duernie said.

"An accident," Kemal repeated dully. "A stupid, pointless accident."

Tix came over and stood by him, trying to find words to say. All he could manage was, "Kemal, I'm sorry."

Kemal stared through Tix, as if he didn't see him. Then something in his eyes hardened. "I'm tired of this," he said. "All the lies and secrets! I think it's time I had a talk with my cousin!"

Chapter Fourteen

Dalton sprawled on the throne in the audience hall, leaning against the arm of the chair as he stroked his chin thoughtfully.

The full council sat before him, aligned on each side of the central aisle. Mariposans, Miners, Musicians . . . but no Dancers. He smiled tightly at their obvious absence and hoped the other delegates understood the message implied by their removal.

He studied the delegates as they sat stiffly in silence; their faces were hard, sullen. Few looked at him; those who did merely glanced quickly at him and turned away, frowning.

Good, he thought. Let them fear me, let them hate

me, as long as they *obey* me.

"Ladies and gentlemen," he said finally. "I believe we've all had enough time to evaluate each other at this, our first official meeting. Shall we get to business?"

The assembly stirred uneasily.

"Initially, I'd like to complete a matter begun by my father," Dalton said. "A matter opposed by many of this council. I'm speaking, of course, about the laser—" Several delegates groaned—"and my own contribution to his vision: a treaty with Mars."

A furious mumbling broke out among the delegates. Dalton chuckled softly to himself and wondered how long to let them stew before speaking. Just about *this* long, he decided.

Before Dalton could open his mouth, however, the sound of a scuffle began outside the audience hall. The ornate doors banged open, slamming into the walls, and two guardsmen stumbled in backward. Kemal pushed his way in after them, staring at Dalton as though he could burn him with his eyes.

One of the guards scrambled forward. "Your Majesty, we tried . . ."

Dalton waved him away. "Why, Cousin, what a surprise. Don't tell me my bumbling guards have actually done their jobs and arrested you?"

Kemal stood his ground without a word. Tix and Duernie ran into the hall and stopped short behind him, looking nervously at the assembled delegates.

Dalton's gaze flicked across Tix, then settled on Duernie. "So this is your Dancer," he said slowly. "We've got quite a file on you, Duernie."

"I know about you, too," she said, her voice choked with hate.

Dalton sneered at her, then turned to Kemal. "We have some new customs that might interest you, Cousin," he said. "Terens! Show our visitors the proper way to enter the king's presence."

Terens rose slowly and came forward, walking like a man asleep. Kemal tore his gaze from Dalton's as the arbiter began to sink to his knees wordlessly. Kemal took a step toward him, thinking the courier was ill, but then he saw him pause and bend his head forward. Terens's face was dead, an ashen mask of stone.

Kemal looked at him with horror. "Get up," he said, confused. "What are you doing?"

Terens remained silent, but several delegates jumped to their feet.

"Dalton!" one Miner shouted. "What is—"

"Your Majesty!" Dalton exploded. "You will use my proper title when addressing the throne!"

The Miner drew back in surprise, then glanced at the guards. Slowly he sat down without another word.

Kemal walked to Terens. "Get up," he said again. "Why are you kneeling to this man?" He grabbed the arbiter by the shoulders and hauled him to his feet. "He's a murderer! Do you hear me?"

Kemal turned to the assembled delegates. "Can you all hear me?" he shouted. "Dalton murdered his own father! He killed Garrick!" His voice dropped. "And my father, too."

No one moved. The delegates sat frozen in their seats; the guards stood fixed as the moment drew out into a nerve-racking minute.

Finally Dalton began to clap. "Well spoken, Cousin," he said, laughing. "I see you finally found your public speaking voice. The last time you addressed the council you weren't quite so eloquent."

"I can prove it, Dalton," Kemal said. "I can prove Ossip didn't drown in the greenhouse pond!"

Dalton raised his eyebrows. "Have you been digging around in the medical records? I'll have to do something about that fool Catiff and his mania for old files," he said as if discussing an annoying insect.

Kemal spun around to face the delegates. "Are you all deaf?" he shouted. "Your precious Sun King is a killer who murdered his way to the throne!"

An uneasy silence filled the hall like a tangible presence, but no one said a word or moved an inch. Kemal looked around the room, searching the faces for some sign of anger or disgust, but the delegates turned furtively away from his eyes.

Dalton laughed quietly. "What did you expect, Cousin? Did you think you could come here and accuse me, produce whatever 'proof' you've managed to scratch up, and the entire government of Mercury would be so incensed that the ministers would rise up and arrest me? Carry me away to some filthy dungeon with burning torches?" Dalton rose from the throne and stepped down toward Kemal. The ironic smile was gone from his face, the mockery from his words.

"Grow up, Little Cousin!" he spat with poison in his voice. "More than one throne has been bought with blood! I'm the king! I'm the center of power here! I'm the reason these insignificant worms have their prestige and honor! They don't care what I've done as long as they can stand close to me and play their part in the game!"

Dalton's eyes burned with a fire Kemal had seen before in men facing battle, men who thought they were indestructible and took foolish chances that cost the lives of both friends and enemies.

Kemal involuntarily took a step backward and glanced around the hall. The ministers, courtiers, and council delegates looked away nervously, but no one stirred. Suddenly he felt very alone and vulnerable.

"My guards will be arriving soon," Dalton said, advancing closer. "Before they take you away to your cells, there's still that matter of the proper greeting for your sovereign."

"What are you talking about?" Kemal said.

Dalton's lips curled back, exposing his teeth in a vicious smile. "Bow to me," he said in a hoarse whisper.

Kemal froze, staring at him. "You're insane," he said, more of a realization than a statement.

Tix stepped forward. "Dalton, stop this b-b-before it goes too far!"

Dalton laughed. "Yes, of course," he said. "My brother reminds me that those of royal blood needn't bow. But you, Dancer," he swung around to Duernie, "you will show your respect."

Duernie's face turned a deep red. "I'll die before I bow to you, bastard!"

"My dear, you've got that backward," Dalton chuckled. "You'll bow to me *before* you die, but you *will* make a fitting obeisance."

Duernie's hands shot to her belt and drew her long knife. The two guardsmen started forward, but before they reached her . . .

"*Dalton!*"

Kemal's voice cut through the room like an explosion.

"What, Cousin?" Dalton asked, low and dangerous.

"Leave her alone!"

"I'll leave you all alone when you get to your cells."

Kemal took a step toward Dalton, unconsciously sliding into a fighting crouch.

Dalton walked around him, careful to keep out of arm's reach but still close enough to taunt him. "This scene seems familiar," he said casually. "I remember once in the hall outside you told me 'This isn't the time or place.' " He paused, his face hard. "No one is going to stop us now."

With a guttural growl Dalton threw himself at Kemal. Kemal ducked and twisted away, swinging his fist at his cousin's exposed face. Dalton swatted the blow away effortlessly and began to circle.

The two guardsmen looked at each other in confusion, then reached for their weapons. Tix put his hand up silently; the men stopped for a moment, then looked to Dalton.

"Stay back!" he shouted at them. "I've been looking forward to this for a long time!"

The guards shrugged and stepped back as a handful of palace soldiers arrived at the doorway. The captain peered into the hall as Kemal jabbed at Dalton, then snorted with a look of disgust and waved his men aside. "Let them go," he said in a bored voice.

Kemal felt his blind anger fade, replaced by the cool, calculating reflexes of a warrior. Warily he circled Dalton, feinting to try to draw the bigger man into a rash move. Dalton was the larger of the two, massive in his chest and shoulders with a measurably longer reach; Kemal nodded grimly to himself. That's could be *his* advantage, he thought. Such a big man was probably slow and less experienced, though both had been trained in military academies. Kemal quickly leaped up and kicked at Dalton's head.

With lightning speed Dalton spun aside and shot his hand up. Kemal felt an iron grip lock on his ankle and jerk him off balance. He came down hard on his back, grunting as the force of the fall knocked the air from his lungs. Before he could recover, Dalton was on him, yanking Kemal's leg up to a position where he could break the knee.

Wildly Kemal kicked with his other foot and struck Dalton's shoulder. Dalton's grip loosened slightly, and Kemal twisted free. So much for the idea that he's slower, Kemal thought.

Dalton moved in quickly, swinging his right fist at Kemal's face. Kemal blocked with his left and counterpunched; he felt his fist land solidly against

Dalton's cheek. He followed it immediately with a quick jab to his mouth.

Dalton staggered back and raised his hand to his lip. He glanced at the red on his fingertips and smiled. "Congratulations, Little Cousin," he said. "First blood goes to you."

Dalton rushed him, roaring. Kemal raised his arm to fend off the attack, but Dalton grabbed his wrists and swung him around. He threw Kemal down the aisle between the seats, where he rolled out of control for a few feet until he crashed into a seat, then scrambled to his feet, swaying dizzily. Dalton was already closing on him. Before Kemal could defend himself, Dalton grabbed him in a bear hug, pinning his arms and threatening to crack his spine. Without thinking, Kemal snapped his head forward, smashing his forehead into Dalton's nose.

Dalton screamed and let go, reeling back with his hands clapped to his face. A gush of blood flowed between his fingers. Kemal lowered his head and charged, butting the big man in his stomach. Dalton's breath exploded in a loud gasp as he flew backward. He hit the throne with a loud *crack* and went down in a tangled mass of broken wood and bent metal.

Kemal leaned against an empty seat and tried to catch his breath. He looked around the hall to find the chairs all deserted; the delegates had fled to the side walls, where they huddled behind the last row of seats. Kemal quickly scanned the faces for Duernie and found her standing by the great doors, surrounded by guardsmen. He almost moved toward her, but the guards didn't seem to be holding her; instead they were leaning against the wall, watching the fight with an almost bored curiosity, as if the outcome didn't really matter to them.

A sound from the throne drew Kemal's attention.

Dalton had shaken himself free of the debris and was struggling to his feet, an expression of insane rage twisting his features.

Dalton lunged at him. Kemal tried to dodge away but was too late by a fraction of a second; Dalton's shoulder caught him on his chest and spun him around. For an instant he saw a massive fist rushing toward his face, then everything exploded in a blinding flash of agony.

There was no more pain after the first blow; he felt only a series of bone-wrenching thumps that came too fast to escape. The last blow lifted him off his feet, and he had a momentary sensation of weightlessness as he hurtled backward. The wall hit his back and everything went black for a split second.

Kemal shook his head, but his vision was still too blurred to see. Something hot and wet ran down the right side of his face and burned his eye. He put his hand up and felt the whole side of his face covered with blood from a gash on his brow; his nose was a formless mass of painful flesh.

His vision started to clear as he struggled to raise himself on his elbow. Somewhere far away he heard a scream, a woman's scream, and the thought drifted through his mind that Duernie might be in trouble. The idea was too abstract to mean anything.

As he forced himself into a sitting position, Dalton strode up. "Well, Little Cousin," he said, "you put up quite a fight. Let me help you." He grabbed Kemal by his shirt and yanked him to his feet.

Kemal blinked some of the blood out of his eye and focused on Dalton. His mind was beginning to work again, and he could feel his strength returning. Dalton shook him, leaning closer.

"Had enough, Little Cousin?" he jeered. Kemal noticed with grim satisfaction that one of his teeth had been knocked out. Weakly he put his hand against

Dalton's chest and pushed with a fraction of his strength.

Dalton laughed at the feeble effort. "Feels like you've had enough!" He slammed Kemal against the wall and let him go. Kemal crumpled to the floor, watching him carefully.

Dalton turned to one of the guards and jerked the man's mono knife from his belt. The rainbow-hued laser flicked to life along its edge as he turned to Kemal.

Before he could take a step, Kemal hooked his foot around Dalton's ankle and kicked at his thigh. Dalton's leg flew out from under him and he sailed backward with his arms windmilling helplessly. He hit the ground hard and skidded as Kemal started to rise.

"Kemal!" Duernie shouted. "Here!" Something metallic landed with a clatter by his foot.

It was a knife—a Dancer knife! Twelve inches of steel curved in the form of a thin crescent, with a blade honed to a razor-sharp edge.

Kemal grabbed the weapon and jumped to his feet as Dalton rose. Both men paused, studying the other. Dalton stood erect, his mono knife grasped firmly in his right hand, both feet planted solidly on the ground. Kemal crouched, his knife held slightly forward, constantly shifting his weight from foot to foot. He felt better with the knife in hand; he had practiced with the weapon for long hours among the Dancers and felt he had an advantage over Dalton now.

But it was a thin advantage at best. The mono knife's single-molecule edge could cut through the hardest stone without effort. If the blade even touched him, Kemal knew he would be maimed.

They began to circle each other. Dalton made a wild slash that Kemal easily sidestepped. His face broke into a wide grin.

"A little out of your depth, aren't you, Cousin?" Kemal said, stabbing abruptly. Dalton jerked gracelessly away, then recovered himself. A thin film of sweat broke out on his forehead.

"Guards! To me!" Dalton shouted, backing away.

No one moved.

Kemal chuckled. "I don't think you're a very popular man." He tossed the knife easily to his other hand and slashed at Dalton's stomach. The big man leaped backward. "They don't seem to care if you live or die." He lunged forward, forcing Dalton back another step. "In fact, I'll bet they're hoping for a change of government!"

Dalton gave an inarticulate growl and shook with anger. "I don't need them to kill you!" he snarled and rushed forward.

That's it, Kemal thought, stepping aside. Get mad! Get so furious you make a mistake!

"I'll gut you!" Dalton hissed. "I'll see you dead at my feet . . . like your father!"

Kemal froze. Dalton's face split into a hideous grin. "You were right about that, Cousin. I did kill your father. Oh, it was an accident, to be sure, but it was my first lesson in power politics," he said with an infuriatingly casual tone. "Would you like to hear about it?"

Kemal felt his face flush, and his grip on the knife became slippery with sweat. He's goading me, Kemal realized, trying to make me do something stupid.

"I was exploring—playing really—in one of Hielo's fusion plants, all very forbidden. Well, I got stuck on a catwalk and Ossip arrived first. I was frightened, panicky, and I kicked him accidentally. He lost his balance and grabbed a high voltage cable. Fried him right in front of my eyes. It was traumatic, Kemal. I was scarred." Dalton smiled, enjoying the story.

"If it was an accident, why did Gordon cover it up?" Kemal said.

"Well, that's the lesson I learned. You see, my father realized that the accident made him king. In one frightened move I caused a change in the ruling house of Mercury! Gordon was afraid such an accident in my past would affect my succession to the throne, so he packed me off to school on Mars and had Catiff concoct that story about Ossip drowning. But I learned from that, Kemal—I learned how a throne is bought!"

Kemal felt red rage well up within him and he had to fight against the impulse to rush blindly against Dalton. That's not the way to fight, he told himself and shook his head.

In that split second of distraction, Dalton moved. He lunged ahead, swinging his mono knife before him. Kemal felt a searing pain along his ribs. He twisted away and lashed out; his blade sank into flesh and he heard Dalton howl.

Kemal quickly looked at his chest—an eight-inch gash ran across his ribs. Fortunately, Dalton's stroke had been glancing; the gash ran long but not deep. Dalton clutched at his leg, trying to staunch his own wound.

Both men smiled grimly at each other as their blood began to spatter the floor at their feet. Kemal staggered as a spasm of nausea washed over him; he fought against the rising bile in his throat and blinked his vision clear. His right eye was already swollen shut and the whole side of his face was an agonizing ruin. His breath rasped painfully in his lungs. Dalton was reeling as well; his nose was shattered and both eyes were red and puffy. His upper lip had swollen grotesquely and a trickle of blood dribbled from the corner of his mouth.

Kemal knew the duel would end soon; either one of

them would kill the other or they would both pass out from pain and loss of blood.

Dalton must have had the same thought. Suddenly he screamed and charged Kemal, his mono knife arcing toward his neck. Kemal raised his blade to fend off the stroke, but the mono knife sliced through the steel knife, snapping it in two.

Kemal stepped back, looking with numbed surprise at the five inches of his blade remaining. Then a shattering blow landed on his jaw and his knees buckled. He could see Dalton standing before him, but he couldn't stop his legs from giving way beneath him. As he sank, Kemal slashed with the remains of his knife, but his arm swung wide, bringing the blade behind Dalton's legs.

Dalton's breath hissed between his teeth as Kemal's blade cut into the tendons behind his knee. The leg folded up and he toppled to the side. Kemal remained kneeling as he stared at the bloody knife in his hand with dull, uncomprehending shock.

Dalton forced himself up into a painful crouch. "This has . . . gone on . . . long enough!" he panted.

Kemal looked up and raised his knife weakly as Dalton threw himself at him. Kemal felt the bulk of the man smash into him and carry him backward. They rolled into the center of the floor and lay still.

No one in the hall moved. No one even seemed to breathe. Finally Duernie tore herself from the wall and ran toward the two motionless figures. A guard grabbed her before she reached them.

"Let me go!" she screamed, twisting in his arms. Three guardsmen were already running to the king.

Duernie pulled away from the guard as one of the soldiers pried Kemal out of Dalton's grip. He came away limp, his face and chest covered with blood. She caught her breath as the guard pushed him aside and rolled the king over. Dalton flopped on his back, the hilt of Kemal's knife jutting out of his chest. His eyes stared blank and glassy.

"Kemal!" she cried and ran to him as he began to stir. She cradled his head in her lap and tried to brush some of the blood away from his face. "Are you all right?"

He opened his eyes and started to smile, then abruptly lurched away. "Dalton . . ." he croaked.

She grasped his shoulder firmly. "It's all over," she said.

"Is . . . Dalton . . . ?"

"Yes," she said. "It's finished."

He grimaced in pain and tried to stand. "Help me up."

She put her hand under his arm and pulled as he fought his way to his feet. The delegates began to come forward, muttering to each other and staring at Dalton's body.

The captain of the guard approached, followed by four of his men. He stopped in front of Kemal, fidgeting uncomfortably.

"Prince Kemal Gavilan," he began uncertainly, "you just . . . killed the king."

The absurdity of the statement almost made Kemal smile, but he knew what was coming next—detention, a trial, possible exile or execution.

"Captain," Tix said abruptly, his voice sounding stronger than Kemal had ever heard it, "your men won't be needed here. You saw what happened here today. This wasn't an assassination. There'll be no arrest."

The captain looked at Tix for a moment, then relaxed. "Very well," he said and made a gesture to his men. The captain paused before Kemal as though he wanted to say something, but no words came. Finally he reached out awkwardly and clapped his hand on Kemal's shoulder, then turned away and disappeared into the crowd.

Kemal looked around at the wreckage, the shattered seats and ruined throne. His head spun but he remained standing, mostly by force of will. Tix rushed to his side and took his other arm when he swayed. Kemal looked down at the broken, lifeless body of Dalton and felt his stomach churn. He started to turn away.

A soldier in the uniform of the radar corps ran into the hall holding a report, then stopped at the sight of the devastation. He glanced at Dalton and blinked with confusion. He looked around until he saw Kemal with Duernie and Tix, and came forward.

"There's been a sighting," he said hurriedly. "The radar . . ."

"What?" Kemal said thickly.

The radar officer frowned and went on. "A RAM battler-class ship just came on the screen," he said. "It's closing on Mercury!"

"A battler?" Duernie echoed. Kemal groaned.

"At its present speed we have about eighteen hours before it arrives." He thrust the report at Tix. "What are your orders, Your Majesty?"

Tix took the report in numb fingers. "M-m-me?" he said.

"We *are* in range of the surface scanners, aren't we?" Quinto asked over the radio.

"We've been within range for ten minutes," Tabibi answered from his ship.

"Where are the interceptors?" Black Barney growled.

"No idea," Tabibi said. "There's no unusual activity on the surface, no alerts on any military frequency. I don't understand."

The surface of Mars grew second by second in front of them as the six ships approached. Actually there were only four ships visible; two NEO troop transports with Tabibi and Quinto flying beside them.

Barney's *Free Enterprise* and Ochoa-Varilla's *DaVinci* both were fitted with state-of-the-art stealth technology—designed by Ochoa-Varilla himself—and were flying well ahead of the others to meet the expected interceptors. At least that was the plan.

"I don't like this," Barney said grimly. "Unidentified aircraft intruding into Martian airspace and they don't care?"

Huer materialized beside Barney. "I don't like it either. We're ten minutes away from the lab on the Plains of Elysium. They've *got* to know we're here."

"Maybe they're waiting for us to get close enough to use ground fire," Barney said.

"We'll know in two minutes," Huer said.

"Entering ground fire range," Ochoa-Varilla announced unnecessarily. "I'm releasing the ghosts."

Ochoa-Varilla's "ghosts" were half a dozen small robot satellites covered with a special reflective coating he had invented, which fragmented radar; the satellites created a radar "illusion" of more than a hundred ships for RAM's ground lasers to lock on to. With any luck, the computer-controlled lasers would waste time shooting at the "ghosts" long enough for the Barneys to land with the NEO troops. At least that was the plan.

"There's no ground fire!" Quinto exploded.

Huer thought there was more than a little disappointment in Quinto's voice, as though he was looking forward to starting the battle as soon as possible. He glanced at Barney, who scowled at his console.

"I don't like this," Barney rumbled again. "Smells like a trap."

"I agree," Huer said. "Something's wrong here. Do you want to abort the raid?"

Barney turned to him, staring with genuine puzzlement. "Just because it's a trap?" He started to laugh, a frightening sound that began as a deep rumble and swelled to a deafening roar in the ship's small cockpit. "That will just make a better fight!"

Huer stared at the battle clone for a moment and felt something like an electronic chill spread through his circuits again; Barney was not human in any real sense, but was a single-purpose clone designed and conditioned for only one reason: to fight.

"We're approaching the lab," Huer said, just to change the subject.

Barney grunted and set the autopilot on landing mode. He swiveled away from the console and stepped back to the debarkation hold. Huer followed him back and watched as he finished putting on the last of his battle armor.

Barney's armor was a sleek, black outfit made entirely of a compound that combined the flexibility of plastic with the molecular density of forged steel. The suit was virtually impervious to anything but a direct hit by a laser rifle; it could even withstand a minor explosion. As the *Free Enterprise* settled to the ground, Barney slipped his helmet on.

Like the rest of his armor, the helmet was black, totally smooth and without any decorative frills or ruffles that could catch a laser shot. The eye guards were rounded, multifaceted sensors that enlarged his visual range. His own genetically engineered eyes could already see into the infrared spectrum, but the goggles extended his vision into x-ray frequencies.

The ship began lurching as it entered its evasive zigzag landing sequence. Barney calmly finished adjusting the helmet's seals and braced himself in front of the hatch.

Huer heard him say, "Ready?" and nearly answered yes when he realized Barney was talking to the other warrior clones through his radio.

At the first touch of ground, Barney hit the hatch's explosive locks and the door blew off its moorings.

Barney dove out and rolled a few yards, coming up in a full-speed run even before the ship had settled.

Quinto was out of his ship as quickly as Barney, followed seconds later by Tabibi and Ochoa-Varilla. The NEO troops were still opening their transporters while the Barneys were already spreading out in a fan formation.

The RAM lab was a complex of buildings spread out over acres of land. Situated on the desert plains of Elysium south of the Boreal Sea, there was no need for fences or barricades; no one could approach the lab without being seen miles before arrival. The entire complex consisted of single-story shelters, except for six guard towers rising above the ground around the perimeter.

There seemed to be no one in the compound.

"Tabibi!" Ochoa-Varilla shouted over his radio. "Where are the guards? Even a lab has to have some guards!"

"I don't know," Tabibi said. "Maybe RAM pulled the laser out of here!"

"I've got heat readings from the guard towers," Black Barney said suddenly. "That's where—"

Without warning, a dozen ruby beams stabbed from the three closest towers. Huer heard a scream from the NEO men as the Barneys dashed forward toward the towers.

Black Barney and Quinto dodged among the iron supports of the tower nearest to them. Without a word to each other they quickly attached timed grenades to the concrete pilings supporting the structure, their movements smooth and practiced. Within seconds, Quinto dove away from the tower and rolled to one of the buildings, his laser already out and firing at a second tower.

Barney came running toward him a split second later, but the explosions caught him, sending him crashing into the building. Quinto glanced at him briefly as he fell heavily to the ground, but Barney was chuckling deep in his throat.

The grenades blew the supports from under the tower; it dropped like a stone and shattered against the ground. Quinto aimed at another tower's legs, trying to melt the metal; Barney added his laser and within seconds the metal framework glowed red.

"Next one!" Barney barked and Quinto shifted his aim to the closest support.

The tower began to list as its legs melted away. As the guardhouse began to topple, three men jumped from the structure; Barney swung his laser around and followed the men down. They hit hard. One threw his head back in a silent scream, clutching his leg; the other two lay still where they fell, unconscious.

Barney turned back to Quinto and raised a clenched fist. Quinto nodded and stood as Barney touched a button on his wristband uplink.

Huer materialized beside them. "We're going into the complex," Barney told him curtly. "Have the NEO troops mop up those towers, then follow us in!"

"They're already working," Huer said as a series of explosions ripped through the camp.

"Good. Where's Tabibi?"

"Right behind you," Tabibi said as he and Ochoa-Varilla ran to the building.

Barney turned to him, his black helmet covering whatever might have been in his eyes. "They were waiting for us!" he said in a low, dangerous voice.

Tabibi pulled his green helmet off and glared at him. "Yes, they were! So what?"

"How did they know?" Barney demanded.

"They saw us on radar! They watched us land!" Tabibi shouted back. "What are you trying to say?"

Barney lurched forward a half-step but stopped

himself. "Where's the laser?" he finally growled.

Tabibi jammed his helmet back on. "According to my contact," he looked up at Barney defiantly, "it's supposed to be in the center of the compound, in Lab Fifteen."

Without a word, Barney turned and began trotting toward the end of the building. The other clones followed.

As Barney rounded the building, an explosion ripped the corner of it away, knocking him halfway across the walkway. A barrage of lasers lit up the street as the gennies threw themselves back and scrambled for cover.

Barney rolled with the force of the blast and came up with his own laser cutting a deadly arc through the darkness ahead of him.

"Where are they?" he shouted.

Ochoa-Varilla raised a grenade launcher. "The alley between those huts," he said quickly as he fired.

The dark gap between the buildings lit up with an orange flash for an instant; Barney caught a glimpse of several figures running toward the next street before he turned back to his companions.

"They're all over the compound," he said. "We're going to have to fight every foot of the way."

"And face an ambush at every corner," Huer added.

There was a buzz of excitement from the battle clones.

Huer raised his eyebrows in dismay. If the Barneys became more interested in fighting than destroying the laser . . .

"Gentlemen," Huer said quickly. "I admire your enthusiasm, but we can't take the time to fight a pitched battle every few yards."

"What do you want us to do?" Ochoa-Varilla asked. "Fly over the buildings?"

"Where is the lab from here?" Quinto interjected.

Tabibi looked up. "I think it's three or four huts directly east." He pointed to his right.

Barney suddenly turned to the building beside them. In one movement his laser withdrew into his sleeve and a grenade launcher protruded from another barrel on his wrist. The launcher fired point-blank at the wall as Barney started forward, and the grenade exploded against the building a fraction of a second ahead of Barney.

With a fierce shout, Barney burst through the wall in a fiery blast. He broke into the building, shaking fragments of burning wallboard from his shoulders.

Quinto began to laugh as he jumped in after him. Huer watched the other gennies follow and shook his head slightly before disincorporating his hologram.

The building they broke into was deserted. The lights were still on and the equipment overseeing the experiments still hummed. Ochoa-Varilla became fascinated by the lab they had entered. He noticed a large zero-gravity chamber along one wall that seemed to have some kind of crystals growing inside. He tried to study the chamber, but Barney was already crashing through the lab in his direct, straight-line fashion.

Ochoa-Varilla sighed and looked at the destruction caused by the warriors. All that science—smashed. He shrugged and pushed over a delicate assembly as he hurried to catch up.

Barney shot another grenade at the back wall and blew half of it away. Across the short walkway, the next building had a door, which at least made the pirate's entrance less noisy.

As the battle clones poured into the entrance, Quinto noticed the building was different from the last. It wasn't a laboratory, because, instead of holding scientific equipment, the room was full of desks and computer terminals. This was an administrative office building.

Quinto quickly looked around the walls, scanning the charts and maps before Barney began destroying everything. There, he thought, catching sight of a large outline map etched on plastic.

"Barney! Everybody, hold on!" Quinto called. "I've got a map. Tabibi, come here."

"No time," Barney growled. "RAM troops are all over."

"He's right, Barney," Ochoa-Varilla said, coming to Quinto's side. "Tabibi, you said the laser was in Lab Fifteen?"

Tabibi joined them at the map. "That's what my contact told me."

"These buildings are labeled by number and function," Ochoa-Varilla said, tracing his finger over the map. "Here's the one we were just in—" He pointed at a box labeled *S Crys Farm,*—"and we're here now, in *Off & Adm.* There's Fifteen." He stabbed at the map.

"There's nothing about a laser," Quinto said shortly and turned to Tabibi.

Tabibi whipped his green helmet off and peered at the map. "I don't understand."

An explosion rocked the office.

"Barney!" Ochoa-Varilla shouted. "Quit blowing everything up and come here! We may be lost."

"May be what?" Barney bellowed and rushed over.

"What happened to your 'contact?' " Quinto demanded.

"I don't know," Tabibi said.

"For someone who knows so much about RAM operations, you certainly don't know much," Quinto said harshly.

"What do you want from me?" Tabibi shouted. "I told you what I heard, that's all! Maybe my people got it wrong." Suddenly he pointed at the map. "There! Look at the next building, Lab Sixteen!"

The building outline on the map bore the inscription *Whd Las XIV.*

"Warhead Laser XIV," Ochoa-Varilla read. "That's it! But it's in the wrong building!"

"How do you know?" Tabibi said. "Maybe they moved it since the map was made!"

"And maybe it's a trap," Quinto said. "They've known about us every step of the way."

"The question is: Who set us up?" Ochoa-Varilla said.

Tabibi turned on them. "Maybe RAM heard I was asking around. Maybe my people double-crossed me," he said grimly.

"Maybe they did . . ." Quinto let his voice trail off, leaving the rest of his sentence unspoken.

"We're wasting time!" Barney broke in. "Let's check Fifteen, then we'll know!" His black helmet with its insectlike eyes swung around on Tabibi for a second, then turned away.

Quinto dashed to the rear door and stuck his head out. "Clear," he said and ducked out to the right.

Barney followed him to the right, then Ochoa-Varilla and Tabibi came out to the left. The four gennies flattened themselves against the wall.

"If there's anyone in there waiting," Quinto said, drawing his grenade launcher, "let's wake them up!"

The clones raised their weapons and fired at the same moment.

Half the wall of Lab Fifteen erupted in a sheet of flame. Black Barney charged forward into the darkened building, followed seconds later by the others.

Suddenly the room lit up with floodlights and lasers licked out of the corners at them.

Barney flung himself to the floor and rolled until he bumped into a counter. Tabibi was already crouching behind it, swinging his laser in a blind arc over the top. Barney gingerly raised his head above the cover, but the glare of the lights made it difficult to see clearly. He felt something carom off his helmet and ducked down.

Ochoa-Varilla threw something and shouted, "Eyes!"

A magnesium flare exploded ahead of them. Instantly Barney leaped over the counter, trusting his helmet goggles to protect his eyes, and opened fire with fragmentary explosives. A rain of deadly metal shards spread through the room, smashing the floodlights. A chorus of screams began, followed by the sound of running.

Barney chased the RAM men into a corridor, with Tabibi a few steps behind. They came in sight of the soldiers as they ducked through a doorway; Tabibi got one shot off, but missed.

Barney reached the door just as it was closing. Tabibi saw him turn his shoulder to it and put on an extra burst of speed.

"Wait, Barney!" he shouted. "You don't know what's—!"

It was too late. Barney hit the door with shattering force and disappeared inside.

Tabibi rushed to the doorway and pulled up short. The door opened onto empty space; there *had* been a stairway, but Barney's entrance had knocked it off its moorings. Barney stood on the ground twenty feet below, tangled in a mass of metal steps and railings, with three limp RAM men twisted like toys at his feet. He held a fourth man above his head and flung him away as Tabibi stared. The man landed fifteen feet away with a sickening thud.

Tabibi looked around the cavernous room—a huge factory, actually. The ceiling was crisscrossed with rails that held pulleys and electromagnets. The floor was cluttered with various tools and mechanical arms; at least the outside edges of the floor were covered with gear. The center was clean, as if something large had been sitting there. A path had been cleared to a large freight elevator at the rear wall.

"Something was here," Tabibi said. "Something big."

Barney glanced at the empty room and gave a dismissive snort. "Whatever it was, it's gone now," he said shortly. "Come help me with this ladder."

Tabibi stepped back from the doorway. "I'll call the others."

"Already did," Barney growled. "Now come—"

An explosion in the corridor cut off his words. Tabibi bounced forward, grabbing the doorjamb desperately to regain his balance. Another bomb went off and his grip loosened. He fell heavily to the pile of rubble beside Barney.

Ochoa-Varilla's helmet appeared in the doorway, looking down. "Are you okay?"

"The laser was here," Barney said, ignoring the concern. "They moved it."

Ochoa-Varilla looked at the equipment in the workroom. "I don't think the laser was here," he said. "This is an assembly plant, not a storage facility. Look at that tread rig. The laser doesn't have treads. And those mechanical arms. Whatever they were building here has nothing to do with the laser."

"Get us out of here!" Tabibi shouted. "We'll check Sixteen!"

Quinto came up beside Ochoa-Varilla. "There's still a lot of RAM troops in here. We gotta go!"

Ochoa-Varilla glanced down at Barney and Tabibi. "Meet you in Sixteen," he said hurriedly.

Barney tore a device from his wrist. "This is Huer's uplink," he said, tossing it up to Ochoa-Varilla. "Get him to the laser, quick!"

"How do we get out of here?" Tabibi shouted.

"Use the elevator," Quinto pointed to the rear wall

and disappeared.

Barney headed for the back wall, striding across the littered floor with his inhumanly long steps. He paused beside the elevator, studying the control buttons as Tabibi caught up with him. Barney reached out to the buttons, but before he could touch one, the elevator began to hum.

Both clones looked at each other for a split second, then flattened against the wall beside the doors.

Barney made a small noise to catch Tabibi's attention. When he looked at the pirate, Barney's arm twitched and a small grenade dropped into his palm; he raised the explosive to show Tabibi, who nodded and turned his armored back to the doors.

The elevator cracked open and Barney drew his hand back, but before he could toss the grenade, a small disc dropped through the opening and erupted in a blinding flash of orange and crimson flame.

For a brief, disorienting moment, Barney felt himself flying backward until his arm caught a chain dangling from one of the ceiling pulleys. Instinctively his hand snapped shut on the chain; the jolt nearly dislocated his shoulder, but he hung on and dropped to the ground as five RAM Terrines ran from the elevator and spread out in perfect formation. Barney caught a glimpse of Tabibi's green helmet peering around a stack of boxes in the corner. Barney started to call him, but Tabibi disappeared as the Terrines started to move toward him.

Barney tossed the grenade in his hand at the closest Terrine and followed it with two more from his wrist launcher. The grenades exploded, enveloping the Terrine in smoke and fire. As the thick haze cleared, the Terrine stepped toward Barney, its arm dangling in a ragged mass of flesh; its other arm reached for Barney.

"Theta!" a sharp voice barked. "Stand off!"

The damaged Terrine stopped abruptly and moved back to let three whole ones pass. Barney watched them come; within his helmet, his lips curled back in a smile of battle-fever at the thought of facing Terrines at last.

The Terrines were the most feared warriors in RAM's military arsenal. They were grown for one reason—to be the most effective killing tool in the solar system. Genetic engineering sharpened their reflexes and enhanced their cardiopulmonary efficiency, but it diminished their capacity for independent thought. Shark genes provided sandpaper-like skin and hardened plates of cartilage over critical areas. Their skulls were bald and heavily armored with extra-thick cartilage, with brow ridges protecting catlike eyes. Hard spurs of horn projected from the heels and elbows, and the hands and feet were tipped with retractable talons. Fangs and large, cupped ears made them appear even more catlike.

There was little humanity left in the Terrines—they were simply berserk, fighting monsters.

Dracolysk's line of Barney clones were designed to be a step beyond the Terrine unit in that they were single-purpose battle gennies with enough mind left for independent thought and initiative. Barney had always wanted to test himself against the Terrines.

Barney leaped forward to meet the three that approached him now. The closest one reached out with lightning speed and smashed a fist against Barney's chest. He felt his armor buckle under the blow, but the plate remained intact. Barney wrapped his hand around the Terrine's wrist and put the full pressure of his own grip plus his gauntlet's servojoints into the hold. His fingers sank into the beast's armored skin and he jerked with all his strength. The arm pulled free of the shoulder, but the Terrine didn't flinch. Its other fist crashed into Barney's helmet and knocked him aside.

"Iota! Gamma! Close!" the sharp voice barked. Barney looked up and realized the fifth Terrine wasn't a Terrine after all, but was a squad commander sent to oversee his troops.

The two Terrines came at Barney from opposite sides; each lashed out at the same moment. Barney managed to block one blow, but the second smashed into his side. His armor protected him from the worst of the impact, but it still staggered him. He swung at the Terrine who had hit him, but the beast's enhanced reflexes carried him out of the way.

Barney felt another impact at his side as the other Terrine hammered at his body armor. He locked his elbow and jammed backward, hitting the Terrine in the face. The head snapped back with enough force to break a man's neck, but the monster righted itself and lunged forward with barely a pause. It brought both its arms up in a pincer hold on Barney's neck. He felt the seals of his helmet crack.

The other Terrine began battering Barney's side, until that armor, too, broke under the strain. Steel fingers dug into the open seam of his torso plate and ripped the armor away. Barney clasped his fists together and drove them into the face of the Terrine holding his neck. The whole right half of the monster's face tore away, exposing layer upon layer of cartilage and skin. The Terrine's grip held firm.

Barney felt the other's fist smash into his body and felt and heard his ribs crack. Involuntarily his head snapped back and a roar escaped his lips. The Terrine with half a face released his neck and swung his fist in a windmill blow that cracked Barney's helmet.

Without his armor, Barney knew he couldn't withstand many more of the Terrines' blows. Desperately he looked around the room and saw a green blur beside the elevator.

"Tabibi!" he shouted.

Tabibi stepped away from the wall; the movement distracted the Terrine pummeling Barney's chest. It dropped to its knee and drew a laser.

"Iota! Hold!" the squad commander yelled. "Not the green helmet! Finish the black helmet!"

Barney froze as the commander's words sank in. "Tabibi!" he roared and took a step toward him.

The Terrine behind him smashed his helmet again, further breaking the seals and twisting it around to partially obscure his vision. Barney ripped the helmet off and flung it at his clone brother. "*Tabibi!*"

Seeing his exposed head, the Terrine Iota punched at him. Barney dodged aside and drove his fingers under the beast's rib plating and ripped up; he fired a grenade from his wrist launcher into the gap and tossed the Terrine away as the explosion detonated.

"Gamma! Get . . ." the squad leader began.

Barney spun on the remaining Terrine as it reached for him. Blind with rage, he grabbed the monster and flung it at the commander. The Martian screamed as the heavy trooper fell against him, crushing him. Barney limped to the Terrine as it struggled to free itself of the commander's body; without new orders, the Terrine fought to complete its last instructions and made an awkward grab for Barney's leg. The pirate drew back, then kicked the Terrine on the side of the head. Its neck snapped with a loud *crack*.

As Barney turned, a pain lanced through his chest. "Tabibi!" he shouted.

Tabibi stepped out of the shadows. "Barney, you don't understand!"

"You betrayed the Oath!"

"That's not what he meant! I didn't . . ."

"You betrayed *us*!" Twin daggers slid from Barney's arm sheaths as he stepped forward.

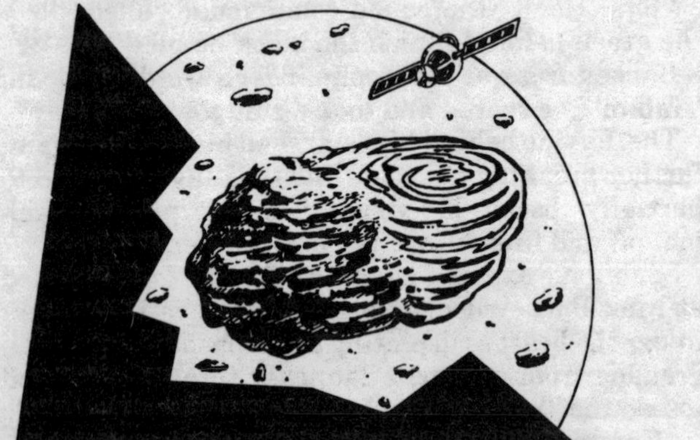

Chapter Sixteen

Parsonawitz activated the imaging program and chewed a fingernail nervously as the RAM battleship's computer fed in the hologram data; in a moment, the familiar sequence began.

Flecks of colored light quickly resolved into a three-dimensional image of a flat plain ringed by bare mountains; Parsonawitz shifted the viewpoint forward and the plain became a blur of sand and melted rock. He punched in a set of coordinates and the rush slowed to a stop over a deep fissure that sank straight through Mercury's crust to a deep black.

The Eye of Phidias, Parsonawitz mused as he smiled tightly and adjusted a visual-enhancement system to infrared; the heat-sensitive picture revealed the Eye as a vent that ran a quarter of a mile straight down, illuminated by a river of magma at the bottom.

Parsonawitz tipped the viewpoint down and had the stomach-wrenching sensation of falling into the Eye. The computer image began to fade as the enhancement reached the limits of its resolution. Parsonawitz slowed the moving viewpoint and stopped it in front of a large, dark crevasse in the side of the vent.

"Parsonawitz, you've been tying up the computer with Ardala's recon pictures for the last three weeks," said Killer Kane, finally impatient with Parsonawitz ignoring him. "There's nothing new you can see there."

The Martian adjusted the hologram generator to enhance reflected light. The darkness lightened slightly, outlining a deep cavern with irregular shapes on the floor and walls.

"I'm sure these forms are sun crystals," Parsonawitz said, ignoring Kane further. "See, this cavern runs—"

"Yeah, it connects to the Phidian Basin, and those *are* crystals," Kane interrupted. "The RAM mainframe computer analyzed her pictures in fifteen seconds. You haven't added a thing to what we know."

Parsonawitz snorted as he turned his seat around to face Kane. "Her pictures are just two-dee flats! I can't change any angles, I can't follow any curves! What do you want of me? These are all but useless!"

"I *want* you to leave the ship's computer alone for an hour!" Kane exploded. "We're approaching Mercury, we've got six hours before a major war starts, and I'm getting tired of you fussing over recon pictures we've all seen until we're sick of them!"

Parsonawitz frowned and twisted his hands in his

lap. "I hardly think this raid can be considered a major—"

"Raid!" Kane shouted. "Parsonawitz, we're riding in the RAM fleet." He swung his hand back toward the living quarters in the aft. "There are five battalions of troops on this ship. That's a thousand men, including two hundred Terrines. Does that sound like we're going out to snatch some prospector's asteroid? This is an invasion, Parsonawitz! We're going to conquer a planet!" Kane stepped into the hologram map and stood above Parsonawitz, glaring at him.

The Martian cringed and wrapped his arms around himself. "Mister Kane," he said, looking down, "you're standing in my projection. I . . . I need to study the target planet."

Kane stepped back, a smile spreading across his face. "You're frightened, aren't you?" he said slowly, as if realizing this for the first time. "You're scared!"

"What's going on, boys?" Ardala said as she entered the bridge. "Some prebattle nerves?" She wore a parody of the RAM military uniform—a black-and-white mottled fatigue suit designed by Mars's top fashion house; but whereas a soldier's uniform would have had pockets and snaps for equipment, Ardala wouldn't dream of allowing anything bulky to mar the smooth lines of her hips or legs. She did, however, carry a hand laser.

Kane grimaced and stomped back to the pilot, scouring the control panel for some detail to complain about.

"Don't mind him," Ardala said with a laugh. "He always gets edgy before a battle."

Parsonawitz cleared his throat. "And you? Have you gone through so many of these raids that you are inured to the anxiety?"

Ardala laughed lightly. "Joachim, you become so eloquent when you're nervous."

Parsonawitz winced again and turned back to the computer control board. Ardala watched him for a moment, her smile fading until her mouth was a tight line of tension. She swallowed once and shook her head, forcing a smile.

"So, tell me, Joachim," she said carelessly. "Where are we supposed to land?"

Parsonawitz touched several keys, activating another simulation program. "Mister Kane and the military commander worked out a plan, and I made a sim of it," he said, nodding behind him to the hologram.

As Ardala watched the flat plain, small versions of several transporters appeared and settled to the ground. "We're going to land several hundred yards south of the Eye of Phidias and march the troops to the crystal field."

Ardala saw a stream of tiny figures pour out of the hologram simulation ships and organize themselves into five phalanxes that began to move toward the deep chasm.

"What happens after we reach the crystals, I don't know," Parsonawitz began.

"After we reach the crystals, your part in this begins," Kane said abruptly, stepping to the hologram. "You're here as an expert on the laser, to oversee the loading of the crystals and to make sure they get back to Mars safely. That's all!"

Parsonawitz glared at him, his eyes burning at having to take orders from a man such as Kane. "If you're just going to snatch the crystals, this is merely a raid," he said. "And you're no better than one of those pirates skulking in the asteroid belt!"

Kane smirked at him. "Oh, there's a great deal more than that. But we are going to have to act as quickly as one of those pirates you feel so superior to. We will reach the Phidian Basin during planetary night, and we'll have only three hours to secure the crystal field before the sun rises and we have to leave. After that we can concentrate on Hielo, but we must make sure the crystals are in our hands. When faced with a battler and forty-three fighters, I think Dalton will become very amenable to any suggestions we might have about his government."

"A puppet regime?" Parsonawitz asked. "When I brought up this invasion to the RAM board of directors, the understanding was that we were mounting a . . ."

"Your suggestion to the board was meaningless until Ardala brought those recon pictures!" Kane shouted. "Parsonawitz, you're a bureaucrat—a cog in a machine. Leave the planning and fighting to those who know how!"

"I will not have you speak to me like that!" Parsonawitz suddenly stood, towering over Kane. "You pretentious little Terran thief!"

Kane made a strangled cry from deep in his throat and lunged forward, but Ardala quickly caught him by the arm and swung him away from the Martian. "I believe I've had enough shoptalk for one day, darling," she purred at Kane. "Shall we get a drink in the rec room and relax while the ship finishes its approach?"

○ ○ ○ ○ ○

"To tell you the truth, I'm not certain the Mariposans will help," said Kantar, plant manager of the largest Mariposa station orbiting Mercury. Tall and thin, Kantar stood in the audience hall amid the members of the council facing Tix as he fidgeted on the throne.

The Mariposa stations were orbiting solar energy plants, most of which were owned by the Gavilan family; the workers had no right of representation in the council, but in the face of the invasion Tix had called for Mariposans to attend the emergency session to add their counsel. Instead of helping, the Mariposans seemed determined to use the crisis to free themselves from Gavilan control. In fact, they seemed to want to disassociate themselves from Mercury entirely.

"I'm sorry," Kantar continued, "but I really don't see how the problems of the Dancers affect us. The Mariposa stations are—"

"This is n-n-not just a Dancer problem," Tix said, exasperated. He had repeated this point for ten hours, speaking with the delegates individually, by groups, and now in full council. "This affects all M-M-Mercury! If the RAM troops land and take the crystal f-f-fields, there is nothing to stop them from capturing Hielo!"

"And how would that effect us?" Kantar broke in. "The Mariposa stations virtually support Hielo with the power we draw from the sun and export. The majority of the Mariposans believe—rightly or wrongly—that they would do very well indeed without Hielo, Tix. Or should I say, Your Majesty."

There was a barely stifled laugh from the Miner delegation, but Tix clamped his lips tightly and pretended not to hear. "I don't care w-w-what you call me, just so we c-c-can agree how to face the Martian invasion!"

"There's only one way to face an invasion," Lomar of the Miners said, standing. "To fight! The Miners have long been allied with the Dancers, and we *will* help our friends! We will stand by the Dancers in the Phidian Basin, even if we get no aid from these . . ." the Miner paused and Tix felt his scalp prickle in fear of what Lomar might call the other delegates, "these more cautious folk." He nearly spat the words.

Tix closed his eyes and slumped as the Mariposan leader leaned forward angrily. "The tone of your voice belies your politic words, Miner," Kantar said aggressively.

"I had another word in mind," Lomar answered. "A much more blunt word."

Kantar started forward and three of his Mariposan representatives leaped up to follow him. Lomar roughly shoved aside the seat in front of him and jumped to the central aisle with two Miners behind him.

"Gentlemen!" Tix shouted, fighting to keep despair out of his voice. "We are f-f-facing an emergency! We can't l-l-let our personal feelings interfere—"

The great doors of the audience hall suddenly burst open and the delegates started around to stare. Kemal, a mass of bandages and bruises, limped into the room. Both his hands were wrapped in gauze that showed faint bloodstains over the knuckles; his tunic bulged with a rib pack over the gash he had received from Dalton; blue and purple bruises stained his face, and the eyelid of his right eye was swollen almost shut.

The delegates froze as he walked in; Duernie ran around the doorway a moment later, breathless. She started for him but drew back as she saw the council staring.

"What, in the name of the planets, are you doing?" Kemal rasped, his voice scratchy and painful.

The Miner and Mariposan delegates looked away quickly as if embarrassed to be caught brawling. "We were . . . discussing our differences," Kantar said, glancing up to Kemal's ruined face.

"Your *differences?*" Kemal raged. "Mercury is facing an invasion by RAM and you are so caught up with your squabbles that you dithered away half a day arguing!"

"I hardly think one ship—even a battler—can be considered an invasion," Kantar offered.

"Besides," Omeran of the Musicians said, "I don't think what happens on Hielo has that much effect on the surface. We Musicians have lived happily in our warrens without interference from here." He swept his hand around to indicate the palace. "It makes little difference to us if the Gavilans hold Mercury Prime or some anonymous board of directors from Mars."

Kemal gritted his teeth and spun around to the Musician, clenching his fists at his side. Duernie quickly put her hand on his arm. "Kemal, don't," she said softly.

Kemal looked at her, then nodded curtly. "You're right," he said quietly. He tried to smile, but the movement of his face muscles made him flinch. He patted her hand, then pulled away gently.

"Have you been to Earth?" Kemal turned to face Omeran. The Musician looked flustered. "Has anybody here been to Earth?"

A few nodded, including Kantar. "I have," the Mariposan said. "A filthy, decaying planet."

"It was," Kemal said, "five years ago. You wouldn't recognize it now, Kantar. The Terrans are rebuilding their old cities. They're founding new communities. They're *growing!* They're backward and provincial now, but they've found the energy again that sent them into space five centuries ago and founded the cultures that spread through the solar system."

"That sounds very little like the Earth I saw," Kantar said dryly. "The Terrans I knew were thieves and beggars, living off the bounty of travelers like myself, or preying on one another. What brought this miraculous change in them?"

"They fought a war against Mars," Kemal said.

"They threw off the 'anonymous board of directors' and regained some dignity, some confidence in what they could do! And now you're putting yourselves in the same position as the Terrans. You're going to let RAM come here and make us a colony! Do you want to live with RAM's laser in orbit around our world?" He turned to Omeran. "Do you want RAM security forces patrolling your warrens? Do you want a Martian board of directors deciding your solar energy production?"

The delegates glanced at one another, then broke into a hurried buzz of whispers and muttering. Kemal shook his head and looked at Duernie; she tried to smile but couldn't. She nodded toward the throne, where Tix sat leaning forward expectantly.

Kemal strode to the throne. "What's going on?" he asked.

"It's b-b-been like this all day." Tix sighed. "They argue and threaten each other as if they had n-n-never heard of RAM. The Mariposans absolutely refuse to f-f-fight. The Miners are willing to help, but the Musicians don't seem to c-c-care at all."

"Why aren't there any Dancers here?" Duernie asked.

"They w-w-wouldn't come," Tix said miserably. "I rescinded the arrests and l-l-let them go. I even offered them a ship."

"What happened?" Duernie asked.

"They b-b-burned it. They stole some ground transport vehicles and w-w-went to the Phidian Basin."

"The Eye of Phidias," Kemal said. "Are there any other Dancers there?"

"Fourteen track c-c-cities have arrived in the last six hours."

"Let me talk to them," Kemal said.

Tix pointed to the recording computer beside the throne. "There's a comm link. You should b-b-be able to contact them."

Kemal hurried to the computer and switched on the communications channels. "Kemal Gavilan calling *Renaissance Gold.* Is Corianne still with you? Come in."

The comm link crackled for a moment, then the monitor brightened with the image of Corianne. "*Renaissance Gold* here, Kemal. I greet you." Her face darkened with concern when she saw his bandages. "You are hurt?"

"Everything hurts, Corianne," he said in a whisper. "I'm tired. I want to come home and rest."

Corianne's eyes flickered to Duernie, then to Kemal. "There is little rest here. We are preparing to meet the RAM ship."

"I know. One more battle," he said. "Sometimes it feels as though I have been fighting all my life. Fighting with NEO against Mars, fighting my own family, fighting RAM. If I have to fight again, I want to fight for my home."

"Then come home, Kemal," Corianne said. "We await you."

Kemal switched off the comm link and turned around. Tix, Duernie, and most of the delegates were staring at him. He wondered if everybody had heard him, then decided he didn't care. "Tix, can you arrange transportation to the surface?"

Tix nodded wordlessly. As if that was a signal, the delegates began filing out of the hall, even though the new Sun King hadn't officially concluded the assembly. Tix looked at the council straggling out with an expression of pain in his eyes.

"Kemal," he said softly.

Kemal stepped closer to him. "What is it, Tix . . . uh . . . Your Majesty?"

"That's the problem," he said. "I'm not a k-k-king."

Kemal glanced at Duernie. "You're the only king

we have," he said lamely.

Tix shook his head and looked down. "You saw what happened in the council. I c-c-couldn't make them work together, and RAM will take the planet because I couldn't."

"You'll learn, Tix. You'll do fine," Duernie said.

"I don't want to learn," Tix said, looking into her eyes. "I watched Dalton, s-s-saw how he acted."

"Dalton was mad," Duernie interrupted. "You aren't like that!"

"No, I'm not. That's the point. Dalton could make p-p-people obey whether they wanted to or not. I saw him! They may have hated him, b-b-but they *obeyed.* I can't *make* anyone do what I want, even if it's for their own good, like t-t-today."

Kemal frowned and nodded. Despite his feelings for his cousin, he knew Tix was right. "What are we going to do?"

"You could be k-k-king," Tix said quietly.

Kemal started back a step, horrified. "I don't want to be!"

Tix smiled faintly. "I know. But that's n-n-not the question. You *could* be king—people would follow you. Whether you want to or not, you can lead. You are your father's son, after all."

Kemal closed his eyes and unconsciously rubbed the bridge of his nose, wincing as he touched the painful bruises. "I don't know, Tix. I can't think right now. I just want to go to the surface."

Duernie put her arm around his shoulder and led him away. "We'll talk later, Tix," she said over her shoulder.

Tix watched as they left the hall. "If there is a l-l-later," he said under his breath.

Chapter Seventeen

One more battle, Kemal thought as he stepped down from the cruiser. The jolt as his foot hit the ground sent such a wave of pain through his chest that it made him dizzy. One more battle . . .

He felt Duernie step beside him and take his arm, but he could see nothing in the blackness. "Are the track cities here? I can't see any lights."

Duernie clutched his arm tighter. "Kemal, your helmet is on opaque," she said with fear in her voice.

"Oh." He touched a toggle on his wrist and his faceplate cleared. A line of brightly lit track cities came into view, their floodlights illuminating an army of Dancers working beside the treads.

"You shouldn't be doing this," Duernie said. "You're too weak."

"One more battle, Duernie. That's all," he said, and grimly took a step toward the *Renaissance Gold.*

Corianne appeared out of the darkness and hurried to them. "Duernie, Kemal, I greet you," she said. "We have little time, I'm afraid. The RAM ship is no more than an hour away."

"Looks like the Dancers have made good use of their time," Kemal said, surveying the line of people filling sandbags to construct barricades and setting large laser drills in fortified embankments. "That's more than we accomplished on Hielo."

Kemal adjusted his visual scanners to infrared and looked at the flat plain stretching out before them. He saw several heat sources moving on the basin. "Who's out there?" he nodded toward the activity.

Corianne glanced at the plain. "Miners," she said. "They're preparing traps and planting thermal flares to confuse the invaders' scanners."

A Dancer came running to Corianne. "Madame, something is happening to the battler!"

"What?" Kemal shouted, a dim spark of hope brightening in him.

The messenger looked at him, then back to Corianne. "The ship is at the edge of our radar, but it does seem to have fragmented. Maybe it hit a meteor."

"Is there a comm link that can reach Hielo?" Kemal asked urgently.

Corianne nodded. "Thorian, give Kemal the radio."

The messenger raised his hand, but Kemal grabbed his arm and turned him quickly to the track city. "Show me!"

Thorian led him to a command station beside the *Renaissance Gold*; Kemal leaped at the radio set and opened the link.

"Mercury Prime, this is Kemal Gavilan! Can you

hear me? Come in—urgent!"

The monitor instantly lit up with the face of a communications officer. "Mercury Prime here, Kemal. His Majesty Tacitus has been trying to reach you."

Kemal frowned and nodded. "Put me through."

The officer reached out of the field of vision and the monitor image dissolved in a scattering of static, then reformed into the face of Tix.

"Tix, I really need to talk to the radar officer. Something happened to . . ."

"The battler, I know," Tix interrupted. "I wanted to t-t-tell you. It released a squadron of fighters and five troop transports!"

Kemal stared at the monitor. "It didn't break up?"

"No," Tix said. "We're under attack, or will be in a few m-m-minutes."

The faint hope died. Kemal cut the link as Corianne and Duernie found him at the radio. "It's starting," he said. "Tell the others to get ready."

❍ ❍ ❍ ❍ ❍

The transports glided to the surface in silent grace and hovered a moment before settling to the ground. The doors swung open at the same instant and soldiers scrambled out into the Mercurian night.

The Terrines came first and laid down a blanket of laser fire before the other troops followed. Outside their ships the soldiers stopped abruptly, looking around in confusion. Their infrared scanners showed the entire Phidian Basin alive with movement. Thousands of heat sources crawled along the basin floor and on the surrounding mountains.

The soldiers hesitated, bewildered, until a dozen laser beams stabbed into their midst. Three men screamed and crumbled as the others dodged away, peering around for the source of the fire.

Field commanders turned toward the transports, listening to orders, then grabbed men and shoved them ahead. The soldiers quickly formed ranks and started toward the Eye of Phidias.

The front line of men suddenly disappeared as a huge pit opened beneath their feet; the troopers behind them stopped abruptly, teetering on the brink. More lasers darted among them and five more soldiers tumbled into the pit. The others hustled around the trap and started forward again. After a few yards, the ground suddenly erupted with a score of Miners lying in shallow pits; they raked the soldiers with laser fire and quickly dove back into the ground, scrambling into a labyrinth of tunnels. A squad of Terrines rushed after the Miners and stumbled into another line of pits.

❍ ❍ ❍ ❍ ❍

Parsonawitz swiveled his chair away from the console and looked to Kane and Ardala with desperation. "The men are being cut to pieces!" he wailed. "I'm monitoring the military broadcast frequency, and they're in trouble!"

Ardala looked up from the holographic sim before her. "Joachim, do relax, won't you?" she said calmly. "The simulation shows a much clearer picture, and we're not in any trouble to speak of."

Parsonawitz jumped to his feet. "Have you heard what's going on down there? The soldiers can't see anything, and the basin is mined with tunnels!"

Kane snorted in disgust. "Shut up!" he barked. "We've lost maybe fifty soldiers, that's hardly a disaster. A landing is always like this at first: unfamiliar terrain, traps. Let's use the fighters to soften up the area before the troops move any farther."

"We can't," Parsonawitz said. "There are so many

thermal flares on the ground that the ships can't fix on any targets!"

Ardala smiled and swept her hand over the hologram. "Then tell the fighters to blanket the whole basin," she said lightly.

Parsonawitz swallowed hard and looked at her as Kane reached for the comm link to the fighters.

○ ○ ○ ○ ○

"They're going to strafe!" someone screamed as a swarm of fighters appeared at the far side of the Phidian Basin, heading straight for the Eye and the track cities closest to it. "Get down!"

The Dancers flattened behind their barricades as the fighters reached the forward line of the advancing RAM troops. As soon as the ships cleared, the soldiers began shooting a fan-pattern of pellet missiles. As each missile hit the ground, it erupted in a shower of small metal chips that tore open the pit traps and ripped open the protective suits of Miners waiting in ambush.

Kemal watched the line of fighters approach the track cities. Duernie tugged at his arm and he flung himself behind the barricade as the pellet missiles exploded. The metal shards tore into the sandbags, knocking over part of the barricade and digging through the chinks in the improvised wall. A woman shrieked in agony as a fragment ripped her suit, but the cry was cut short. Kemal glanced behind at the track city, watching the pellets rend its outer hull.

Duernie rolled over, staring at the pock-marked arcology. "They're gone," she said, her voice tight.

Kemal peered over the barricade. "Not them." He nodded toward the advancing line of RAM troops.

The Martians came on—slower now that they had to pick their way around the open pits and holes that gaped in the basin floor—continuing to move toward the Eye of Phidias. Lasers shot red streams from the Dancer lines into their ranks; occasionally the RAM men returned fire, but they couldn't see enough of their enemies to aim effectively.

The sides of the surrounding mountains then came alive with Miners pouring from tunnels and crevices. The RAM troops saw them coming, but before they could react, a barrage of grenades and laser fire cut down most of their flank.

The troops faltered for a moment; the flank facing the Miners dropped to the ground and began returning fire as the front line resumed its methodical advance. The surprise attack from the mountains was supposed to halt the RAM soldiers and allow the Dancers to storm their position so that they were fighting on two fronts.

But the Martians were too well trained to be diverted. Kemal watched them advance and realized what a weak plan it had been after all; the RAM forces were a professional army while the Mercurians were miners and nomads who fought haphazardly, with little forethought or training.

The Martian flank was holding against the Miners while the frontline troops continued to move forward. The Dancers' battle plan had been broken. Kemal saw Corianne talking intently to Vamir, the *Renaissance Gold*'s control ace. They both gestured wildly, pointing at the RAM men, the Miners, and their own Dancer positions.

Kemal crouched behind the barricade and scuttled to them. "Corianne, we've got to move soon!"

She turned away from Vamir. "The Miners didn't stop their advance. We need to formulate a new—"

"We don't have time!" Kemal insisted. "The troops will be here in minutes. We've got to attack!"

"I agree," Vamir said bluntly. It was clear from his

tone that he had been arguing for such a move.

Corianne sighed and let her shoulders slump. "Very well. Give the order, Vamir—you're the military commander tonight."

Vamir nodded and barked "Go!" into his radio.

The Dancers rose as a wave and leaped over the barricades. Kemal had a dizzying memory of a similar charge by Dancers that resulted in a slaughter, but then as now he could do nothing to prevent the deaths. He rose and started for the barricade.

"Kemal, wait!" Vamir shouted.

He turned impatiently. "What?"

"Don't go," Vamir said. "We need your experience as a soldier who fought against Mars."

"You need my laser out there more," he said, nodding at the basin. He looked back for Duernie, but she was already gone.

Corianne put her hand on his shoulder. "Don't be foolish, Kemal. We need your knowledge."

He shrugged her hand away and vaulted over the barricade. The jolt of landing jarred his chest so painfully that he nearly passed out. He started to run and saw Duernie's scarf ahead. He wanted to call her but knew that would only distract her.

He caught up with her in a few steps. She glanced at him and they exchanged weak smiles, then concentrated on staying alive.

Kemal saw a group of Dancers on his left firing wildly, their laser beams sweeping the ground ahead of them in erratic arcs. They hit nothing and made themselves good targets for the RAM troops.

"Pick your targets!" Kemal shouted into his radio. "Short bursts, and keep moving! Don't let your beams make you a target!"

The Dancers continued to fire carelessly. Kemal shook his head and stared ahead into the darkness. In the distance he could make out vague forms moving, so he shifted his visual scanner to infrared. The thermal flares still burned, making the basin seem alive with heat, but he could see some of the heat sources running. He dropped to his knee, took careful aim, and fired. The movement stopped.

Two men beside Kemal screamed and fell. Crimson streaks darted past, followed by other cries.

"Down, down, down!" Kemal bellowed, dropping to the ground. "Lie flat! Everyone, use the thermals for cover, they can't see us!"

The line of Dancers dove for cover, scrambling into the shallow pits or just hugging the ground.

Kemal looked forward; the heat sources glowed, but he couldn't see any movement from the Martians. Apparently they also were lying low.

Duernie rolled closer to him. "See anything?"

"No," Kemal replied. "Everybody's down, for now."

"Did you see those strange heat sources?"

"What do you mean?"

"There's something really hot out there, besides the flares."

Kemal drew a deep breath. "Must be Terrines. They're genetically altered soldiers with high metabolisms—very hard to take down. If they have Terrines, we're in trouble."

"Kemal, Duernie, are you well?" he heard Corianne's voice on his radio.

"We're here," Duernie said. "About fifty yards south of your position. No one's moving."

"You mean you've stopped the RAM troops?" Vamir asked.

"Temporarily," Kemal said. "But they're not going to give up. And we can't hold them for long."

"In two hours, it'll be sunrise and the surface temperature will rise so high that they'll have to leave," Corianne said.

"But they'll be back."

"Kemal, we're holding them," Vamir said. "The Dancers are holding RAM soldiers!"

"These are civilians!" Kemal broke in. "They'll never hold highly trained troops back. Corianne, RAM wants those crystals, and we aren't going to be able to stop them!"

The radio went silent for a long moment, then Corianne's voice came on, sounding tired. "Those crystals again. Those damned crystals. They've been nothing but grief for us since we found them!"

Kemal raised his eyebrows in surprise. Hearing Corianne swear was enough of a shock itself, but to hear her curse the crystals was unthinkable. He glanced at Duernie; her eyes were moist, as though she were on the verge of crying.

The crystals had offered the Dancers the only hope of breaking out of the grinding poverty that had dogged the nomads for generations. The crystals were the only commodity on the surface of Mercury that were valuable to anyone else in the solar system. They had been discovered by the Miner Madog, but the Dancer Ubrahil Carrera had first seen the commercial possibilities of crystals that could focus and increase the power of every laser, from industrial models to surgical laser-scalpels. With proper development, the Sun Crystals could lift the Dancers from homeless nomads to a community in control of its destiny. The crystals had become a symbol of hope for the desert dwellers—and a source of grief.

"Corianne, this affects all Mercury," Kemal said softly. "The crystal field must be destroyed."

"I know, Kemal," Corianne said slowly, dragging each word from her soul. "I shall take the matter up with the Dancer council."

"Quickly," Kemal said. "We don't have much—"

A compression grenade exploded behind the Dancers, cutting his words off.

Chapter Eighteen

Huer crouched in front of a NEO lieutenant and thrust his face near him. "Wilson, what are you doing with your men here? The laser is five buildings over that way!" He pointed toward an area lit by red flames.

Wilson and his men were huddled in the shadow of a building with another contingent of NEO troops across the narrow walkway in front of them. RAM troopers on the roof across the street had stopped their advance and kept them pinned with laser fire.

A spray of laser beams scattered through the night, piercing Huer's image and sizzling along the ground at his feet.

Wilson reflexively lunged out to grab Huer, but his hand had as little effect on the hologram as the lasers. And since the hologram was being projected from an uplink unit on the soldier's wrist, the image migrated with Wilson's movement. "Dammit, Huer!" Wilson yelled. "There are five hundred RAM troops out there to my hundred and fifty!" Another laser beam drilled through Huer. "And unlike you, my men die when they're hit!"

Huer's face wavered slightly, as if the effort to concentrate on the battle raging around him drained his ability to maintain the projection. It was a computer version of worry, Wilson thought.

"You're right," Huer said. "I'm sorry, but the Barneys may need help."

"The Barneys? Huer, *we* need help! Do you know there are Terrines here?"

"Well, do something!" Huer said desperately. "Shoot back, or . . ." Another burst of laser fire stabbed through Huer's image.

"Don't tell me my job," Wilson growled. "And please get out of the line of fire! It's unnerving to see you getting shot!"

Wilson turned to his men. "Red Squad! Blue squad! Grenades . . . keep 'em tight!"

Fifteen men raised grenade launchers and fired at the building across the street. The roof exploded with flame as debris and bodies arced into the sky.

"Now move!" Wilson was on his feet and dodged around the corner as his men scrambled to follow.

They cleared two buildings before an explosion knocked Wilson off his feet. He rolled away from the ruined building and looked up as three Terrines dashed out of a doorway and headed for him. The NEO men fired continuously at the Terrines, but their lasers had little effect.

"Jacobs! Cendars!" Wilson roared as the two men

raised their portable rocket launchers to their shoulders. They fired simultaneously, and the three Terrines were engulfed in a crimson ball of fire and smoke. One of the Terrines broke through the wall of flames, still running toward the NEO men, though it limped badly and its arm hung in tatters at its side.

Wilson rolled over and covered his head with his hands as a dozen NEO lasers licked at the one-armed Terrine. It stumbled and fell to its knees beside Wilson as a dozen Earth soldiers leaped at it.

The Terrine's arm swung out with inhuman speed, smashing into the helmet of one of the NEO men; the man's head snapped over sharply and he crumbled, his neck broken. Two men jumped on the Terrine, wrapping their arms around its chest to pin its hand to its side. The Terrine shook itself violently and the men flew off, crashing into the other soldiers. Wilson threw himself at the gennie's back, knocking it flat, and drew a dagger from his boot. Before he could strike, the Terrine jabbed its elbow into his stomach and flung him backward.

Wilson landed heavily on his back, his breath rushing from his lungs in an explosive burst. As he gasped for air, he became aware of a hissing sound and realized his suit had torn. Frantically he ran his hand over the suit until he found a two-inch rip in the fabric and clamped his hand over the breach. Accustomed to Earth's atmosphere, Wilson began to feel his head throb and his chest burn from the thin Martian atmosphere; vaguely he heard a muffled explosion somewhere close by, but thought it might just be his ears. Darkness swallowed him.

Wilson felt himself being roughly hauled to his feet. He looked at the man helping him and recognized him as Chen. He drew a ragged breath but didn't get enough air.

"Take it easy, lieutenant," Chen said. "Your suit

couldn't seal this big a hole and lost pressure, but I fixed it." Wilson quickly reached for the tear and felt a bulky patch. "It's just a temporary fix, so don't move around much."

"The Terrine," Wilson gasped. "What happened to it?"

"Did you black out, sir?" Chen asked. "Sergeant Yates killed it with a grenade. Damn, those things are hard to stop!"

Wilson looked at the ground and saw the dead Terrine, along with nine of his own men.

Yates stood inside the next building, shooing the soldiers around the corner. "Go, go, go!" he shouted, slapping them on the shoulder as they passed. "Huer said it's the next building down! Keep moving!"

Wilson took a step and stumbled against Chen.

"It'll take a couple of minutes for your suit to build pressure again, sir," Chen said. "You want to rest here?"

"No, keep me on my feet," Wilson said as they hobbled after the troops.

Huer materialized beside them, again projected from Wilson's uplink unit. "Are you wounded?"

Wilson glared at him for a moment, then turned away. "Where'd you come from? I didn't call you up."

"I fed in a code myself to activate all the uplinks so I can participate in the whole battle simultaneously. It gives me a unique overview."

"How many casualties?" Wilson asked.

"Twenty-seven dead, thirty-two wounded, including yourself," Huer replied. "We lost captains Kerr and Newall. That leaves you in command, lieutenant."

Wilson shook his head. "Better find someone else," he said.

"He'll be all right," Chen broke in. "He just needs a few minutes for his suit to build air pressure again.

He's fine, really."

Huer looked at him closely, then shrugged. "See you at Building Sixteen," he said and disappeared into a shadow.

Wilson turned to Chen. "Thanks," he snarled.

Chen smiled and gave his shoulder a squeeze. "You'll be okay, sir."

"Any more good news?" Wilson groaned as Chen stumbled.

They caught up with the rest of the NEO troops as the squad crouched beside Building Sixteen. Yates nodded as Wilson approached, and pointed at three men. "Morgan, Taylor, Sanchez, get in there and tell me what's happening. It's too quiet, and I don't want any more men walking into a trap."

The three backed up to the door and opened it slowly.

A heavy *thump* shook the wall. The man looked around, confused by the sudden noise, but couldn't see anything. Another shock hit the wall and it began to bulge outward. Yates leaped away and shouted, "Everybody, move, move, *move!*"

The soldiers scattered away as the wall began to crack. The bulge grew as the men stared, until finally the wall buckled with a loud *crack* and burst in a shower of flame and dust.

❍ ❍ ❍ ❍ ❍

"I don't like this," Quinto said, crouching against the wall inside Building Sixteen. "It's too quiet!"

Ochoa-Varilla nodded beside him. "This is the only building in the whole camp that isn't crawling with RAM troops. I've got a bad feeling. Can you hear anything? Breathing, movement?"

Quinto stood still, listening. "No, nothing. And I don't see any heat sources on infrared. Shall we take a look around?"

"After you," Ochoa-Varilla said. His hand patted along the wall until he found a light switch and turned it on.

The room lit up with powerful floodlights. Quinto whistled softly as he stared at the cavernous chamber that dropped three stories under the Martian surface. A graded ramp led down to the floor below. Ochoa-Varilla took a step onto the ramp, staring transfixed at the huge device hanging from a pulley near the roof. A receiving dish almost touched the center of the floor; above that a sphere sprouted two solar collector panels.

"Is that it?" Quinto asked, awed. "Is that the laser?"

Ochoa-Varilla mumbled something and continued down the incline. Quinto frowned as he watched him, then began looking around. He didn't believe RAM would booby-trap every building in camp *except* the one that contained the laser. Something had to be wrong.

Ochoa-Varilla reached the bottom and walked silently to the laser, oblivious to the clutter around him. Several large metal boxes lay scattered over the floor, but Ochoa-Varilla saw nothing but the laser.

"Get Huer," Quinto called. "Hey, we've got a job! You can admire the scenery later."

Ochoa-Varilla started, as if waking up, then waved to Quinto. "Sorry," he called. "I just got caught up with the science." He touched the uplink Barney had given him and watched as Huer's image formed out of the swirl of lights.

Huer stared at the laser towering above him, frozen by the sheer magnitude of the scale.

Quinto sighed impatiently. "If you guys are done being impressed, can we blow that thing off the face of this planet?"

"Eh?" Huer said, turning to Quinto. "Oh, yes, of course. Pardon me, I was just—"

"Yeah, caught up with the science, I know," Quinto said. "Is that really the laser we're after? Not just a model?"

"As far as I can tell, it's a working laser," Huer said, then his face brightened. "If you want to be absolutely certain, you could feed my program into the computer and I could crawl around inside it for a while."

Ochoa-Varilla started to laugh. "That sounds like plain old scientific curiosity to me! But I have to admit, I've wanted to get inside a few circuits myself just—"

"Do you two know we have a war going on outside? People are dying while you stand around admiring that bloody thing!" Quinto barked.

Huer looked down, embarrassed. Ochoa-Varilla coughed and turned to the ramp. "Okay, okay," he said. "Get some grenades ready."

"Is there some machinery active in here?" Huer suddenly asked.

"Not that we know of," Quinto said. "Why? Are you picking something up?"

"I'm getting a reading . . . something just activated on the floor."

Ochoa-Varilla turned just in time to see one of the metal crates abruptly unfold and a steel arm telescope toward him. The claw on the end clamped tightly around his leg and yanked him off his feet. The arm began drawing him back toward itself as a turret sprouted from the top; several sizes of muzzles sprang out of the turret and swung around to focus on Ochoa-Varilla.

Quinto's laser rifle snapped to his shoulder as if by its own will. "Move!" he screamed.

Ochoa-Varilla began twisting and rolling, Huer's

image following him like the end of a whip. The turret spat a quick laser beam that struck the floor beside the gennie's head; another muzzle shot out and a second shot followed, grazing his shoulder.

Quinto fired. His beam struck the mechanical arm but reflected away harmlessly. "What is that thing made of?" Quinto asked Huer as he shifted his aim to the turret. Again his beam had no effect.

Quinto let his rifle drop and pulled up his grenade launcher.

"Don't!" Huer called. "He's too close!"

He'll be dead anyway, Quinto thought and fired a grenade.

It hit the turret beneath the laser barrels and exploded. The metal box rocked back with the impact as the turret was torn away. Ochoa-Varilla scrambled forward, the claw still clinging to his ankle. Another telescoping arm shot forth and skittered along the floor, groping blindly for the Barney. Quinto shot two more grenades at the gap left by the turret. They hit the hole and erupted in a volcano of sparks and electrical fire. The mechanical arms twitched across the floor, then slowed to a stop.

Quinto leaped down from the doorway and ran to Ochoa-Varilla. The back of his armor was torn, but his breathing was regular. "Can you walk?"

Ochoa-Varilla groaned and turned to face him. "What for?" he asked irritably.

Quinto grinned and pulled him to a sitting position. "I just thought you'd want to give RAM a moving target."

Ochoa-Varilla stood. "Damn!" he rasped, falling against Quinto. "That thing almost ripped my foot off. I think it tore a tendon. What is it, anyway?"

Huer's image finally stabilized. "I've never seen that kind of weapon before," he said. He actually sensed things only through scanners on his hosts' uplink units. "It's made out of some kind of titanium alloy—very hard, and it's covered with a mercury compound that is highly reflective. It has an albedo of point nine plus, almost perfect reflectiveness. Lasers won't have any effect on it. It's probably just a guard device."

Quinto swallowed and looked nervously around the warehouse. "Let's get out of here before something else shows up. Can you get up that ramp?"

Ochoa-Varilla looked up the incline. "Sure," he said uncertainly. "Give me a hand."

Quinto put his arm around Ochoa-Varilla's back and started up the ramp, then something under their feet started to move.

"Did you feel that?"

"Yes!" Quinto shouted and pushed Ochoa-Varilla off the ramp. The incline began to open under Quinto's feet. He grabbed at the receding doors as he started to fall, but his fingers only brushed the edges.

He felt himself falling and flexed his knees so he would land softly. As soon as he touched down, Quinto flung himself to one side and rolled to the back wall, then dodged quickly away, moving with manic speed in case someone was taking aim at him.

After a moment, Quinto saw no one was shooting at him and stopped his random zigzagging to look around. He was in a small room with a wire mesh floor; Quinto noticed machinery through the metal grating—some kind of elevator, he thought; this is probably a storage shed, now a trap.

"Hey!" he called. "Are we in trouble?"

"Nothing major," his clone brother answered casually. "But you might want to come back on the floor and say hello to our new friends."

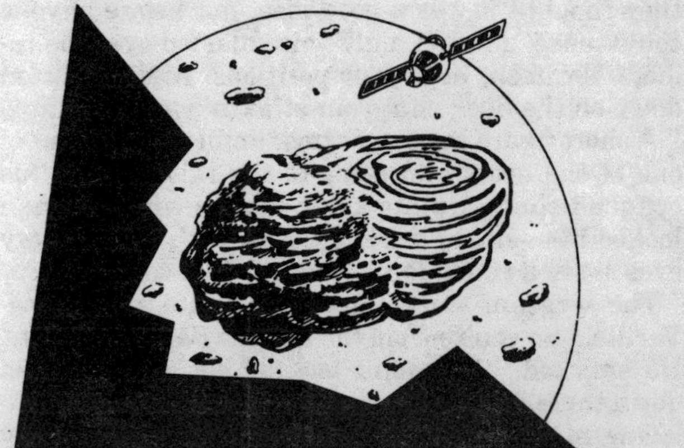

Chapter Nineteen

Quinto sighed and glanced at the opening above him, about fifteen feet, he estimated. He flexed his legs, felt his suit's servomotors activate, and jumped. He caught the edge of the ramp and swung himself over in one motion, landing in a tight crouch.

Two dozen RAM soldiers lined the overhead walkway, looking very nervous despite their complete battle armor and laser rifles trained on Ochoa-Varilla. Several men flinched and took aim on Quinto at his sudden appearance.

Ochoa-Varilla took a step forward and looked at the men as their weapons followed him. "Gentlemen," he began, "you could save yourselves a great deal of trouble if you'd simply step back and let us continue with our business. We won't be long, I promise."

A couple of the soldiers looked at each other as if they thought it was a good idea, but before anyone could move, a harsh, ugly voice blasted over the radio, "You men, hold your positions! And you scum down on the floor, shut your stinkin' yaps!"

A short figure in heavy armor ambled slowly out of one of the doors and came to the rail. Despite his opaque helmet, Quinto knew exactly what the man looked like—heavy-set and fleshy, with small, piggy eyes set in a ruddy face, a typical field sergeant.

The sergeant stared down at Quinto and Ochoa-Varilla. "So you're from the famous Barney project." He smirked. "You don't look so hot now, trapped down there and facing real men!"

One of the soldiers sidled closer and nervously whispered to the sergeant.

The sergeant brushed his hand away impatiently. "Why? What're they gonna do? You afraid they're gonna leap up here and chew you into little pieces? They're just more gennie trash that bit off more than they can chew."

"Excuse me," Ochoa-Varilla said, his voice light and jocular. "I have work to do." He took a casual step toward the supports holding up the catwalk. Quinto began to edge toward the great laser.

"Sarge," the soldier said again, "these guys are *good*. You shouldn't—"

"Shut up!" the sergeant bawled. "If you're so concerned about how good they are, finish them!"

The troopers looked at each other for a moment. The man beside the sergeant fidgeted. "But they're trapped, they can't—"

"Damn you! I said burn them!" The sergeant grabbed a rifle from one of his men and turned toward the floor.

Ochoa-Varilla leaped under the cover of the catwalk as Quinto dove at the laser and somersaulted to his feet. Three laser beams flicked the floor near his feet but weren't even close enough to count as misses. Quinto huddled close to the huge laser, watching the RAM men. They stopped firing and began a confused buzzing of questions on their radios.

That's a break, Quinto thought. They can't shoot the laser.

"You dance pretty good, clone," the sergeant shouted. "Think you could do another step for us?" Quinto heard him guffaw again.

Quinto scanned the shadows under the walkway until he saw Ochoa-Varilla's dim form hunched over some kind of console. "Hey how about a hand out here?" he called.

"No can do. I'm afraid that guard-bot twisted my foot so badly that I can't dance a step." Ochoa-Varilla then chuckled in his radio. "But I found something you might want to see."

Quinto glanced at the twenty yards between himself and the sheltered area under the walk—a flat, bare floor with no cover and two dozen armed men watching his every move. He slipped his laser up into shooting position and sighted on a trooper who was gesturing helplessly at the next man.

Somehow he couldn't bring himself to waste the shot. These soldiers didn't seem to have their hearts in the battle; most of them looked as if they wanted to be as far from the Barneys as possible—except for the sergeant. Quinto withdrew his laser and brought up a grenade launcher, then fired a flash-and-smoke bomb onto the catwalk.

The small explosion startled the troops; the men closest to it bolted blindly away, running into comrades. The sergeant started bellowing orders, but no one paid attention.

Quinto took advantage of the confusion to dash across the floor. A few crimson beams stabbed at him, but the shots were so wild that he didn't even bother to dodge as he ran. He stumbled and looked up to see the sergeant following him with a laser rifle.

Ochoa-Varilla grabbed his arm and yanked Quinto into the shadow of the walkway as the sergeant howled in frustration.

"Getting a little arrogant, aren't you?" Ochoa-Varilla laughed.

Quinto winced as he felt around the small hole seared into his leg. "Yeah, well, I'm paying for it." He rubbed his calf gingerly, but he knew his enhanced metabolism would heal the wound quickly. "What did you find that's so interesting?"

Ochoa-Varilla patted the console beside him. "This is the control panel for the equipment in here, including the laser."

"Does Huer know?"

"He's inside now," Ochoa-Varilla said, as Huer's holographic image suddenly swirled into view.

"This is it," Huer said hurriedly. "I can set the laser's capacitors to discharge internally."

"Then why didn't you?" Ochoa-Varilla said.

"Because the capacitors are empty and I need your flesh-and-blood fingers to initiate the recharging program. Now follow my fingers on the keyboard." The hologram started punching buttons slowly, so Ochoa-Varilla could copy his movements.

Huer stepped back as Ochoa-Varilla finished the last of the code. "It'll take about twenty minutes for the capacitors to recharge. Now input my program to the computer and get out of this building!"

Ochoa-Varilla quickly fed Huer's digital personality program into the computer as the hologram beside him dissolved. He looked up as a fine pinprick of light poked through the catwalk above and began cutting a thin line across the platform.

"Looks like we're going to have to do something about them," Ochoa-Varilla said, hefting his laser.

"Is that really necessary?" Quinto put his hand on the weapon.

"Getting squeamish? That's not the Quinto I know."

Quinto shrugged. "These are just kids."

Ochoa-Varilla lowered his rifle. "OK, have it your way, but I want a private talk with that sergeant." The sarge's voice erupted over the radio again, screaming abuse at his men.

"I'd like that, too," Quinto agreed, and pointed to the synthetic pillars beside them that supported the catwalk. "Shall we? I think he's right overhead."

Ochoa-Varilla nodded enthusiastically and grabbed the nearest pillar. "I've got this one."

"Right," Quinto said, moving to the next column.

Ochoa-Varilla gave him a high sign and the two clones tore at the supports. The metal shrieked as it was ripped free of the floor. Simultaneously Quinto and Ochoa-Varilla pulled down on the dangling pillars, and the walkway overhead buckled. Several men tumbled to the edge and scrambled to hold on to the railing. The two Barneys shook the pillars until one man fell off and crashed to the floor with a string of curses.

The sergeant looked up as Quinto and Ochoa-Varilla released their pillars and took a step toward them. He slid away from them, then began crawling wildly for the center of the room.

Almost casually Quinto strode across the floor and picked the sergeant up, holding him at arm's length toward the remaining men on the ruined walkway. "Now be careful, boys," he said. "You don't want to do any wild shooting with your beloved sergeant in the line of fire."

Two of the men immediately raised their rifles to take aim, but their comrades stopped them. Most of the soldiers began backing toward the doors.

"Where the hell are you going, you gutless . . . ?" the sergeant screamed. "Get back here and fight!"

Quinto shook the man violently and opened his mouth, but before he could get a word out, Huer walked calmly onto the floor from Ochoa-Varilla's uplink.

The room fell silent as Huer's impressive figure approached the sergeant and stopped in front of him. "You should tell your men," Huer began in a voice loud enough to be heard by everyone, "that I have just set the Warhead laser's capacitors to discharge internally. That means it will explode with the force of a K-cannon shell in fifteen minutes. This building and a quarter of the entire camp will be destroyed."

The sergeant looked up at his men. "Don't listen to him!" he shouted. "It's a bluff!"

Huer shrugged. "I just wanted you to know," he said and looked at Quinto and Ochoa-Varilla. "That goes for you, too."

"Gotcha, Doc," Quinto said. "We'll be out in a minute. We just want to clear up a few disagreements with the sarge."

The sergeant kicked wildly at Quinto but couldn't connect. He turned to the catwalk as his soldiers were pushing and shoving to get through the doors. "Come back! I *order* you . . ."

"Don't worry, Sarge," someone called back, "we'll see you get put in for a decoration for this."

Ochoa-Varilla laughed as he neared Quinto. "Now, Sergeant, I believe you were commenting on our heritage?"

Quinto reached over with his other hand and dug his fingers into the man's helmet. With a quick twist, the seals broke; Quinto flicked the helmet away.

Yes, he thought, looking at soldier's face, I was right—little, piggy eyes.

"Lousy, stinking mutant gennie crud," the sergeant spat.

Ochoa-Varilla's hand shot out abruptly, his thumb hooking into the sergeant's mouth. "Really, you should do something about your mouth." He gave the man's lower jaw a gentle tug, nearly ripping it off. "Why, Quinto, look at that! This poor man is suffering from severe dental deterioration."

"You mean he has cavities?"

"Certainly." Ochoa-Varilla snaked his fingers into the sergeant's mouth. "See?" Quinto heard a *pop* as Ochoa-Varilla pulled out a small, white tooth. The man's eyes bulged as a choked moan escaped from him.

Quinto laughed. "Old man, you're getting blind. There's nothing wrong with that tooth."

"There isn't?"

"Look at it! You got the wrong one." This time Quinto reached quickly into the sergeant's gaping mouth and yanked. An incisor came out as the man's eyes filled with tears and he started kicking helplessly. "It's a good thing we found this in time, or we might not have been able to save it."

"You better get your visual enhancers checked, you worthless gennie." Ochoa-Varilla laughed. "That's a perfectly healthy tooth."

Huer suddenly threw up his hands and glared at them. "This building is going to explode in a few minutes and you two are wasting time torturing some poor soldier? I give up! You can both stay here and get your molecules disassociated." His image started to fade.

Quinto nodded seriously. "He's right. Let's go. Let's take the sarge to Black Barney. He's always been much better at dental work."

"That's the ticket!" Ochoa-Varilla replied as the sergeant began flailing with his arms.

"Oh, have you heard of Barney?" Quinto asked as they started toward the ramp. Ochoa-Varilla swung his grenade launcher up and fired three percussion grenades at the wall—just for show.

O O O O O

Quinto and Ochoa-Varilla strode through the flaming hole, laughing as they held the semi-conscious sergeant between them. NEO men stared at them open-mouthed as Quinto shook his prisoner, then carelessly tossed him aside.

Lieutenant Wilson was the first to recover. He limped forward. "Are Black Barney and Tabibi in there?" He nodded to the warehouse.

"No," Ochoa-Varilla replied. "We left them in Building Fifteen. As far as we know they're still . . ."

An explosion cut off his words. Quinto quickly looked up to see a wave of RAM troopers pour across the street toward them. His grenade launcher came up in his hand in one motion, and he laid down a blanket of grenades while the NEO men scrambled for cover.

The Martian soldiers crossed the street and battered Wilson's men down before the smoke from Quinto's grenades cleared. Fighting at close quarters made grenades useless; Quinto withdrew his launcher into his sleeve and glanced around the melee, his hands twitching with the exhilaration of combat.

Two RAM men were backing the wounded NEO lieutenant against the building, a pair of ugly knives waving before them. With a long step Quinto shouldered between them and grabbed each by the nape of his neck. Quinto flung the startled men in opposite directions and reached out to support Wilson. "You all right?"

"So far," Wilson panted.

The lieutenant's portable uplink began to glow a vivid red as Huer started to materialize; he stepped toward Wilson even before his image finished forming.

"Lieutenant, you've got to get your men out of here!" he said urgently. "This whole area is going to blow in a few minutes!"

"What about the laser?" Wilson asked.

Huer stomped on the ground impatiently. "Don't worry about the laser! It's gone! Just get your men back to the ships!"

Wilson limped to his squad. "Yates!" he shouted. "Round 'em up!"

Ochoa-Varilla rushed over and began hauling Quinto toward the street. "Get out here!" he yelled. "Terrines!"

The word galvanized Quinto. He bolted away from Ochoa-Varilla, running eagerly for the sounds of battle ahead.

He turned the corner in time to see a huge Terrine lift a NEO soldier over its head. The man screamed once before the Terrine broke his back and tossed him away. RAM troops fanned out behind the Terrine, shooting at the Earth men as they tried to escape the Terrines' onslaught.

Quinto rushed forward with a howl of rage and battle fury, his grenade launcher sliding from his sleeve into firing position.

The Terrine turned on him, and before he could raise the weapon, Quinto felt the Terrine's hand clamp on his shoulder. Its fingers dug deeply into his body armor, and with a bone-wrenching yank the Terrine tore the entire arm unit—including the weapons systems but minus a protective inner layer—off his shoulder. For a split second Quinto stared at his naked arm, too stunned to be grateful it was still attached to his torso.

The Terrine swung a blow that landed squarely on Quinto's chest, knocking him back against the building. Instinctively, Quinto kicked at the battle gennie's midsection, but the Terrine's reflexes were faster than even his enhanced muscles. The Terrine's hand clamped on Quinto's ankle, stopping it dead. Quinto balanced precariously for a moment as the Terrine raised its hand in what seemed like slow motion.

The Terrine's fingers curled into a fist and snapped down on Quinto's leg. An explosion of agony burst below his knee as Quinto collapsed, fighting against the wave of darkness that threatened to engulf him.

He could see the Terrine leaning down, its hands reaching for his helmet. Quinto tried to roll away, but knew he was too slow.

A speeding blur suddenly crashed into the Terrine, sending it sprawling into the area between the buildings. Quinto looked up as Ochoa-Varilla stood up and looked into the alley. "Get Barney," Ochoa-Varilla snapped. "If we're fighting Terrines, we're going to need him!" He disappeared into the alley.

Quinto looked at his leg in numb shock. His armor was shattered completely, exposing the torn flesh of his shin. A jagged bone protruded from the bloody tangle of muscles. He stared at it with almost professional admiration; the Barney clones' bones had been engineered to be virtually unbreakable, yet the Terrine smashed through his armor and leg with a single blow. He wanted to find that Terrine again . . .

Huer materialized beside him via Quinto's own uplink unit. "Quinto, we've got to leave! The laser is going to explode!"

"I know, I know," Quinto growled. "I have to find Barney first. Do you know where he is?"

"He gave his uplink away," Huer said. "I can't access him without you."

Quinto stood on his good leg and took a painful hop/step toward the next building. A series of explosions blew a column of orange-red flame out of the alley in front of him. He could hear the raucous roar of Ochoa-Varilla's laugh on his radio as the smoke cleared.

Quinto tried to walk, but his leg wouldn't support his weight and he fell heavily.

Huer quickly kneeled beside him. "You're hurt," he said, disbelief in his voice. He reached for the clone, but his hand passed through Quinto's shoulder.

"Forget it," Quinto snapped. "Just get me to Building Fifteen."

"It's right here." Huer pointed to the structure next to them.

Quinto dragged himself to the building and began scrambling along the wall, looking for the entrance.

He saw the door, about ten feet in front of him, and tried to get to his feet, but his broken leg kept slipping out from under him.

"Barney!" he screamed into his helmet radio, his voice more shrill than he intended.

The door flew off its hinges and cartwheeled across the walkway. Tabibi's green helmet peered around the door frame, then he dashed out, his hand holding Barney by the collar of his black suit. Quinto noticed Barney was clawing at his black helmet as if trying to rip it off.

"Is he hurt?" Huer asked him. "Look how Tabibi is holding him!"

"There's something wrong with his helmet," Quinto said. Then he saw the great crack that split the right side of the helmet. "Barney!" he called, waving. "Get out!"

Tabibi glanced at him briefly, then ran to the end of the building with Barney in tow. Without stopping, they rounded the corner, into the middle of the assault on the NEO men.

Quinto saw two Martians level their laser rifles at Tabibi, then quickly raise them again without firing. Tabibi swung his arm around and flung Barney at the soldiers.

"*Tabibi!*" Quinto screamed at the top of his lungs. Huer stood beside him, frozen with shock.

The RAM men immediately turned their rifles at the battle clone and opened fire. Barney tore at his helmet and squirmed out of the way of the crimson beams dancing around him. One struck his leg and Quinto could hear his howl of pain. Quinto rolled away and smashed his fist into the wall; Huer just stood there for a moment, then took a step forward.

Another scream cut through Quinto's radio; his face screwed itself up in pain. Again he struck the wall and felt the wallboard crumble. He dug his fingers in and drew himself up a few inches. His hand reached higher and he hammered his palm against the surface until the material cracked. He pulled himself into a crouch. The tissue in his leg tore as he rose to his feet, but at least the pain drowned out the sound of Barney screaming.

He forced himself to turn and look. Huer walked slowly into the open street as lasers stabbed through his image. He didn't notice the beams; his eyes were fixed on the form of Barney as the clone writhed on the ground, still clawing at his helmet.

Quinto saw another RAM soldier raise his laser and fire at Barney. Barney jerked to the side as the beam struck him, then lay still. Screaming with rage, Quinto reached for his grenade launcher, but the weapon was gone. The sense of helplessness choked him as he limped along the wall, clutching at boards for support.

A burst of fire exploded ahead of him. He looked up

as a squad of RAM men with a plasma thrower swung the muzzle toward him and fired. Quinto threw himself away from the wall as the bomb struck, splashing the building with flaming jelly. He stumbled across the walkway to the warehouse and reached the corner as Tabibi burst through a ring of RAM soldiers that had pinned the last NEO troops down.

Quinto found a laser pistol on the ground and gingerly picked it up, settling it on his wrist as he aimed at the green helmet.

Wilson's hand suddenly clamped on the laser and tore it from his grip. "What are you doing?"

"Give me that!" Quinto roared, reaching for the gun, his voice a harsh croak. "He killed Barney!"

Wilson grabbed his shoulder and spun him around. "Come on, man! This whole place is going to blow up any second!" He shoved Quinto away.

Unable to respond, Quinto crashed to the ground, clutching at his leg. A dark wall of agony swirled around the edge of his vision as he fought to hold on to consciousness.

"Damn me!" Wilson said, kneeling beside him. "I didn't realize you were wounded! Let me help you up . . . We've got to get out of here!" He grabbed Quinto under his arms but couldn't budge the huge battle clone.

"Quinto!" Wilson gasped. "Come on, make an effort! I can't lift you by myself!"

Quinto struggled to his feet with Wilson's help. The lieutenant slung the clone's arm over his shoulder and sagged with the extra weight. Wilson started forward, pulling him along. Quinto moved his legs, but the motion was purely autonomic.

Quinto was only dimly aware of the jostling movement; the pain from his shattered leg ran through his body and exploded in his head with every step. He could hear the sound of other feet running and opened his eyes to see NEO men scrambling ahead of him. Off to the side . . .

He saw Tabibi's green helmet, blurred and indistinct. Quinto shook his head and tried to focus his eyes. It *was* Tabibi!

Quinto jerked away from Wilson and grabbed the lieutenant's laser pistol. Wilson spun around as the clone raised the gun and sighted on Tabibi . . . then the sky went red.

The night blew up in a scarlet blaze that washed over the camp. The building behind them came apart and rushed over them like a berserk wave. Quinto watched the destruction around him with a part of his mind, as if he had stepped outside himself and become simply an observer, a disinterested viewer of a badly made video show . . . that got to the end . . . and went black. . . .

○ ○ ○ ○ ○

Quinto felt a soft jolt to his face. It didn't hurt, it was just a vague pressure that was there for a second, then gone. He felt it again.

"Come on, Quinto, open your eyes," someone called to him from across the abyss of space.

Quinto forced his eyelids open. The face of one of the NEO medics leaned over and smiled. "How do you feel?"

"I feel . . . I don't feel anything," Quinto said thickly.

"Doesn't surprise me. We filled you up with enough anesthetics to stop a battalion. Don't try to move for a while. We have to get the rest of the troops loaded and leave Mars as fast as possible."

Mars. The word brought back the memories of the last few hours and he started to rise. The doctor put his hands on his shoulders and pressed him gently back. "Don't try to move, I said," the doctor told him firmly. "Your leg is mangled from all that running around. If you weren't a Barney, you'd have lost it. Even with your remarkable recuperative powers you'll need to rest a couple of days." The doctor pursed his lips grimly. "I wish the others had been as lucky. I've got some other people to look after, but I'll be back." He rose and walked to an adjacent bed.

Quinto looked around. He was in a blinding white room, lying on a cot with the wreckage of his armor scattered on the floor. Whoever had peeled it off him had done it in a hurry. The rest of the room was packed with makeshift beds holding wounded Terrans. The smell of disinfectant and medicine stung his nose.

"Hey, Quinto, glad you're awake," Ochoa-Varilla called to him from the next cot. "You okay?"

Quinto turned to him. "I'm all right," he said. "Probably feel this in the morning, though."

Ochoa-Varilla laughed. "Yeah, maybe we're getting too old for this kind of work."

Quinto let his eyes wander across the clutter of armor, clothes, and weapons that littered the floor. He caught sight of a green helmet crushed beyond recognition.

"Tabibi!" Quinto blurted. "Where . . . ?"

"He's dead," Ochoa-Varilla said grimly.

"Good!" Quinto snarled. "The bastard killed Barney!"

"What?" a deep, rumbling voice growled.

Quinto saw the familiar face rise into view a few beds away. Black Barney, his chest a mass of bandages, glowered at him. "Barney! You're alive!"

The pirate scowled, a look of impatience on his face.

"I saw Tabibi push you into the RAM men . . ." Quinto started.

"That was *him,*" Barney spat. "I took his gear, made him wear mine. They were aiming at the helmets."

"What are you talking about?" Quinto asked.

Barney glared at him a moment, his eyes burning. "He betrayed us," the pirate finally said.

"You mean to RAM?"

Barney looked away. "He betrayed us," he said again and sank back on his cot. Quinto knew that was the last thing Barney would ever say about Tabibi.

The intercom made a sharp, crackling sound. "Secure all stations," the crisp, metallic voice said. "Emergency liftoff procedures beginning."

Huer appeared between Quinto and Ochoa-Varilla from an uplink unit on the floor. "I'm glad to see you two made it," the hologram said. "Don't worry about your cruisers. I've assigned men to pilot them back to the asteroid belt."

"Thanks," Ochoa-Varilla said. "How many did we lose?"

"Out of the one hundred fifty men that went in, eighty-three came back," Huer said, his face tight.

Ochoa-Varilla whistled softly. "Almost half died?"

"What about the laser?" Quinto asked.

"Destroyed," Huer answered.

Quinto felt a wave of dizziness sweep over him. He tried to call Huer, but the effort didn't seem worth it. He closed his eyes and sank into darkness.

Chapter Twenty

Parsonawitz looked up from the computer. "There's a message coming in," he said, awed.

Kane gave an exasperated snort as he stared at the combat sim hologram. "So put it on the monitor," he snapped.

"It's not on a comm link," the Martian said. "This is a communique directly from Pavonis. Highest level security code."

Ardala rushed to him. "What does it say?"

"I don't know yet," Parsonawitz said. "It's coming in on a military channel and needs to be unscrambled." He watched the console as the message LED flickered erratically.

Ardala leaned over the computer impatiently. If Pavonis was communicating on the highest security channel, the upper levels of the RAM hierarchy were concerned, and the board rarely took a hand in a simple military operation.

"It's in," Parsonawitz said and began punching in the scrambler code.

"What's it say?" Ardala repeated.

"Give the program a chance to work," Parsonawitz said. "Okay, here it is. Kane, you should see this."

Kane ignored him and continued to study the sim. "Just give me the highlights," he growled, trying to stay as far as possible from the cowardly, infuriating, presumptuous Martian bog worm . . .

A square-faced RAM commander came up on the monitor. He frowned at the camera and coughed, obviously uncomfortable with the message. "This is Commander Talbot. Mars is under attack by NEO forces," he said in a flat, emotionless voice. "A squad of gennie clones and Earth troops have landed on the Plains of Elysium. Your ships and men are needed immediately. Withdraw your forces from Mercury and return to Mars." The monitor went black.

"*What?*" Kane raged.

"Mars is under attack and we've been recalled," Parsonawitz said with no small relief. "Do you want me to replay the tape?"

"Shut up!" Kane shouted. "You strutting, pompous . . ."

"Be quiet, both of you!" Ardala snapped. "We've got to think! Why would NEO invade Mars? And why land on the Plains of Elysium?"

Parsonawitz cleared his throat nervously and looked down at the console, busying himself with a knob beside the dark screen.

"What is it?" Kane demanded, striding to him in three long steps.

"Er . . . nothing," Parsonawitz said quickly, too quickly.

Ardala sidled up on his other side. "Now, Joachim," she said with a silky purr, "you know *something* about this." She reached out to him, running her fingers along his cheek.

Parsonawitz pulled away from her fingernails and bumped into Kane. He looked at him, then at Ardala. "The laser is at Elysium," he admitted finally.

Kane chuckled harshly. "So that's where you hid it."

"I thought," Parsonawitz began, then added quickly, "that is, the RAM board of directors felt the laser would be safer in a laboratory, where we could study and test it further."

"NEO isn't invading Mars," Kane interrupted. "That's a hit-and-run operation to destroy the laser."

"And they're probably finished by now," Ardala said. "We'd never get back in time to do any good."

"But the orders," Parsonawitz said, motioning to the monitor.

"Shut up," Kane told him and turned to Ardala. "There's a little more than an hour until sunrise over the Eye. If the troops can reach the crystals before then, we can hold them no matter what RAM says."

"You know, RAM was never really in favor of this invasion." Parsonawitz shook his finger at Kane. "When you proposed this, most of the board disapproved."

"Shut up!" Ardala snapped. "This has nothing to do with RAM or the board! Everything about the invasion has been arranged at a level far above the board."

Kane groaned. "Is this the work of the Great Manipulator again? Ardala, I'm starting to worry about you!"

Parsonawitz rose half out of his seat and gaped at

her. "You're talking about Holzerhein, aren't you?"

She frowned but otherwise ignored him. "I don't know what he's after. He set up this invasion, and now he's calling us off." She shook her head. "There are too many pieces missing. I can't tell if he really wants us back on Mars or if he expects us to go ahead and take the crystals."

Kane smashed his fist on the console. "Dammit, Ardala! What difference does it make what he wants? We've got a planet at our fingertips and you're worrying about some computer spook's dreams of godhood! I lost the laser because you were trying to second-guess him. I'm not going to throw this planet away because of you!" He turned from her and grabbed the radio microphone.

"Kane! Stop and think! You might be playing into his hands!"

"And he might be playing into mine! I don't understand this obsession you have for ruining Holzerhein's plans. We could become the most powerful people in the inner planets if we work with him."

"I don't mind working with him, but I'm damned if I'm going to work *for* that bloodless nethead! I'm not going to let him run me through a maze like some lab animal, and if the only way to stop him is to tear this whole project apart, then I will!"

Kane opened a comm link to Mercury's surface with a vicious blow to the console. "Ardala, whatever you're trying to prove, I won't let you ruin my chances on this planet!"

Parsonawitz stood and backed away from Ardala, his eyes wide with horror and disbelief. "Am I to understand you're actually *trying* to ruin Holzerhein's campaign? Holzerhein's?" He breathed the name with awe.

Ardala and Kane both turned on him and shouted, "*Shut up!*"

○ ○ ○ ○ ○

Kemal slapped the Dancer on the back. "Okay, you understand what you're supposed to do?"

The man nodded. "I got it."

"Good. Tell the others," Kemal waved at the half-dozen Dancers dug into the basin's floor around them. "And remember, don't use the radio—RAM's probably monitoring our communications. Use the intersuit link."

The Dancer raised his hand and clenched his fist in affirmation. Kemal turned and scuttled away in a low crouch. He risked lifting his head to scan the landscape for Duernie, but she was lost in the darkness as she passed the new plan among the entrenched Dancers.

Kemal heaved a deep sigh and crawled behind a boulder to rest. The last hour had been a whirlwind of activity, making plans and spreading the word among the Dancers. Since the thermal flares were dying out, RAM's grenades and lasers were striking with more accuracy and more frequency. There was more activity going on behind RAM lines, too: scrambled radio communications and shifts in troop positions. Something was about to happen. With sunrise so close, it didn't take much military acumen to guess the Martian troops were preparing for one more push.

His radio crackled in his ear. "Kemal, come in. This is—"

"Corianne, why are you breaking radio silence?"

"We have an important transmission for you. Where are you? Can you get back here?"

Kemal scanned the horizon until he saw the dark shadow of the track cities against the mountains. "I'm about a hundred yards north of *Renaissance Gold*."

Corianne made an impatient noise. "It would take too long for you to come back. We'll feed the transmission directly to you. Stand by." The radio began a quiet hiss.

"Wait," Kemal said. "Who wants to talk to me?"

A burst of static came on, then an unfamiliar voice said, "Kemal? Kemal Gavilan of Hielo?"

"This is Kemal, but I wouldn't say I was 'of Hielo' anymore. Who is this?"

There was a brief pause. Kemal could hear an excited babble of voices on the other end of the comm link. Finally he heard, "This is Corocan of the Mariposan assembly. Where are you right now?"

"Where am I?" Kemal exploded. "I'm in the middle of a battlefield with RAM troops all around me! What's so important that you have to break radio silence?"

Corocan coughed nervously. "Well, I won't interrupt you anymore. Good luck, and, well . . . signing off." The radio went dead.

Kemal frowned and activated the link again. "Corianne, were you listening? What was that all about?"

"I'm not sure," she answered. "I think the Mariposans are just curious about you."

"About me? This is a rotten time to indulge in idle curiosity."

"I don't know if you're aware of it, but you've become the object of a great deal of discussion since your last appearance on Hielo."

"Well, can you cut off the curiosity seekers until this is over?"

"Kemal, I think that call was important," Corianne began.

A barrage of mortar fire drowned out the rest of her words. Kemal flattened himself against the boulder and peered around its edge. The RAM troops were moving.

The Terrines came first, darting forward even before the mortar barrage ended. RAM regulars followed more cautiously, allowing the Terrine troops to clear the way.

The Dancers made an effort to fight, but they had nothing that could stand against the Martians. The Miners' great drilling lasers didn't have weapons-grade power, and the few hand-held lasers among the Dancers had no effect on the Terrines' armored bodies.

The Mercurians began to fall back.

The Miners scattered back to the hills, and the Dancers retreated toward their track cities. Kemal watched the RAM forces catch their first scent of victory; the regulars picked up speed, running almost as fast as the Terrines. Behind their advancing line he saw a group of men bringing up a portable missile launcher.

Kemal pushed away from the rock and sprinted toward the Dancer barricade. "Fall back!" he shouted into his radio. "They're bringing up missiles! Fall back!"

The first shell streaked over his head and tore into the *Hermes Trismegistus,* the track city directly in front of him. The missile ripped through the arcology's hull, rocking the huge desert ship. The air within it fed an explosion in a vivid orange flash.

Kemal tried to change direction but tripped. He scrambled to his feet as another rocket smashed into the city. The *Hermes* tilted dangerously, its port treads lifting off the ground. A split second later, two more missiles hit the mobile arcology and it crashed over into the dust, a volcano of flames shooting out of the jagged hole in its hull.

Kemal rose to his feet slowly, staring at the track city as its treads gradually ground to a halt. The *Hermes* was dead. He had never heard of a track city being destroyed, and the thought burned inside him.

A crimson beam flashed beside Kemal, startling him out of the shock. He twisted aside and dashed toward the barricade. He dove over the embankment as the sky behind him suddenly lit with a blinding glare of white.

Kemal whirled around in time to see another blue-white bolt of lightning crash into the ground far behind the RAM troops. Even the Martian soldiers stopped to watch the lightning tear an erratic path through the transport ships that brought them to the surface. The bolt struck one of their vessels, and it erupted in a shower of sparks and debris.

Martian commanders began pushing their men forward, and the advance began again. Kemal looked down the barricades until he saw the *Renaissance Gold* and started running toward it.

Duernie was waiting for him when he reached the communication center beside the arcology. Vamir sat at the comm link, barking orders into the microphone as Corianne directed a stream of Dancers carrying equipment away from the advancing Martians.

"Kemal!" Duernie called when she saw him. "Did you see the *Hermes*?" she asked, her voice choked with grief.

"I saw," he said. "Were there any Dancers inside?"

Corianne stepped over to him. "Everyone from the *Hermes* is safe. We're trying to salvage the equipment from it, but the city is gone." Her voice trailed off. In all of Mercury's history, a track city had never been willfully destroyed, and the magnitude of the act staggered the Dancer's imagination.

But a war raged around them. "Corianne, what happened to the RAM ships? What was that lightning?" Kemal asked.

"That came from a Mariposa station," she said. "They've adapted their microwave transmitter to discharge in an arc. They can't aim the energy bolt with accuracy, but it is very destructive."

"The Mariposans did that?" Kemal asked, puzzled. "But they didn't want anything to do with this war."

Corianne shrugged. "Whatever you said must have been more eloquent than you knew. We've even received a call from the Musicians offering to send troops."

"They won't arrive in time," Kemal said.

"That's not the point," Corianne replied. "The important thing is that the factions of Mercury are united now—behind you." She paused, staring at him with her unnerving directness, then added softly, "Your Majesty."

Kemal swallowed and gaped at her wordlessly.

"Look, I hate to interrupt this momentous scene, but we do have a problem," Duernie said, nodding toward the RAM soldiers.

Vamir stood up from the makeshift communications center. "Let's go!" he shouted to the Dancers around him. With a gallant gesture, he offered Corianne his arm; she put her hand lightly on his elbow, then they both broke into an awkward run toward the mountains.

Duernie grabbed Kemal's hand. "Come on, Kemal! Wake up!"

Kemal looked at her, then at the advancing Martians as if he had just become aware of the chaos around him. They started running at the same instant.

"Do you think they'll follow us?" Duernie asked as they broke through the end of the track cities.

"No," Kemal answered. "They want the crystals more than they want us. They'll head for the Eye of Phidias—for now."

"I wish I could see their faces when they get there," she said with a ferocious grin.

○ ○ ○ ○ ○

"They're pulling back!" Parsonawitz crowed with a laugh of pure delight. "See, look at the sim!"

Ardala and Kane quickly ran to the hologram simulation and looked as the infrared filter showed a straggling of heat sources scatter toward the mountains.

"Wonderful," Kane said, his mouth set in a tight line. "Have you found the source of that bolt of energy that hit the transport?"

"Well, the discharge was very erratic, so I can't trace it precisely, but it probably came from one of the orbiting Mariposa stations," Parsonawitz said. "Why are you concerned with that? We've won!"

"I'm always concerned about a weapon I can't see," Kane replied grimly.

"Maybe we should destroy a Mariposa station as a warning," Ardala suggested.

Parsonawitz glanced up at her, his eyes gleaming. "Yes," he said quickly. "A lesson on the consequences of resistance! If we destroy a few stations, they wouldn't dare repeat the attack." He almost licked his lips in anticipation.

Kane looked away in disgust. "I don't think that will be necessary," he snarled. "The crystal field is what we came for."

"Yes, yes, of course," Parsonawitz agreed. "Still, I'll just fix the coordinates of a station and feed them into the weapons system, just in case we need to make a point." He huddled over the console, his hands playing over the controls.

Kane shook his head and turned back to the holographic sim to watch the progress of the troops. They'd already reached the line of track cities and passed beyond them to the last stretch of land before the Eye itself.

Ardala came to the sim and turned her back to the scene. She stared at Parsonawitz as he busied himself at the computer. "That man disgusts me," she said under her breath. "I've been thinking about how nice it would be if we had some sort of accident on the way back."

"My dèar, it amazes me occasionally how similarly our minds work," Kane smiled at her.

She looked at the sim. "Will the troops reach the Eye before sunrise?" she asked, changing the subject.

"Easily," Kane replied. "We'll have a load of crystals in orbit within half an hour. When the laser arrives, we'll have the whole planet."

"If there still *is* a laser," she said.

Kane opened his mouth, a sarcastic retort beginning, but he stopped before saying anything, his face suddenly thoughtful. "Yes," he said seriously. "We need a contingency plan, one that doesn't include him." Kane nodded toward Parsonawitz.

"Hush," Ardala said. "The soldiers are at the Eye!"

"They're there?" Parsonawitz leaped up and rushed to the hologram as the swarm of RAM troops converged on the crater at the end of the Phidian Basin. The three of them crowded around the sim to watch the first men approach the edge of the chasm.

A deep, burning red suddenly appeared on the hologram, glowing deep in the Eye. The crimson wash spread through some underground crevasse, radiating under the map to a cavern. The troops began to scatter back from the boiling Eye.

"What's going on?" Ardala jumped back from the sim. "Parsonawitz?"

"I don't know," the Martian sputtered. "There's active magma below the basin. It may be a volcanic eruption."

"Contact the troops and find out what's happening down there!" Kane snarled.

Parsonawitz scrambled to the comm link and fumbled with the controls. Suddenly his head snapped up. "We're getting another message from Pavonis," he said, his voice shaking.

Kane bared his teeth in a soundless growl of frustration.

○ ○ ○ ○ ○

Kemal paused on the side of the mountain and looked back as the first rumbles shook the ground. Duernie caught his hand in hers and squeezed hard enough to hurt him.

"It's really happening," she whispered, still only half believing.

Kemal nodded, watching. The Eye of Phidias suddenly glowed with a burning orange-red aura. Within seconds the red stain extended outward from the Eye, crawling through the crevices beneath the surface.

The RAM troops began to scramble away from the crater, pushing and shoving at each other in mindless panic. As Kemal watched, a man tripped and was trampled by the retreating army.

From within the Eye an angry red bubble of magma welled up and splashed over the rim. Kemal felt the ground heave under his feet.

Duernie clutched at his arm for balance. "What's happening?" she cried. "The thermal bombs shouldn't be doing this!"

"I think we set off a volcano," Kemal said.

A gout of molten rock exploded from the crater, spraying into the dark sky like a fiery geyser. The Martians scattered from the burning rain as it fell back to the surrounding plain.

Another explosion erupted from the Eye. Kemal slipped as a small avalanche of stones and rubble shook loose from the mountainside. The Dancers and Miners around him lurched and fell as well as the ground shifted.

Kemal looked up as a dome of magma gushed up to the rim of the Eye and spilled into the basin. Within seconds, another wave surged up and over the growing volcanic cone. Kemal's feet slid from under him and he felt himself being carried down the mountain slope in a shower of dirt and stones. He wrapped his arms around his helmet and let the avalanche carry him.

Finally he slowed to a stop after a few yards. "Duernie?" he called.

"Here, beside you," she said. "I think it's over."

Kemal stood up as a large area around the Eye began to crack and sink, sending up a cloud of dust that settled quickly in the airless atmosphere.

Duernie stared at the scene in silence. Kemal tried to see her eyes, but she turned away from him, hiding her face.

The crystals were gone. The hope and future of the Dancer community was destroyed, blown up by their own hands. Kemal felt a swell of pride for their sacrifice, for their vision. At the same time, he ached for the nomads; seeding the crystal field with thermal explosives all but condemned the Dancers to a future of poverty and despair.

Kemal turned away. The other Dancers on the mountainside had stopped running and were staring at the fiery glow from the Eye. No one moved for what seemed like an eternity, each Dancer lost in his or her private thoughts.

Finally a man's voice came through Kemal's radio. "They're leaving!"

"Who's leaving?" Kemal asked, searching for the source of the voice.

"The RAM soldiers! They're pulling back! I can see

them through my macroglasses."

"Where are you?" Kemal stood.

"Where are *you*? Oh, I've got you. I'm about thirty paces to your left."

Kemal grabbed Duernie's hand and started running toward the man. They almost ran him down in the darkness.

"Whoa, slow down!" he said. "You're here already. Kemal, isn't it?"

Kemal brushed aside the man's question, then asked, "May I borrow your viewer?"

"Sure, take it!" he said, handing Kemal the device. "I just wanted to meet you and shake your hand." He extended his palm. Kemal took it absently.

The man pumped the prince's arm with a vigor that surprised Kemal. "My name's Ondrah Canabar!" he said, grinning hugely. "Pleased to make your acquaintance!"

Kemal tried to retrieve his hand, but Ondrah wasn't about to let go. "That's not a Dancer name, is it?" Kemal asked, anxious to look at the RAM troops but not wanting to be rude.

"No, I'm a Miner," Canabar said proudly. "Been scratching around these mountains for a hundred and fifty years. This is the first time I've felt like I was part of something bigger than just me. I wanted to thank you for that."

Kemal cleared his throat uneasily. "Well, you should thank RAM then."

"Not for all the beryllium in the inner planets, I wouldn't thank them!" Canabar snorted. "You're the one who did this, got all the factions to stand together. There's a lot of talk about you, Kemal. What you did up on Hielo to that sand-eater Dalton, then coming down to the surface to fight with us. Well, I'll let you go now." He released Kemal's hand. "I just wanted to say I met you."

Kemal stared at him for a moment, then looked at Duernie. She smiled at him and shrugged. He shook his head, then brought the macroglasses to his faceplate.

"They *are* leaving!" he cried, watching the tiny figures run from the Eye.

"Let me see." Duernie tugged at his arm.

"Oh, sorry." Kemal handed her the viewer. "Tell me what they're doing." He and Canabar turned to the basin floor and stared into the darkness.

Duernie raised the glasses. "They're still running . . . past the track cities . . . the transports are moving up to them and . . ." She lowered the macroglasses and looked at Kemal, tears in her eyes. "They're really leaving!"

"There!" Canabar's finger stabbed ahead. "Did you see?"

Kemal followed his hand. Through the darkness he could see a sudden flare as a transporter's engines ignited.

Another bright flare lit the basin, then another.

Kemal felt his legs begin to shake as the tension broke inside him. He swayed to the side, and Duernie grabbed his arm.

"Are you all right?" she asked, staring into his faceplate with concern.

"Fine, I'm fine," he said. "I just need to sit a minute." He sank to the ground gratefully and let a deep breath escape.

His receiver erupted in a cacophony of laughter, cheers, squeals, whistles, and howls of delight. Kemal smiled and tried to work up the energy to join the riot, but found he only wanted to rest.

It was nice to hear the sounds of celebration again; he smiled and took Duernie's hand. Canabar clapped him on his shoulder softly and beamed a wide grin.

Slowly the chaotic noise began to resolve into a

word. It took Kemal several seconds to recognize his name being repeated over the radio.

"Kemal . . . Kemal . . . Kemal . . ." the chant gained power as more voices joined until finally it seemed the entire basin reverberated with his name.

Through the noise Kemal heard a garbled voice trying to break through the racket.

". . . this is Hielo. Can you hear me, Kemal? Come in."

Kemal boosted his transceiver. "Kemal here, Hielo. I read you."

"You're all right, K-K-Kemal?" He recognized Tix's voice.

"I'm fine."

"We've been monitoring the radio, and it s-s-sounds like the whole planet is calling your name."

"I hear it," Kemal said weakly.

"Kemal, you can't doubt it now," Tix said. "This is your w-w-world. They want you. I'm going to abdicate the throne in your favor."

Kemal nodded within his helmet, too numb to care that the gesture couldn't be seen. "Yes," he said thickly.

Chapter Twenty-one

The barber flitted around to Kemal's right side, snipping at a strand of hair he had worried over for ten minutes. "Can Your Majesty turn his head slightly to the left?" the barber asked.

Kemal scowled and tilted his head.

"Ah, perfect!" the barber cried gleefully as he busily cut and patted the offending hair into place. "Now, if Your Majesty can look down."

"That's enough!" Kemal blustered. "My hair looks fine as it is! I don't want to spend the whole day like this!"

The barber bowed and backed away. "As Your Majesty wishes. If I may be so bold—has Your Majesty thought about growing a beard? It would lend a dignified—"

"My dignity is fine," Kemal snapped. "Your services have been excellent, thank you. You may go."

The barber bowed again, clasping his hands in front of him as he bobbed backward to the door. "You're very gracious, Your Majesty. If you need anything else while in Mozart, please allow me . . ."

Kemal sighed through clenched teeth. "Yes!" he shouted. "I will! Thank you!"

The barber disappeared through the doorway as Kemal jerked a towel from around his neck and threw it on a chair. He paced furiously across the suite, kicking at the very expensive furniture of the most luxurious hotel of the Mozart warren.

Tix and Duernie came in from an adjacent room, carrying the Sun King's ceremonial robes. "Let's try a f-f-final fitting," Tix said, holding the outfit up to Kemal's chest. "The alterations l-l-look fine."

Kemal brushed the clothes away with an impatient gesture. "Will you stop hovering over me!" he bellowed. "For the last three days everybody has been fussing over me, poking at me! I'm getting sick of it!"

Tix looked at Duernie, then back to Kemal. "Why are you b-b-being so difficult?" he asked. "You insisted your c-c-coronation take place planetside instead of on Hielo, where everything is—"

"Oh, damn the coronation!" Kemal snapped. "I didn't think the whole thing would be this much trouble. I haven't had a moment's peace since I agreed to be king. Everybody's haunting me, telling me what to do, how to act. You know, Terens grilled me for days about proper etiquette! Is this what the rest of my life is going to be like?"

Duernie smiled wryly at him. "You're not getting cold feet, are you?"

"I'm getting something," he said, frustrated. "I'm

getting sick of all this is what I'm getting!"

She nodded, setting aside the costume. "I know," she said gently. "It's a big day—for all of Mercury."

Kemal opened his mouth but shut it again and began pacing without a word. Finally he said, "Look, the coronation isn't for six hours. I'm going to get out of here for a while, go for a walk or something."

"You want some company?" Duernie asked as he turned to the door.

He stopped and looked at her, smiling. "If you don't mind, I think I'd like some time alone."

She winked at him. "Go ahead. I'll be here when you get back."

He reached out and ran his finger along her cheek, then nodded almost imperceptibly. He turned and hurried from the room.

Tix watched him leave. "Is he all r-r-right?"

"He's just nervous," Duernie said.

O O O O O

Kemal changed into his rocketjock clothes and sneaked out of the hotel. He wandered through the warren for a half-hour before he started to recognize some of the tunnels. Since Mozart had been chosen as the site of the coronation, tens of thousands of credits had been spent by the government on Hielo to spruce up the dilapidated warren—which was Kemal's intent in picking Mozart for the honor. The entire underground city had taken on a new appearance; repairs to the tunnel walls had replaced the crumbling tiles, new lights lined the corridors, and most of the buildings had new facades. The entire community shone, proud of its role in Mercury's future.

Well, almost the whole warren. Kemal paused at a tunnel entrance just off the spacedock complex and peered down the dark corridor. This was the tunnel

Kal Hawker had taken to get to his spacer bar when Kemal had given him the *Sun Spot.*

On impulse Kemal entered the hall. It was deserted now, a shabby, run-down dead end cluttered with rubble and debris from the construction in the rest of the warren.

"Whozat?" a rough voice with a thick Miner accent called from the darkness ahead.

"No one," Kemal said, surprised by the sound. "I was just—"

"Well, if you're comin' in, come in," another man said, "otherwise, buzz off!"

Kemal smiled and stepped into the tunnel. Once his eyes adjusted to the dimness he could make out six or seven people lounging along the walls, a motley collection of Dancers, Miners, and down-and-out Musicians taking their leisure out of the way of the rest of the world.

"Who are you, then?" someone asked.

"I'm . . ." Kemal began, searching for a name.

"He's a spacer," the first man said. "Can't you tell by his clothes?"

"Yeah, probably looking for that bar that used to be here," a raspy-voiced woman put in.

"Used to be?" Kemal asked, walking to the group. "What happened to it?"

"Ah," a Dancer in badly patched robes snorted, "it got shut down. All this prettying up going on . . . I guess the royal architects didn't think this part of town was worth saving."

"Bloody Royals," a Miner snarled, scratching his leg. "Can't leave well enough alone."

Kemal cleared his throat self-consciously and sat next to the Miner. "Yeah, them Royals," he said with more bitterness than he intended.

"Hey, shut up about the king," the Dancer snapped. "My name's Feld, and this surly Miner is called

Techer." Feld gestured to the side. "The big guy's Igor—he's from Mars. Fought in the Earth-Mars war, you know. The rest of these folk . . . I don't know them."

Kemal turned to the Martian. Even in the dark he could tell Igor was huge, tall and broad in the shoulders. "I fought in that war, too," he said. "How come you're not still in the army?"

Igor grunted and stared at him with cold eyes through the dimness. "You were NEO?"

Kemal swallowed, wondering if he had touched a nerve. "Yeah," he said, returning the stare.

Igor continued to glare at him for a moment, then looked away. "Good fighters, NEO," he said simply.

"So, what did you do in the war?" Feld asked Kemal. The others in the tunnel groaned loudly.

"Oh, you know," Kemal said. "Different things. Nobody wants to hear old war stories."

"I *love* war stories," Feld insisted. "They got a lot of heart. Even the lies!" The others against the walls started laughing.

Kemal felt something open up inside him at the sound of the laughter. "Yeah, I got a few stories."

○ ○ ○ ○ ○

". . . and he turned around with his rifle, but the whole barrel was sheared off right at the capacitor assembly." Kemal started to chuckle. "The look on his face!" The others began laughing; even Igor's grim face broke into a humorous grimace.

Kemal felt a rough hand clap him on the back and looked up at Kal Hawker smiling at him, a half-dozen men standing behind him.

"What are you doing here, Your . . ." Hawker began, but Kemal made a quick gesture and he stopped. Hawker glanced at the others and nodded. ". . . old buddy?"

Kemal laughed and stood, slapping Hawker on his shoulder. "Just passing through. How about you? I thought you'd be on the other side of the solar system by now."

"Oh, I heard a story floating around the asteroid belt that there's going to be some kind of coronation here, and we thought we'd come have a look." The men behind him nodded enthusiastically.

"You know anything about this new king? Kemal?" Techer the Miner asked Hawker. "Not that I cares about the damn Royals."

"You shut your mouth about Kemal!" Feld interrupted angrily. "I don't want to hear any of your trash about him! I was there at the Eye of Phidias, and so was he! He wasn't hiding in his cloud city. He was right down there in the dirt with us! So don't you go spilling your bile about *him* to me!"

Kemal glanced at Hawker, who winked at him. "You were at the Eye?" Kemal asked.

Feld nodded. "That's right. I used to ride on the *Hermes Trismegistus,* but it got blown to hell by those Martian bastards!" He quickly turned to Igor. "No offense meant." Igor nodded wordlessly.

"I know what happened to the *Hermes,*" Kemal said, sitting beside him. "It was a good city."

Feld's eyes narrowed. "You were there?"

Kemal shrugged. "I know a lot of Dancers."

❍ ❍ ❍ ❍ ❍

Tix rushed into the suite without knocking. "Duernie! I just got a c-c-call from Huer on the computer!" He gasped, out of breath. "He and Barney have been looking for Kemal and just found him in some miserable closed-off tunnel with a gang of c-c-cutthroats and he doesn't want to come back!"

Duernie looked up from her computer. "Sounds like he's having a good time."

Tix stared at her, flabbergasted. "But . . . but the coronation," he said.

"It's more than an hour away," she said. "He'll be back in time. Or maybe he won't."

"Duernie!" He stamped his foot in frustration. "He's going to be crowned k-k-king today, and instead of g-g-getting ready, he's having a party with a bunch of p-p-pirates and rocketjocks!"

She sighed wearily. "If you want to go look for him, go ahead. Do you know where they are?"

"Down by the spaceport, in an abandoned t-t-tunnel."

○ ○ ○ ○ ○

Tix approached the dark corridor warily, straining his ears to catch even the slightest sound that might mean trouble. He wasn't sure what he would do if there was any, but he felt prepared nonetheless.

Instead of the soft scrape of a knife being drawn from its sheath, or the heavy breathing of a waiting assassin, or the hushed whispers of kidnappers, he heard . . . singing?

He quickened his pace. Indeed, he could hear a raucous song coming from the tunnel ahead, something about blasting through the asteroid belt and plucking a fat merchant ship. There was a loud burst of laughter after the last verse.

Tix tentatively poked his head around the corner, peering into the dim hall. Perhaps a score of rough-looking men sat on the rubble, talking and joking . . . with Kemal in the middle of them!

He swung around the corner and almost tripped over Black Barney, who sat with a huge Martian and a case of ginger beer on the ground between them.

"Tix!" Kemal called happily. "Come in! Have a drink!"

Black Barney handed him a bottle of the amber soda without comment. Tix stared at it with disbelief. Slowly the big Martian stood, glaring at Tix.

"Something wrong with ginger beer?" he rumbled menacingly.

"N-n-no," Tix said, quickly opening the drink. "I love the stuff!"

"Come on over." Kemal motioned to him. "Meet my friends. What are you doing here?"

"Looking for y-y-you. The coronation is going to t-t-take place in an hour, Kemal."

Suddenly the tunnel fell silent as the men turned to Kemal. The abrupt silence startled Tix.

"W-w-what . . . ?" he began.

A shabby Dancer dressed in torn and ragged scarves slowly stood up beside Kemal. "You . . . you're Kemal? Kemal Gavilan?"

Tix watched as Kemal turned away, his face burning with shame. Then he took a deep breath and looked up at the men. "Yes, I am."

The Dancer Feld stepped back. "You were at the Eye with us? That wasn't just a story Corianne told?"

"You know Corianne better than that," Kemal said. "I saw the *Hermes* fall. It took four direct hits from missiles to kill her. She was a good city."

Feld's eyes filled with tears and he looked away.

A short Miner pushed his way to Kemal's side and poked him in the chest with a dirty finger. "If you're a Royal, what are you doin' here, with us?"

Kemal swatted the man's hand away. "I wanted a little time to be a human being before I got dragged into a world I'm not sure I'll like."

The Miner blinked in confusion, then frowned. "And now you've had your fun, you're going back to your palace and forget about us down here?"

The Miner's aggressive tone made Tix break out in a sweat. "Kemal, I think w-w-we better get back."

"Well, what about you?" Kemal demanded of the men around him, his voice angry. "A few laughs, then ship me back to Hielo with those bloody Royals?"

The venom of Kemal's last words surprised the Miner. He started to sneer, but stopped, watching Kemal with a puzzled expression.

Finally Feld said, "What do you want of us, Your Majesty?"

Kemal looked at the men around him, then fixed on the Dancer. "We stood together in war. Can we stand together now, too?"

"What do you mean?" the Dancer asked. "At the coronation?"

Kemal forced a chuckle. "If ever I needed the support of friends, it's now."

❍ ❍ ❍ ❍ ❍

Duernie almost missed the light, nervous tap at the door. "Pardon me for disturbing you," she heard Terens call softly, "but I was wondering if you had heard from Kemal. The ceremony is about to begin."

Duernie opened the door, startling the anxious arbiter. "Not in the last five minutes," she said, trying to keep the irritation out of her voice, "but Doctor Huer said they were on their way. I told you that when he reported."

"Oh, yes, of course," Terens stammered. "I just thought you might have heard something more."

A clatter from the lobby below interrupted him. Duernie cocked her head to one side. "That's probably him now," she said, smiling.

Terens grimaced. "Oh, I hope not!" he wailed and hurried to the stairs down to the ground floor.

He froze halfway down at the landing. The doors of the elegant hotel stood open, one hanging from a broken hinge. A horde of . . . *savages* dressed in filthy rags swarmed into the lobby, poking and grabbing at the expensive sculptures and pictures that decorated the room. Delegates and ministers stood in shock as the army of riffraff shouldered past them and trod over the exquisite carpet with their dusty boots.

"Here . . . here now!" Terens sputtered, starting downstairs. "What do you think you're doing?"

Two of the men laughed at him, but the rest simply ignored him as they spread throughout the lobby. One short, squat Miner had cornered the Miner delegate Lomar and was gesturing wildly; Lomar's face turned a bright red as he listened, then swung his fist at the interloper. The grubby Miner ducked, then charged the delegate, his arms swinging madly. The two crashed backward, upsetting a vase, and fell against the minister of solar energy production.

Terens groaned and turned to the door as Kemal walked in with Tix and Black Barney beside him.

"Kemal!" Terens cried. "Thank the stars you're here! Help me get these . . . creatures out of here!"

"Get them out?" Kemal cried. "I invited them! They're my friends!"

"Your . . . your . . ." Terens tried to say something but noticed Kemal staring at the stairs behind him. Terens turned to see Duernie on the landing.

She stepped past him, holding her hand to Kemal. He took it and hugged her as they both laughed.

"Excuse me, Your Majesty," Terens said, "but the coronation is about to begin, and we need to . . ."

"Let's get on with it!" Kemal cried, and started walking to the doorway leading to the ceremonial platform facing the public square.

Terens's shoulders sagged. Oh, my, he thought, I can see there are going to be some changes at court.

Epilogue

Parsonawitz fidgeted nervously in the cold, dark chamber, shifting his weight from foot to foot, playing with the collar of his shirt. Kane heaved a deep sigh of exasperation and jabbed him sharply with his elbow.

Ardala tapped her heel impatiently and stared into the murky green light that seemed to have no source in the room deep within Holzerhein Crag.

"How long will you keep us in this deep freeze?" Ardala asked the darkness.

"I was thinking of leaving you here," a harsh voice whispered from nowhere. "At least that would clear the field of three incompetents."

"Incompetents?" Kane shouted.

"Yes, incompetents!" Holzerhein thundered, and the small room shook. Parsonawitz clapped his hands over his ears and sank to his knees, moaning.

The three watched as a flicker of light began to grow in front of them. The hazy green glow began to form into the shape of Holzerhein, sitting behind a massive desk. His normally harsh features took on a harder angularity, giving his face a more predatory appearance than he normally had.

"Forget it, Kane," Ardala said carelessly. "You can't outshout him. He's got too many amplifiers."

Kane smirked and folded his arms across his chest. "What's the point of all this?"

"I'm still deciding," Holzerhein said softly. The implication hung in the tomblike room. Parsonawitz groaned and started to rock back and forth.

Kane swallowed hard and glared at the hologram. "I don't much like being grabbed at the spacedock by your Internal Affairs thugs and dragged to your—"

"And I don't much like having a well-planned invasion ruined by bumbling fools who can't even use the tools they've been given! You had five squadrons of men, fighters, and a battler!" Holzerhein's harsh whisper rose to a grating crescendo. "And even with those resources you still failed to take an insignificant backwater planet such as Mercury!"

"And what about you?" Ardala shouted at him suddenly. "The most powerful person in human history, and you couldn't hold the laser, on your own world! With all RAM's resources at your command!"

Holzerhein rose from his seat, his holographic stare burning into Ardala's eyes. She took a step forward, her jaw jutting out defiantly.

"Admit it, Holzerhein," she said. "You played the game as well as you could, and you still lost!"

Holzerhein sank back into his seat, steepling his

fingers over his chest. "I . . . lost," he said quietly, as if the admission cost him dearly. "I lost the first hand, but there's always another deal."

"Well, I'm not in your game, so don't waste your cards on me!" She thrust out her chin aggressively.

"Oh, Ardala, you will always be a player," the hologram said, his thin lips curving into a tight smile. "You add a certain piquancy to the game."

Ardala's eyes glittered. "Then you will lose," she hissed. "You bloodless vampire!" She spun around and stalked to the elevator door behind her.

Kane looked at Holzerhein, then quickly strode to her side, praying the doors would open. To his surprise, they did.

Even more surprising, the elevator began rising. Kane started to laugh. "Well, my dear, did that feel good? To tweak the bear's nose in his own den?"

She started to chuckle. "Yes, it felt good!" she said. "It was *delicious!*"

"Why do you suppose we're still alive?"

Ardala tossed her hair lightly. "Who knows? I suspect we have value as players. After all, I still have the laser plans."

Yes, Kane thought, smiling to himself; I may need a few cards as well.

○ ○ ○ ○ ○

Parsonawitz gaped as Ardala and Kane disappeared into the elevator. Still on his knees, he began to scramble toward the doors, but they remained uncompromisingly closed. He glanced nervously back at Holzerhein, still at his desk.

"Are . . . you done with me?" he stammered.

Holzerhein turned his iron gaze on the RAM executive. "I am very definitely done with you."

Parsonawitz's Adam's apple bobbed as he tried to

swallow, but there was nothing to choke down. "M-m-may I go?" he ventured hesitantly.

Holzerhein chuckled with a horrible rasping sound. "It gets lonely here in my citadel. Sometimes I need a companion to wile away the decades."

Parsonawitz blanched and scrambled at the unmoving elevator doors. "You need me for the game!"

"You aren't much of a player," Holzerhein replied, his image beginning to fade along its edges.

"No!" Parsonawitz howled. "You still have the laser plans, and there are other crystals."

"The Dancer sculptures are useless," the hologram said, its colors growing ever paler.

"Not Dancer crystals, Venusian!"

Holzerhein's image stopped its diffusion and began to solidify again. "What about Venus?"

"The Miner who brought the first commercial plant to Mercury came from Venus," he said quickly. "He was working with Venusian crystals when he found the Sun Crystals on Mercury were better. But the Venusian crystals . . ."

Holzerhein's eyes went blank for a minute, as if his consciousness had fled into some maze of circuits. "There are records . . ." Holzerhein said slowly.

"Yes, yes, the crystals are crude, but they can be altered on a molecular level."

"Then do so," Holzerhein said shortly.

The elevator doors opened. Parsonawitz stared at them, only half-believing his eyes. "It might take years to cultivate the crystals and make them usable."

"You'd better begin, then," Holzerhein commented.

"Of course, of course," Parsonawitz babbled and scrambled into the elevator.

Holzerhein watched the doors close and let his mind wander through the many possibilities. There's much to be done, he thought, then smiled.

Clone Warrior

A strain of bigger, stronger, faster, and more savage clones than any in the solar system has evolved in a secret RAM laboratory. One clone with tremendous abilities emerges from the rest. When Black Barney's vicious creators aren't looking, he rallies his warrior siblings in a deadly revolt. Freed by an unexpected ally and eager for revenge on RAM, Barney dedicates himself to a life of piracy, doing what he can to steal more than just the megacorporation's thunder.